DISC DESTRUCTION

A GUARDIANS OF THE BONES NOVEL

K.J. JACKSON

First Edition: May 2022
ISBN: 978-1-940149-69-1

K.J. Jackson Books

Historical Romance:

Hold Your Breath
Stone Devil Duke
Unmasking the Marquess
My Captain, My Earl

Lords of Fate
Worth of a Duke
Earl of Destiny
Marquess of Fortune

Lords of Action
Vow
Promise
Oath

Revelry's Tempest
Of Valor & Vice
Of Sin & Sanctuary
Of Risk & Redemption
To Capture a Rogue, *Logan's Legends*
To Capture a Warrior, *Logan's Legends*
The Devil in the Duke

Valor of Vinehill
The Iron Earl
The Wolf Duke
The Steel Rogue
The Christmas Countess
The Devil Baron

Box of Draupnir
The Heart of an Earl
The Blood of a Baron
The Soul of a Rogue

Exile
Exiled Duke
Wicked Exile
Dangerous Exile

Guardians of the Bones
Discreet Destruction
Shadows of Scandal

Paranormal Romance:
Flame Moon
Triple Infinity, *Flame Moon #2*
Flux Flame, *Flame Moon #3*

Be sure to sign up for news of my next releases at
www.KJJackson.com

DEDICATION

– As Always,
For my favorite Ks

{ CHAPTER 1 }

Verity scooped up the cane from the muck of the ground and swung the heavy silver head of it directly at the knees of the cutthroat behind her.

That he'd reversed course from charging down the alleyway to join in on the attack on Declan meant she wasn't as silent as she would have liked.

The first man she had gotten to had screamed as he went down. A dagger across the back of one's thigh tended to do that. But the brute was too bloody tall for her to attack the throat. Luckily, after the blade across his leg, his cane was easy to rip out of his hand and knock across his jaw.

Where in the hell was Jack?

The cane slammed into the knees of the brute coming at her and she glanced past him. At the far end of the alley, Declan was engaged with two of the three cutthroats that had jumped him—one was already face down on the ground—but he didn't need two more rushing him.

"Bitch." The word was part swear, part howl.

His knees busted, the brute in front of her crashed into the brick wall, then slipped to the mud. She slammed the heel of her boot into his temple.

Best Declan didn't come down the alleyway to investigate. With any luck, he didn't hear the man's scream through his own battle.

She tucked her blade into the pocket of her apron and crept into the shadows of the alleyway, moving closer to Declan.

One of the men he'd been fighting was in a heap against the brick of the building to her left and Declan was dodging the blade the last cutthroat was waving about.

To the left. Down. To the right. Declan flew while the other man lumbered, grunting.

Damn, he was quick.

She'd seen him fight many times, and every time, she was jealous. Fast. Strong. Smart. Levelheaded. Moves that were unexpected. So *sure* of himself. She wouldn't want to go up against him. Ever.

But she did enjoy watching him.

Quick as the snap of a whip, Declan's hand snatched the cutthroat's wrist and he cracked it, the blade falling from the man's hand.

A knee into the brute's gut and then Declan slammed the cutthroat's head back into the building behind him.

The man sank, slowly, crumpling into himself. Third one down and still air permeated the alley.

"Verity?" Declan's look swung her direction.

Hell, she thought she was enough in the shadows. Close, but not too close. Damn the white apron she hadn't had time to strip off.

He'd seen her and it was no use hiding. She stepped forward, nodding, just as a new cutthroat charged at Declan from behind.

She jumped, feinting fear, pointing as she held out the heavy cane in her hand to him. She would have offered a terrified scream if it had been plausible.

A quick glance behind him at the threat and he coughed out a, "Thanks," then grabbed the cane from her hand and turned and swung.

The brute was out in an instant.

Declan spun back to her.

"You shouldn't be out here, Verity. What are you thinking? You know these streets aren't safe—and especially the alleys. Get the hell back to the Alabaster." His irate words rained down on her.

Her head bowed, hiding her face, but she nodded, silently contrite. She moved forward, sliding past him as she picked over prone bodies and headed toward the lights of the street that led to the Alabaster.

Five steps past him and his voice cut into the night. "Verity—I'm sorry. I didn't mean to yell at you. Scare you."

Her feet paused and she half turned back, gave him a quick nod, then ducked her head, scurrying the rest of the way out to the main street.

"I can walk you back." Declan's voice was directly behind her. He moved too fast. He always did, popping up over her shoulder when she wasn't prepared for him.

Not looking up at him, she shook her head, her steps quickening, and the sound of his boot heels faded behind her, stopping until there was no echo of them.

Off on her own.

A scared little mouse, on the run.

That was her job. Her *real* job.

A scared little mouse that was actually a *deadly* little mouse.

~ ~ ~

Verity hadn't spoken in two years, four months, three days.

It was easy to keep track, for every day she awoke, she had to remind herself where she was. What she was doing. How deep she was in.

Two years, four months, three days of living with this farce of being a maid at the Alabaster gaming hell, and now she was staring at the end.

"You have to find a way out of it. Without answers, you are useless and you need to get out." The long line across Hector's forehead that was always present—from temple to temple and starker than the many other wrinkles creasing his skin—deepened with his aggravation.

She shook her head, her mouth pulling to a tight line. She would explain if she could, but she couldn't speak. If she broke now, she didn't think she could ever slip back into the pretense of her life.

Hector knew exactly why she wasn't answering, but that didn't stop a long sigh from exhaling from his lungs. Fingertips met fingertips in front of his mouth, making a steeple, and the sides of his forefingers tapped on his lips as he stared at her. "You're going to have to give me more to go on, Verity, or I will be forced to pull you from the job. Put someone in your place that can find the answers we need."

She leaned forward, picking up the quill on Hector's desk and then stabbing the nib into the inkwell. Holding in a growl, she scrawled the point across the paper, ink smearing.

You cannot. I am trusted. No one is in a better position. Not even Jack. I cannot lose this post.

Hector's hands dropped away from his face, his left fingers curling into a fist that landed atop the desk, the weathered wrinkles along his knuckles stretching to white. "Then make a bloody exception and speak to me. Tell me something—anything. I haven't heard words from you in two years. You've done well on the job, but this current threat is not acceptable. And you won't even talk to me. Explain it. Three attacks in one month cannot be condoned."

She shook her head and scratched more words onto the paper, then spun it toward him.

You know why I cannot speak. I have this handled.

"I never should have put you on this job." His head shook, more to himself than to her. "Never should have listened to Jack on the matter." His fist uncurled and he sucked in a deep breath, leaning back in his chair. "You give me no choice. I have to pull you from the job."

She jumped to her feet, her head frantically shaking as she slammed her knuckles onto his desk. Her left hand flew up, palm to him as her right hand grabbed the quill, dashed ink onto it and scrawled more words onto the paper, the last letters mere scratches in the paper for lack of ink.

I will find the source. I am close, I know it. I took care of the other threats well enough. Please don't do this—you know why.

He stared at the paper for several long heartbeats. His dark blue eyes, aged almost to silver, lifted to pin her.

"Then find out who is attacking Mr. Rudderton. That is part of your job. Threats like this will not be tolerated."

A stay of execution.

For now.

With a nod, she set the quill onto the desk gently, belying the desperation making her fingers twitch.

He would notice that. The slight shake along her pinky.

Hector liked that she didn't flinch. Didn't hesitate. Didn't show fear. It was why he chose her to begin with.

Another farce that had been hard to keep up with for the past three years.

For she did flinch.

She did hesitate.

And she was absolutely, definitely afraid.

But all of that had to remain hidden. From him, from the world.

She nodded to him again. A promise with her look, if not her words, that she would find who was threatening Mr. Rudderton.

Hector accepted it with an incline of his head.

She turned, walking out of his office and into the night, her black maid's dress letting her disappear into the darkness, into the shadows along the streets.

She made it halfway to her boarding house before the tears of frustration started to fall.

Rarely did she let the pitiful, desperate core of her bleed out with salty tears. But it had been so long—so long since the last time she had cried—that she couldn't quite stop the tears as she usually did.

She *had* to find the threat against Declan, or all would be lost.

Her brother was counting on her.

And a noose was waiting for her.

{ CHAPTER 2 }

Her hands twitching, Verity looked through the sinking darkness to the end of the alley and across the street to the next tunnel of darkness. Coaches, wagons, and horses passed by, blocking her view again and again, but her stare stayed pinpointed on the corner of the alley across the way.

She was deep enough into the shadows to not be seen, but close enough to the street to spring at any moment. Her nose twitched at the coal dust she'd sprinkled across her face to hide her white skin in the shadows. No apron tonight. No silly mistakes.

The last three attacks on Declan were connected—she knew that just as well as Hector did. Verity had recognized one of the attackers that had managed to escape the fate of his partners multiple times, yet still he kept coming for Declan with more cutthroats. The idiot was for some reason determined to take down one of the most brutal rulers of the rookeries.

It made sense—Declan would always be looked at with salivating tongues, a king on the top of the heap, needing to be sliced down. Too much power, and power bred danger.

The slippery eel that kept escaping her dagger or Declan's fists was a stocky, barrel-chested man with two missing front teeth and a fat nose that was so crooked, it didn't even matter that she had broken it with a fire poker the first time she'd saved Declan from him in an alley. The

man was either stupid, or had far more resources at his disposal than someone of his lowly station normally did.

For he kept coming after Declan.

That meant the brute was the key to finding out who was ordering the attacks on Declan.

She just had to make sure the cutthroat would try again. And soon.

She needed bait.

And she wasn't above using the man she was paid to protect as said bait. Which meant getting Declan out of the Alabaster, his main gaming hell, and into the neighborhood in the middle of the night.

An easy enough task, as she had gone to him, drawn pictures of a man beating a woman in front of the Seasweep Boarding House. A drawing which Declan instantly deciphered as old man Lewis beating his wife again.

Declan had a soft spot for Mrs. Lewis, who housed most of the sailors that cycled through the Alabaster or one of Declan's other gaming hells on their way in and out of London. Their coin at the tables was too lucrative to lose, and Mrs. Lewis knew how to take care of all the men in the best way possible. She also knew how to pass along to Declan all the overheard comments, plans, and schemes that were discussed by the sailors at the Seasweep.

It kept Declan's pulse on any lucrative deals, and that was how he worked. He was cunning, charming. He had his portion of the rookeries run with a wink and a smile and a fist one didn't see coming.

Though at the moment, Declan was on a fool's errand, for Mrs. Lewis wasn't currently being beaten by her derelict husband—Verity had seen the vagabond passed out in the walkway three streets away.

True to his code of decency, Declan didn't send one of the Alabaster guards for the job—no—Mrs. Lewis was far too important to his enterprise. Declan needed to be sure Mr. Lewis personally got the message that he was dispensable, his wife was not.

Declan was on the move minutes after Verity had alerted him, striding out from the well-lit alleyway along the side of the Alabaster and charging down the street.

She'd barely had time to get herself into position before he came into view.

Also true to the efficiency that strummed in his veins, Declan veered to the right into the dark alleyway opposite the street from her.

Predictable. Always in such a hurry, he would, without fail, take the shortest path. Even if it meant shadows and darkness and danger.

Declan had far too much arrogance for his own good.

There had been nine attempts to club and rob him the last two years. Five of those attempts were specifically on his life—three within the last month alone. She'd helped thwart all of them—though in four of the instances, Declan was already engaged in the skirmish and she just skirted about the edges of the melee, cutting the number of attackers to a manageable amount that he could dispose of without much problem.

It wasn't that Declan couldn't handle himself. It was that the odds were often stacked against him and no one had his back.

She did.

He just couldn't know she did.

Even if it put her in peril.

Over the years she'd had to come up with excuses for the bruises, the broken fingers, the cuts across her face, the limping after she turned her weak ankle once again. Which was easy enough to do when one didn't talk, when one always kept her head down and her hands busy.

When one was a mute.

There. Three men poured out from a hack across the street, slinking into the shadows behind Declan. The middle one stocky and barrel-chested with the crooked nose she'd met before.

Verity darted out from the alley and skirted across the road, dodging horses and carriages.

By the time she vaulted herself into the opposite alleyway, she heard a grunt and knew the brutes had caught up to Declan.

The two at the front had attacked and Declan was already engaged.

Knuckles hitting flesh. Bones crunching. Flashes of bodies flying back and forth and into the brick buildings confining them.

Not enough space for all three cutthroats to attack at the same time and the third brute hung back, waiting for one of his partners to fall out of the way.

A grunt of pain echoed into the night and was instantly followed by a growl in Declan's low voice—so low, it shook her chest.

Through her open pocket, she pulled free her dagger from the sheath strapped to her thigh and had it up and ready and slicing across the third brute's throat before he could even react to her hand grabbing the thick of his hair.

Small. Quiet. Deadly. As she'd been trained.

Declan might leave those other two alive. She was another matter.

Threats had to be extinguished.

She'd learned that long ago, in the most painful way, that mercy was for the stupid. For those willing to forfeit their own lives—or the lives of their loved ones.

She'd left mercy behind long ago.

She shoved the man forward and he staggered away from her, holding his throat, bouncing between the brick walls and crashing into the back of one of the other cutthroats. The brute sank to the ground just as Declan slammed the head of one of the attackers into the building to his right.

That left one man standing and Declan could handle him.

Verity slinked backward into the shadows, but kept a wary eye on the outline of the man still standing, picking his moment to lunge at Declan. Close enough to spring forth should Declan need help. Though he never did—especially when it was one-on-one.

Like always, she planned to sneak out of the alley and disappear into the night before the last body hit the ground.

That Declan had seen her in that alleyway a week ago had been a mistake she didn't plan on replicating. With

Hector keeping a close eye on her, the last thing she needed was Declan to become suspicious of her.

With any luck, both of the men Declan took down would still be alive, though she truly only needed one of them to survive—hopefully the stocky one, as he appeared to be the leader of this inept crew. She could be back with rope, a wheelbarrow, and Jack within ten minutes and the cutthroat would be turned over to Hector for interrogation. They just needed to scoop up the rubbish of the man before the night watchman came through—not that the watchmen did much of anything in the rookeries. These areas of London, they were ruled by men like Declan and his partner, Talen. Watchmen were just a wink to the farce of law and order.

Aimed at Declan's face, a blade flashed silver in the sparse light from the street, and Verity stilled her retreat, her weight shifting to her toes.

Declan jumped back, dodging three swipes of the cutthroat's blade before he ducked and tackled the man in the chest, slamming him against the wall. The blade clanged into the brick and thudded into the muck of the alley.

One swift knee to the brute's stomach and his body flew up, then collapsed downward. He dropped to the ground and Declan sent a boot across his jaw.

The last one down. So quick and ruthless, it froze Verity in place. She knew the violence Declan was capable of. But to see him in action made her chest tighten. Tighten in ways it shouldn't.

He was a job.

A job that kept her brother safe. A job that kept her from swinging at the end of a rope.

She had stilled for too long, for in the next instant, Declan was charging at her.

In black from head to toe—even her face covered in coal dust—she'd thought she was well hidden in the shadows.

Except for that damn blade in her hand.

She spun, running, only to have his arm slam around her waist and send her legs flying out from under her.

"Who are you? Are you with them?" The brutal growl in his voice was unmistakable. He would crush her without a blink.

He slammed her against the brick wall, pinning her in place with his arm across her waist, her toes not touching the ground. His face only an inch away. "Who in the hell are you?"

She crushed her head back against the brick as she tried to turn her face away from him.

"Verity?" The sudden shock in his voice sent her look to him.

At that second, a hard mass slammed into both of them from the side, sending them sprawling into the mud of the alleyway. Her dagger went flying.

Scrambling, Verity tried to free her limbs from under Declan even as the two men jumped on him, swinging, hitting anything they could.

She kicked away from the brawl, her hands frantic in the muck and dirt, and she found her blade. Crawling back toward Declan, she spotted the open neck on one of the

men attacking him and she dove, slamming the tip into the brute's throat. So focused on hitting an artery, she didn't see the boot coming at her temple.

A boot that sent her flying.

Lost to blackness before she hit the ground.

{ CHAPTER 3 }

Declan sat at his desk, fuming, the nib of his quill tapping on the wood as he pretended to look at numbers on the ledger in front of him.

Hell, he wasn't even pretending. His glare was focused on one thing.

Verity strewn across the settee in his office at the Alabaster, the surgeon busy with a hooked needle and thread, closing up the wound at her temple.

Bloody fucking hell.

His throat tightened at the fresh blood still seeping from the wound as the surgeon put in the last stiches.

True, it was hard to see in that dark alley and those cutthroats could have very well not seen exactly who he was. They could have thought him some moronic fop that had lost his way in a dark lane, ready to be flipped and picked. It had happened before. It had happened last week.

But this was different. Those imbeciles had attacked him. *Him.*

He ruled this part of the rookeries and he'd just been attacked on his streets. *His* streets.

Not only that, they'd hurt Verity.

Poor, innocent Verity, who had probably been chasing after him to help with Mrs. Lewis.

He ran an exhausted hand down over his face, his palm rubbing his eyes for a long second. Ever since his partner, Talen Blackstone, had stepped away months ago from their

business to handle the estate he'd inherited along with the title of viscount, Declan had been in charge of their enterprise.

Solely in charge.

The full of it—the Alabaster, the five other gaming hells, the shipping, the smuggling, the general business of everything in their expanding empire that ran from Covent Garden to the river.

Too much. Not to mention he'd been attacked in a dark alley more than once in the last month.

It was a tough go, not having his best friend at his back. Talen had always taken care of the numbers and, by his surname alone, had set fear into any that opposed them. Declan had always taken care of the people—their men, the families within their borders. Both had taken care of any threats to their enterprise, their battle-honed skills enviable after growing up in the hardscrabble of life on the seas.

But Talen was now absent.

Not that Declan could blame him. Talen now had something to lose—namely, his new wife, Ness.

Declan heaved another sigh for effect, prodding the surgeon across the room to speed along so he could look at Verity.

She was one of the few people in his organization that he trusted implicitly. And she could have very well been killed tonight.

Killed, when he needed her.

She was mute, true. Couldn't read or write. Those assets had always meant that she could tell no tales of the

Alabaster and of the business. But she was solid. Always at his call. Always a step ahead of what he needed.

Hired as a maid, she'd become much more than that in the last two years, somehow running the entirety of the inner mechanics of the Alabaster without saying a word to any of the other staff. Yet they all followed her directions in some concocted sign language around gestures they'd developed.

The one thing that worked smoothly in his life—the Alabaster—and he'd almost lost the woman that made it so.

He slammed the quill onto his desk and stood, striding across the room to hover over the surgeon's shoulder as he snipped the end of the thread now embedded into Verity's skin.

"Has the blood stopped?" The stitches along her temple were mostly hidden just inside her hairline. Dark red hair that Declan had never quite realized she possessed, for the black cap that was partially pushed up across her head always covered her hair entirely. The rich hue of it hid the drying blood.

"It has." The surgeon, Mr. Damus, nodded. He glanced up over his shoulder to Declan. "What was she doing in that alley?"

"I don't know. I imagine she was following me from the Alabaster to the Seasweep to help with Mrs. Lewis."

The right side of Mr. Damus's lips lifted in a snarl. "Mr. Lewis is at it again?"

Declan shrugged. "I never got there. I sent Jack to take care of it."

"Lewis is worse than a steaming pile of dung."

"Aye."

Mr. Damus looked back to Verity's face. "Who attacked you?"

"Not sure." Declan exhaled a sigh. "I imagine it was some ruffians from Bloodwater's crew. I don't know where he pulls those idiots from."

"Again?"

Declan nodded. "They haven't taken to the message to stay on their side of the Thames. I'll be sending out another reminder tonight to Bloodwater."

Mr. Damus stood from Verity's side, bending to put away his instruments and close his bag. He stood, pointing down at Verity. "I'd stay and observe her, but I was on my way to the Den of Diablo to look at a leg mangled by a carriage."

"Whose leg?"

"Rufus, I believe."

Blast. Rufus was one of the burliest men that watched over the women at the brothel—dumb as a rock—but he would die for each and every one of those women. He would have to remember to send two of his men over to help until Rufus was healed. If he healed. "Will he lose the leg?"

Mr. Damus moved toward the door. "Possibly."

"Then why did you stop here first?"

Mr. Damus stopped with his hand on the door handle and looked back to Declan. "It was you." His look twitched down to his patient still dead to the world on the settee, his eyes lingering on her for a bit too long. "It was Verity."

Why in the hell was Damus looking at her like a lovesick puppy?

Declan moved to his right, blocking the man's view to Verity. While he appreciated the loyalty, he didn't need the man to get any ideas about Verity. "Best get to it, then."

Mr. Damus's look lifted to Declan. "Make sure you have someone clean the scabs around the wound to make certain the blood stops. Sometimes blood continues to seep underneath and no one is aware."

"Aye. I will do so. Thank you."

Mr. Damus nodded and left the room.

It took Declan five full seconds before he could turn around to Verity.

He protected all the innocents in his territory, but he'd failed Verity on that score tonight. Failed miserably. What the hell had she been doing in that alleyway?

He turned toward her, looking at her sleeping form for a long second before he went to the wash basin in the corner of the room and dunked a washcloth into it, soaking it.

He moved to Verity's head, bending over as he swiped the wet cloth against the wound. She winced every time the cloth settled onto her skin, but didn't awaken.

Declan studied her face, his thumb moving to wipe the black dust from her cheeks. So odd. She was usually a paragon of neatness. Apron, dress and cap firmly in place and never rumpled, much less dirty.

His thumb swiped along her cheekbone and he lifted his hand, looking at his thumb pad that was now caked with black powder. Coal dust? Damus had cleaned off much

of it, but streaks still marred her skin. It was why he didn't recognize her immediately in the alleyway—without her white apron, she'd been a specter, a shadow moving in the night, in black from head to toe.

Had she been cleaning out a fireplace? He had people for that.

He shook his head, using the edge of the washcloth to wipe away the coal dust on the upturned side of her face. More smearing, than actually removing it, but the more he worked at it, the more came off. He dragged off her black cap so he could wipe the black dust off her forehead.

Strands of her dark red hair tugged away from her scalp as he pulled the cap from her head. The cap dropped to the floor as the full of her red hair froze him in place.

How had he never seen her without that black cap tight about her head?

Her dark red hair curled about her head, a braided crimson crown that circled again and again and spoke of a land before man when the gods of old ruled the earth. Thick and lush. The strands that escaped the weave circling her head were wavy, but not curly. How did she fit all of it under her cap?

Why?

He couldn't look away from her hair and he dropped to a squat, balancing on his heels in front of her, staring at her. The answer slammed into him.

She worked at the Alabaster.

Though they didn't offer prostitutes to the patrons, there were no shortage of lecherous men milling about the building. And there were a multitude of rooms furnished with beds and mirrors and accoutrements that were available to the men that brought their own whores to the establishment.

Her head of hair would draw attention anywhere—in the most crowded Drury Lane brothel, in the fashionable shops on Oxford Street, or in the chaos of Seven Dials— attention she wasn't prepared to deal with, being a mute.

He'd always known she was smart, but she also possessed the sort of canniness that kept one alive in the rookeries.

Exhaling a sigh, he ripped his stare away from her hair and looked to her wound. He dabbed at it as gently as he could so she wouldn't wince at his touch.

Had Mr. Damus known about her hair? Was that why he had been staring at her so? How often had the man been around Verity? Too often, he imagined. If anyone was hurt at the Alabaster, any of his men, Verity was always in the room, providing towels and water and comfort. How many hands had gripped onto hers during her years here? How many brows had she wiped?

That answer was easy. Too many.

Verity was always around, a steady, calming presence for not just him, but for everyone in his employ.

Declan studied her face as he swiped away the last of the scab along her temple and tried to remove the coal dust. Nudging his fingers under the side of her jaw, he lifted her face to clean the other side of it.

How had he never touched her face?

Her face was pretty, delicate. Almost bordering on the edge of cracking from holding all that hair atop her head.

Dainty lines of cheekbones, a petite nose, yet her lips that never parted with words were full, the top closing in the center to a soft heart shape. Even with smudges of dirt about her face and the deep purple half-circles under her eyes, she was pretty.

That was what Mr. Damus had been staring at. Pretty, but exhausted.

She was always at the Alabaster. Always working. He needed her to rest more. Needed to get rid of the fatigue on her face. He would tell her that when she awoke.

The coal dust mostly removed, he settled her head back down onto the cushion of the settee.

He glanced down her body, watching her chest rise and fall under the serviceable black dress she always wore. She would be wispy, frail, if he didn't feed her as well as he did at the Alabaster. Even at that, she flittered along the line where she could easily be broken. A delicate finch.

Yet she did everything here at the Alabaster with such efficiency and strength, he'd never really studied her.

Guilt settled into his chest.

She needed more time off. Needed heartier meals.

He had neglected to take care of the one person he needed to keep his empire from imploding.

With a frown on his face, Declan stood and went back to his desk, sitting and staring at the ledger in front of him, willing the numbers to come out balanced, or he'd have another long night ahead of him.

The echoes of the gaming night in full swing below echoed into his office. He should be down there, making the rounds about the main gaming hall and in the private gaming rooms, but he couldn't leave quite yet. Not until Verity woke.

His gaze drifted from the numbers to Verity every couple of minutes.

Jotting a note along the side of the ledger, Declan's head jerked up, his gaze frantic.

Mumbling.

Mumbling coming from Verity.

Her eyes were still closed, but her mouth was open. Her lips that *never* parted, except to eat, curled around words.

The words scattered, muffled. Words he didn't understand, then, "Leave her alone—leave her. Stop. Stop, you cannot. Stop."

Her body twisted with the words, the battle going on in the depths of her mind manifesting in her limbs.

Fascinated, Declan stood and prowled silently to her, staring down at her as her lips moved, talking—speaking.

Her tongue worked.

Her lips, her throat, her breath—they all worked.

She wasn't mute. Not at all.

Two plus years, and she'd never said a word. Not a damn word.

She'd let everyone think she was a mute.

What the hell was her game?

{ CHAPTER 4 }

Her mind slammed back into consciousness.

Not the gentle, *sunlight was streaming in through the window and it was time to rise*, waking. No, it was the brutal, *heavy black boot is stomping through the darkness and smashing into her head*, type of waking.

Gasping, her body flew upright before her eyes opened, panic coursing through her veins.

Light. Bookcases. Desk.

Declan.

Declan behind the desk.

Her mouth clamped tight and she exhaled the panic through her nose, her gaze going down to the wooden floorboards in front of the settee as her fingertips lifted to her temple, searching for the source of the pain thundering through her skull.

There. Just inside her hairline. Bumps. Thread. Stitches?

The boot. The boot flying into her head.

She'd been kicked so harshly she'd needed stitches? Unacceptable.

Heat started to creep around her neck. She'd been knocked into blackness. She hadn't even seen it coming. She'd let them attack Declan.

Fine guardian she was.

"The panic on your face. You are fine, Verity." Declan's deep voice rumbled into her ears and her look jerked upward to him.

She pointed to the wound on her head, then to him and lifted her shoulders.

He nodded. "I took care of them. I am fine."

She nodded, catching her breath. Heaven help her, had she been splayed out, asleep in Declan's office? For how long?

She tilted her right ear upward. Very little noise from the main gaming room below. It was deep into the night, close to dawn.

She needed to get out of here. Her left hand unconsciously lifted to pull down her cap around her head, but her fingers only touched hair. Hair. More hair. Braid that circled her head. Where was her cap?

She looked down about her lap on either side of the dark blue damask settee.

Hell. There was her black cap, crumpled up in the back wedge of the cushions.

Blast. He saw. Saw her hair.

"Verity, you handled that blade well."

What? Muddled thoughts sat like thick soup in her mind and she couldn't get her brain working fast enough.

She glanced up at Declan, not really noting his words as she frantically smoothed out her cap on her lap. She gave him a quick nod, then slapped the cap atop her head, shoving her hair the best she could under the edges, her face now burning hot.

A wretched mess. She was nothing more than a wretched mess.

She jumped to her feet, turned slightly toward Declan with her head down and made motion of pots and food—trying to impart the information that she was disappearing into the kitchens to make sure cook had put the new leeks into a soaking bowl for tomorrow.

Without looking at him directly, she could see his stare was still fixed on her. Cutting through her.

She started to turn to the door to escape, but then noticed his heavily bandaged forearm lying atop the desk.

Rushing across the room, she grabbed his arm, her fingers running over the top of the linen bandages. Her eyes wide, she looked at his face.

"It is nothing." He shook his head, his grey eyes still pinned on her. "Just a cut that sliced too deeply. Those blackguards were not out for a waltz."

She'd failed—failed. They had come too damn close to killing him.

Hector was sure to pull her from the job now.

Her mind racing, she rubbed her fingers along the edges of the bandage, looking for the end of the strip of linen, wanting to see underneath it.

He jerked his arm out of her grasp. "It is fine. Nothing too deep or dangerous."

Her hands dropped to her sides. He wanted nothing more to do with her. She'd been a burden where she shouldn't be.

The heat in her cheeks pulsated, threatening to scorch her from the inside out.

Defeated, her head bowed, she turned from him and walked toward the door of his office.

"Verity."

His voice stopped her at the door and she turned halfway back to him, her eyebrows raised, a faint frown on her lips.

"You were talking."

She stilled, her eyes going wide.

Hell. *Hell, hell, hell.*

Stunned frozen for long seconds, she finally managed to shake her head, her eyebrows collapsing together in confusion.

"You were. I heard it." Declan stood up, his knuckles landing hard on the desk as he leaned forward. "Words. From your mouth. While you were sleeping."

Her head still shook, but it slowed, a pathetic back and forth wave. She was slipping. Everything was slipping away.

His lips pulled tight, his stare on her turning deadly, piercing. "Yes."

He shoved upward from the desk and stalked across his office to her, not stopping until he was inches away, the wide, muscled mass of him bearing down over her. "Words. Came. From. Your. Mouth."

Blast it to Hades and back.

"Now tell me what the hell you're doing here, being able to talk." His words seethed, dripping down on her like molten iron.

Too close. He was far too close.

She needed distance from him. She always did.

Standing next to Declan, too close, she was always at the precipice of breaking. Of opening her mouth. Of letting words escape.

She let that happen and her life would turn into one disaster after another.

Only one card left to play.

Pitiful.

She forced tears to her eyes, looking up at him, her head shaking in fear, her shoulders and hands lifting up and down in confusion.

He blinked, the slightest crack in the steel armor across his grey eyes.

Another blink and his shoulders went back, pulling himself slightly away from her.

The tears had the desired effect.

He shook his head, then took a step away. And another. His hand ran across his forehead. "Forgive me, Verity. I did not mean to upset you."

With a quick nod, she tucked her head down into her chest and ran from the room, down the tight twists of the servants' stairs until she landed in the empty kitchens.

She collapsed onto the roughhewn bench that lined one of Cook's wide tables, her elbow landing on the worn wood as her fingers tightened along her brow, trying to stop the pounding pain that threatened to explode her brain.

Think. Think. Think.

Calm. She needed calm.

But bloody hell—she'd talked in her sleep?

Of all things—*in her sleep*?

When had that started?

She slammed her forehead against her palm. How could she be so stupid?

{ CHAPTER 5 }

It had only been two days since she'd been kicked unconscious in that alley, but Verity had planned this visit a month ago and wasn't going to let anything—even the slight dizziness that still randomly attacked her head several times a day—make her postpone it.

Declan hadn't approached her again in that time, and she had the day off from the Alabaster, with Jack keeping a close eye on Declan while she was away.

Hector hadn't requested her presence at his office, which was a good thing—she hoped. She had reported the latest attack, as was necessary, but her report had left out several pertinent details, namely, that she'd been knocked senseless and had babbled in her sleep in front of Declan.

Any one of the litany of missteps from that night would have her out of a job.

Taking a calming breath of fresh air, she paused as she turned to look up at the imposing red-orange brick façade of Harrow School. She smoothed the front of her cerulean muslin walking dress, then looped closed the frog closure to her matching wool cape with the intricate rose and vine embroidery along the edges.

This was the only clothing Verity had left from the life that had once been hers. And with it on her body, four times a year for these visits, she felt a small slice of sanity return to her bones.

She looked to her left, the smile genuine on her face as she watched her little brother descend the front staircase after grabbing a coat. Ned had wanted to walk with her outside, so she'd moved out to the wide lawn that led up to the front of the building as he fetched his overcoat.

His salty blond-brown hair had grown in length in the front, almost brushing against the top of his eyebrows. His green eyes that matched hers twinkled, as they always did when she came for a visit.

He put on a front. She put on a front.

Neither one of them willing to scratch below the surface of all that crusted around them, all that threatened to suffocate them.

He stopped next to her and she couldn't resist reaching out and brushing a strand of hair away from his eyes, even though she knew he didn't like her fussing with him. "You are almost as tall as me, now."

He laughed, a smirk so arrogantly satisfied crossing his lips she couldn't resist her own chuckle.

"By next visit, I will have grown taller and you will have missed the day it happened." His voice had deepened. Too much time she'd lost with him since her last visit.

She laughed. "I think that is a day that I do want to miss. You realize no matter how tall you grow, you will always be my little brother?"

"Yes, but I'll be able to pick you up and toss you about, so that will soothe my ego somewhat."

Laughter at the impish look on his face played at her lips and she shook her head, her gaze setting forward toward the trail. A pleasant walk, even in the brisk air, the lane followed along a grove of trees on the eastern edge of the grounds.

Their breath puffing in the cold air, they started walking. Remnants of a wintertime chill hung in the air and the cold ground was barren, springtime sprouts not yet appearing.

All levity disappeared slowly from his face as they walked, but Ned waited until they were clear of the main building before he looked at her directly. "When can I come home?"

Home? They hadn't had an actual home to live in for a long time.

Her tongue scraped along the side of her teeth as she bit back words. She forced a bright smile on her face. "You don't—" Her throat revolted, spiking a wicked cough that was so bad, they had to stop and Ned had to pat her back.

It was like this every time she came here. Her vocal cords were not in shape for actual words coming from her mouth, and it took some time to force the words to come easily. She'd used up her quota with those first few sentences.

This was the one exception she made to her rule of not speaking. The quarterly visit with her brother. He would get to hear her talk, even if no one else did. Aside from these few precious days, she couldn't afford to slip and accidently speak, and making too many exceptions to the rule put everything at risk.

She told herself it was for Ned's sake, breaking the rule for him so he wouldn't worry on her work. But it was really for her. For her to have a few hours of normalcy. It was the

only thing that reminded her she'd once lived a different life, had been a different person. A better person.

She cleared her throat, attempting words again. "You don't like it here? Just last visit you said you liked it fine."

"It is tolerable, but I want to be with you. I am old enough to help now. I can work. I was old enough before, truth be told."

She exhaled a sigh, her head shaking. "You know the rookeries will not end well for you. What were we there—two months? And it was already clear there was only one path ahead of you."

It had scared her—scared her to her marrow how quickly the wayward boys of the rookeries had latched onto Ned, forcing him to learn how to pickpocket, roll drunks—all things that were against his very nature. He'd only been ten.

He shrugged, wrapping his arms across his chest. "Then not London. There's got to be somewhere else we can go."

"I am working on it."

"When? When can we leave England?"

"When it's safe." She attempted to keep her voice even.

"When will it be safe?"

"I don't know."

"You never do." He started walking again and she had to hop a step to catch up to him. "It's been like this for almost three years. You don't know when, but you continue to promise we can leave."

Her hand jutted out, wrapping along his shoulders and pulling him against her. Even though he'd grown, he was rail thin and she could still manhandle him. "I know.

I know it seems like more empty promises. But it is not. I don't want us to leave here until I can ensure that we won't wind up in another place that is just as bad as the rookeries—or worse. All of the schooling that you get here helps for where we can go next. It will give you a real chance to make an honest way in life." Her arm tightened along his shoulders. "So please, just hold on. Until we can leave, please, just keep your head down. Please. Please. Please. One foot in front of the other. Head down, grace in your heart. Can you do that?"

They took several more steps before Ned exhaled away the sour look on his face. He offered one gruff nod, then looked at her. "I'll keep on, as I have been."

Her bottom lip jutted upward. He wanted to be with her so badly. And she wanted to give him that—more than anything.

But this was the safest place for him.

Safe for him.

Safe for her.

She forced a bright smile on her face. "So tell me more about Mr. Percival's latest rantings on that naturalist—what was his name? Oh yes, Mr. Lamarck and his theories on organic transformation."

Ned chuckled. "It is amusing to watch Mr. Percival turn a nice shade of purple when speaking on the topic. He has been making us read every publication of Georges Cuvier's to counter the theory."

"Why even bring up Mr. Lamarck's theories if he is so openly opposed to them?"

"He's adamant you need to know the theories in order to dismiss them, so we have gone in-depth on Cuvier's principle on the correlation of parts—every organ has its function and is related to the other organs and, basically, can never evolve or change."

"Which side do you think is correct?"

He shrugged. "They both have merit, I suppose. But I care more about wanting to see Mr. Percival's head explode in front of us, than anything else."

She laughed, reveling in the short time she had with her brother. Walking and talking with him was so familiar, yet the normalcy of it was out of reach, no matter what they pretended.

But pretend she did. Pretend in these hours that she was safe. He was safe. Life was as it had once been.

When it hadn't been for a very long time.

And wouldn't be for some time more.

{ CHAPTER 6 }

"Get in the carriage, Verity." His voice a barely controlled roar, Declan slammed open the carriage door before Jack slowed the horses. That he'd stayed in the carriage as long as he did was nothing short of a miracle.

Just outside of the boarding house where she lived, Verity jumped at his order, spinning around and sending the pretty blue cape with the elaborate embroidery along the edges to fly out wide from her scant frame. Her green eyes looked up at him in the carriage, wide and terrorized.

Caught.

He'd caught her and she damn well knew it.

Her head started to shake, her eyes frantic, left and right, searching for escape. Searching for the hack she'd alighted from just the moment before.

No escape at the moment, little traitor.

Declan would have nothing of her trying to escape him and he jumped from the carriage, grabbing her upper arm before she could dart away. He picked her up, shoving her up and into his coach.

She landed with a thud in the far corner of the cushions and he climbed in after her, slamming the carriage door closed as Jack set the horses forward.

Setting his legs wide to devour all the space in the carriage, Declan sat on the rear cushion opposite her, his elbows on his thighs as he leaned forward, his glare skewering Verity.

Verity in some of the most expensive clothes to ever walk through the rookeries. Clothes that belonged in Mayfair. Not in the filth and despair of these streets. Not walking into a boarding house.

And absolutely not draped on a maid from a gaming hell.

Her hair—her thick red hair relaxed in a soft upsweep with a pert little blue hat at the crown of her head. It showed off her hair in the most glorious way—sinful, even for how he wanted to tear the pins out of it just to see the strands fall about her shoulders.

Sin and deceit. That was what was pinned under those strands.

The woman had been playing a game with him for far too long. *Years.*

It ended tonight.

Verity kept her eyes downcast, refusing to look up at him—a look she'd mastered over the years for he'd seen it thousands of times over. Look down. Look meek. No one questions.

But now he knew better.

She had been just smart enough not to run from him on the street. For if she had…he didn't even want to imagine what he'd do to her. But he suspected he would cross any and all invisible boundaries he lived his life by, and he would go too far.

Especially after what he saw today.

Ever since she'd spoken in her sleep in his office, he'd let her go freely about her business, not giving her any indication he'd thought any more on the matter.

But he had.

He'd become obsessed with it—her—actually. He'd followed Verity, observed her because of the odd compulsion that had latched into his mind with the hooks of a harpoon after hearing her voice. Hearing her *speak*.

Curiosity? Partly. Following a hunch? Mostly.

The first day he followed her everywhere at the Alabaster had been unremarkable. She took care of all the business of the place, from making sure the chambermaids cleaned all the upper rooms well enough, to making sure the hall boys had taken care of every shard of broken glass on the floor of the main gaming room from the previous night, to listening to what Cook was planning for the next evening and shaking her head yes and no until she was satisfied with the fare that was to be offered.

Truly, he had no idea she did so much at the Alabaster. That she commanded as much respect as she did.

All of that respect had vanished the second she stepped out of her room at the boarding house the next morning wearing those clothes. A rich woman's clothes.

He'd followed her.

Followed her to Harrow School. Waited outside, watched and listened from within the tree line as she walked with a boy from the school that was maybe thirteen, fourteen. She walked with him, and *talked* with him. Talked. Laughed. Smiled.

Talked.

Every second, his blood boiling hotter and hotter until he was stripping off his coat and cravat and nothing but rage was pumping through his veins.

What in Hades was her game?

None of it made sense. But she had been playing him, and Talen, and everyone at the Alabaster for the fool. Blatantly lying for the last two years.

To what end?

To steal? She would have moved herself into much nicer accommodations long ago if she'd been stealing from him.

To gain his trust? She'd certainly accomplished that more than a year ago. But she never did anything to that trust, other than solidify it, day after day after day.

To be a diligent little worker and never ask for anything? There wasn't the slightest reason for that—everyone wanted something more. Everyone.

So that left him with one option. She was a spy.

Probably for Bloodwater's crew, if he were to guess. Bloodwater had tried to move into their territory at crucial points during the last year, when they were most vulnerable—when Ness had come into Talen's life and he was preoccupied. When Talen had left. When their gaming hell by the London Docks had burned down.

Bloodwater had been salivating over their territory for years. With Talen scarce, the bastard was waiting for one little misstep to swoop in upon. Bloodwater underestimated Declan. Everyone did, because Declan was the levelheaded one, the kind one, the smiling one. Yet he was just as deadly as Talen and had the capacity to be just as brutal when it was called for.

Bloodwater would discover that if he kept pushing.

But it could be someone else that had sent her—a slippery snake in tall grass, waiting to strike, someone Declan hadn't even considered.

Whoever Verity was spying for, Declan was going to get it out of her, one way or another.

The carriage turned into the service lane behind the Alabaster and stopped at the rear entrance.

Declan opened the coach door and jumped out, then turned back to Verity cowering in the corner. "Get into the Alabaster, Verity."

She shook her head, her fingers clutching onto the edge of the cushion.

He ground out seething words through gritted teeth. "Get into the bloody building before I grab you by the neck and drag you in there."

She stilled, her mouth parting in a gasp.

Good. She should be scared witless at the moment.

Slow—too slow for him—she inched along the bench toward the carriage door. The second she was within reach, he grabbed her forearm and yanked her from the carriage, letting her drop to the ground. He dragged her, barreling in through the doorway, and headed straight for the dark staircase at the left—the one that was off-limits to most of the patrons of the Alabaster.

Gordan was manning the door and his eyebrows lifted when he saw who Declan was dragging behind him, but the man didn't say a word. He paid his men to be smart like that.

Of course, Gordan probably didn't even recognize Verity with her hair showing and dressed in fine clothes.

Declan could feel her body tugging away from his, stumbling on the stairs behind him as he stormed upward, but it only made his clamp on her arm more vicious.

Not until he got to his office did he release her, spinning her toward the settee as he turned to secure the door. "Sit."

She stuttered a few steps toward the settee, then sat, clutching the edge of it, her backside teetering on the front of the cushion. Ready to sprint the first chance she got.

He didn't bother to take a calming breath as he closed and locked the door, then spun around to advance on her. Not fast. Slow and stealthy, a predator set to catch. To kill.

"Who do you work for?"

Her eyebrows went high and she shook her head, true panic setting in. Her eyes started to gloss over, tears at the ready.

He fell for that two days ago. Not this time.

"You're not going to tell me?"

Her head still shook, tears slipping down her face.

He swallowed the last few steps to her with his long strides, his hand jutting out lightning quick, his fingers wrapping around her neck before she could try to dodge away.

He shoved her backward, his grip around her neck, pinning her to the back of the settee. "Don't make me hurt you. For I will get answers out of you one way or another. I saw—heard—you talking to that boy at that school. I *heard* you, you lying little wretch."

She gasped, her throat working against his palm. "You—you were at Harrow?" Words, rough and foreign, fell from her lips.

His hand snapped away from her neck, his breath leaving his chest. He hadn't imagined it. He'd seen— heard—everything at that school. Yet here, in his office, he'd never imagined it.

She could *talk*.

And the true disbelief that she was actually saying words—real words—hit him.

He jerked back, standing straight, his hands folding in and out of fists as he stared at her. "What the hell is your game?"

Her fingers fell to her sides, gripping the cushion as her eyes closed for a long second. Two. Three. Her eyelids opened and her gaze lifted to him, green irises meeting him straight on. "Fine. I can talk." Her voice rough, gravel over her tongue, she had to pause to cough. "I can talk."

He had to take a step back. Another. And another. Halfway across the room, for if he didn't, he wasn't sure what he might do to her.

"Good." He nodded with a sneer. "Now that we have that out of the way, there's one more matter. Not only do I know you can talk, I saw you in the hack on the way to Harrow School with the *Morning Chronicle* in your lap."

Her fingers twisted together atop her thighs. "I—I like the pictures. I like to look smart when I go to Harrow."

A low, rumbling, caustic laugh bubbled up from his chest. In the next instant, fury spun him away from her and he slammed his fist into the wall near his desk. Blood

dripping from his knuckles, he whipped back to her. "Stop fucking lying to me."

Shaking out his knuckles, he glared at her for a long moment, then rushed across the room and grabbed her arm. A yelp squeaked from her mouth, but he couldn't control his grip. He yanked her to her feet and dragged her over to his desk. "Look at this."

Her green eyes were fixed on him, flinching. "Wh-what?"

His hand wrapped around the back of her bare neck and he forced her head to look down at his desk. "I said, look at this."

As he had waited for her outside her boarding house, he'd had one of his errand boys passing in the street run to the Alabaster and have Thomas put this on his desk.

Her hands shaking, she clutched the edge of the desk as she nodded, her look focusing on his desk.

There, in the middle. One piece of paper on the expanse of the wide desk, the words scrawled big.

If you are reading this, you are a dead woman.

She gasped.

"Just as I bloody well thought. You can read as well." It took immense effort not to snap her neck then and there, but he stretched his fingers wide, releasing her. He took a step back, his arms crossing over his chest, his glare flaying her.

Her knuckles turned white as she gripped the edge of the desk, and it took her a long moment to lift her gaze to him. "What are you going to do to me?" The words scratchy, desperate.

"Who sent you?"

She exhaled, a pained look making her eyes crinkle. "I cannot tell you."

In those four words, verification of everything he suspected. She wasn't anything he thought she was. She'd played him the fool—for *years*.

Looking at her made him sick, but his glare refused to leave her face as he stalked a vicious step forward. "Then, frankly, Verity, I don't know what I'm going to do to you. But it won't be pretty. It won't feel good. And it won't be *silent*."

{ CHAPTER 7 }

Declan locked her into one of the upper rooms of the Alabaster.

A small mercy, for Verity was sure he was going to strangle her in his office. She would be dead and Ned would be without her. It was bound to happen one way or another—she just hadn't counted on it being so soon. Though, better Declan's fingers than a scratchy noose.

Instead, a stay of execution.

Verity glanced around the bedroom.

This was a room meant for liaisons with women the patrons of the Alabaster brought with them. She'd always admired that about Declan and Talen—that they didn't run a brothel above the gaming rooms. Didn't own even one brothel in their many businesses.

But the bedrooms were still available for patrons to use. And use them, they did. There was never a shortage of men and women trailing up the stairs, never a shortage of rooms that needed to be cleaned after they left.

In the last two years, she'd stumbled in upon a number of rooms that were supposed to be empty that were not, and that had been its own sort of education. Something she hadn't anticipated when she'd taken on this job.

Despite the elegant room with tasteful linens of a warm blue, Verity could barely take in her surroundings, instead, staring at the back of the door, the dark blue paint

on it gleaming to where she could see the shadow of her reflection in the light from the sconces and fireplace.

How long would she need to wait?

She stood three steps away from the door, listening. It had been five minutes since Declan had dragged her up here and locked her in.

Whether he had disappeared to concoct the ways in which he was about to torture her for information, or he had shoved her in here so that he didn't break and beat her, she wasn't sure.

Declan had a heart of gold for those with loyalty to him. For enemies, though, his heart lost all blood, all compassion. He could be brutal—she'd witnessed that on more than one occasion.

She wasn't planning on being present to find out what he had brewing for her.

She intended to be gone.

Not hearing a thing in the hallway, and only echoes of gruff grunts and a squeaking bed from down the hall, she slipped her right hand down along her walking dress, pulling up the muslin skirt and wool petticoat, and then she bent forward.

Her fingers moved up to her thigh where she always kept a dagger and a small coin purse strapped to her leg. Always ready to escape anything at a moment's notice. That lesson was learned long ago.

She freed the leather purse from the strap about her leg and opened it, pulling free the skeleton key she always kept on her person.

She'd had the Alabaster locksmith make her a skeleton key a year ago when he had come to fix one of the doors. She'd merely had to show him the heavy keyring she had to carry around to get in and out of all the rooms, and he took pity on her, delivering her a skeleton key that opened every lock in the place the next day.

She was getting out of here before Declan killed her.

Not that she was convinced he would actually do so, but she'd betrayed his trust, full and through. For a man like Declan, loyalty was everything...she couldn't take death by torture off the list of options he had for her.

She had to escape and she had to disappear—somehow—before he discovered she was missing.

Ned was the most important thing now—she would get him first. Except, no. Her room. She had to get to the boarding house first to grab whatever money she had hidden in the wall. It had to be enough. It *had* to—there was no other choice.

Money. Harrow School. Then a ship. A ship to anywhere that wasn't here. She could start from nothing once more. People always needed their chamber pots emptied, no matter what part of the world she and Ned ended up in. She would do that—empty chamber pots until the end of her days if it meant that her brother was safe and taken care of.

She moved toward the door, her ears straining for the slightest creak in the boards of the hallway. Silence.

Slipping the skeleton key into the lock, she held her breath.

Clink.

She turned the knob, cracking the door open just a slice so she could peek into the hallway. Empty.

Opening the door farther, she slid into the hallway on her toes, each step as silent as possible. She paused to relock the door from the outside, then skirted along the side of the corridor where the wood didn't squeak underfoot.

Down the servants' stairs and she made it out into the night through a side door that opened into an alley between the Alabaster and the decrepit brick building next to it.

It wasn't until she was a street away that she dared to heave a breath.

Her feet fast, she sped toward the boarding house and was up and in her room within minutes. Several people she knew saw her along the way, but hopefully in her current dress and the dark shadows she'd managed to stay in, they didn't recognize her. Nor would they think to tell Declan about it. At least not until tomorrow.

And by tomorrow, with any pitiful grace fate managed to toss her way, she and Ned would be long gone.

Pulling back the stained and faded fleur-de-lis paper-hanging, her fingernails dug into the edge of the vertical board slightly askew behind it, and she yanked at the wood. The plank bent, just enough to get her hand behind it, and she slithered her arm into the wall until she found the small leather purse she'd hidden in there a year ago.

Every extra penny, every extra coin made it into this purse.

She pulled it free, then pushed the plank of wood back in place and smoothed the paper-hanging over the wood.

Lifting her skirts high, she removed the small satchel clasped to her thigh, emptied the contents of the purse into it, then reattached it to the leather strap about her leg.

One quick look around her room and her eyes landed on her black maid's dress and white apron.

Were her chances of escape better in that dress or in her current dress?

In her current dress and cloak, she was a target, at least until she made it out of the rookeries. No one bothered to rob maids. Maids were everywhere—in and out of every fine home in the city. In and out of the rookeries visiting family. Maids were everywhere. Always.

Blend in—always blend in. Wasn't that what Hector had taught her?

Time she didn't have to spare, but she needed to change.

She quickly stripped out of her cerulean walking dress and shrugged her limbs into her black service dress. Gathering her hair as tightly as she could without braiding it, she secured it with pins and then stuffed most of it under her black cap.

But she couldn't leave her cloak—the one her mother had helped her embroider so very long ago—so she turned it inside out, the black satin lining facing outward having to suffice.

Then she disappeared into the night.

{ CHAPTER 8 }

Declan knew she had a key.

Knew she would escape.

Knew she would lead him directly to the person she worked for.

But this…this he hadn't expected.

He had thought she would run straight to whoever had hired her to spy on him.

His mouth pulling tight, he squinted in the low light flickering from the lamps atop the brick pillars that flanked the end of the main drive into Harrow School.

Verity waved off the hack driver as she stepped down from the old carriage that had been repurposed into a hack. The driver tipped his hat and sent his horses onward.

Back in her black maid's uniform—including the white apron making her look like she was on her way to work—she stood by the tall right pillar at the entrance to the grounds, watching the hack until it disappeared down the street before turning to the lane that led up to Harrow School.

She was after the boy. Collecting him.

Which meant she was running.

She'd been discovered and now she was looking to escape, for she wasn't safe.

His jaw ticked back and forth, his gaze looked on her shadowy form.

Which meant one of two things. She meant to escape him. Or she meant to escape whoever had hired her to infiltrate his business and his life.

Or both.

The rage that had boiled in his marrow since he'd tossed Verity into that room at the Alabaster quieted, if only slightly.

She was scared and she was running.

Not so fast, little imposter.

After two years of lying directly to his face every waking hour, she couldn't run until he said she could.

He slammed his fist onto the ceiling of his carriage. "I'll need your help with this, Jack."

"Aye, sir." The coach shifted as Jack moved from his driver's perch, and Declan opened the carriage door, joining his driver aside his black coach still a good distance away from the entrance to the school.

Declan held out a black sack to his driver. "I'll grab her and you drag this sack over her head as quickly as possible."

Jack's lips pursed for one second. "Is this necessary, sir?"

Declan tore his gaze away from Verity as she started walking up the long drive to glare at Jack. "It is to scare her. Which *is* necessary at this juncture." He looked back to Verity. "And not a word of this to anyone—anyone—do you understand me?"

Jack took the sack from his hand. "Aye."

With his stare trained on Verity, Declan jumped onto the grassy bank that rolled into the brick fence that marked the grounds of the school.

Verity's strides were brisk, purposeful, but it did nothing to speed her away from them. Silently, the two men slipped through the darkness up along the drive and were upon Verity in no time.

The last ten steps to her, Declan ran, surprise on his side, his body in full force as he wrapped his arms around her from behind and locked her hands to her sides as he picked her up.

Jack was right behind him, slipping the hood over Verity's head before she could even scream.

And he knew she could scream.

She struggled against his iron grip for only a minute before she realized the futility of it, and stilled as he carried her down the drive and to his carriage.

She was light. Far too easy to manhandle.

Jack opened the coach door, and Declan stepped up into, stretching his legs wide and sitting down on the bench, Verity still locked within his arms. The smallest bit of her backside caught the bench between his legs.

He wasn't about to let her go—give her the slightest chance to escape—until he had her back at the Alabaster.

Jack set the carriage in motion and they weren't even a third of the way back to the Alabaster when Declan realized the folly of holding her like this.

Even with as still and stiff as she was, her body swayed with the rocking of the carriage, her backside rubbing along him. Enough to make his damn cock wake up and twitch with excitement.

Aware—too aware of her body.

Her *treacherous* little body.

He'd been too damn aware of her since he'd seen her red hair spilling out of her cap in his office the other night. Too damn aware of how delicate her features were. Too damn aware of how full her lips curved.

It was in that moment that something clicked in his brain, and he realized, both in his mind as well as his body, that Verity wasn't just a maid, a keeper of the Alabaster.

She was an actual woman.

She'd taken great pains to paint herself into the backdrop of the Alabaster during the years. Never drawing attention. Doing everything that was asked of her. Keeping secrets of the patrons. She'd become part of the building, an organ in the machinery that kept his empire running. No one looked at her too long or asked any questions of her. Just as she'd designed it.

His left arm was locked across her body, just under her breasts, and it struck him that she actually had breasts— breasts that were straining against the black fabric of her maid's dress more so than he'd ever seen. A weight to them, pressing down on his arm, that was hard to miss.

She'd never had breasts before. In fact, if someone had asked him about her endowments, he would have said she was a board, rectangular, no curves to her at all. Earlier in the day, her body had mostly been hidden under the blue cloak so he hadn't been able to see her shape.

Bloody hell, had she been lying about this too? Binding her chest this entire time?

For her breasts heavy against his arm and her butt pressed against his cock was telling him a very different story about her curves. A very different story than the mute maid he'd come to depend upon had ever given him.

His cock took on the title of the newest traitor, twitching hard again as the coach hit a rut and her body ground against his.

It didn't matter. She was a bloody phony. A liar.

An enemy.

And he picked his enemies apart, piece by excruciating piece.

The ride only grew more excruciating to his shaft, Jack hitting every rut that had ever existed on these scarred streets, and by the time they were back at the Alabaster, Declan couldn't wait to release her. To get a step—or five—away from her.

But not yet. His arms still locked around her, he carried her up to the room he'd locked her in earlier, dropping her down on the bed.

The entire ride, she hadn't tried to escape, hadn't said a word.

Plotting, most likely.

Taking three steps away from the bed, Declan took a moment to drag a breath into his lungs that wasn't filled with the scent of her hair—lemons—the damn lemon scent he'd sometimes catch wafting in the corridors of the Alabaster.

She sat on the edge of the bed, a stone statue, hood still over her head. Peculiar that she hadn't tried to remove it— her hands weren't bound. Her fingers were entwined, her hands on her lap, motionless. Terrified? Or smart—don't fight against something you know nothing of?

One step forward and he reached out and dragged the hood off her head.

Her black cap tumbled off her head with the hood and locks of her red hair fell down past her shoulders with loose pins dangling from the strands. Several chunks of hair landed across her face and she blinked, blinked again, then pushed the annoyance out of her eyes.

Her look found him and her jaw dropped with an exhale. A relieved exhale.

So she *was* running from someone scarier than him.

"You didn't think you'd get away so easily, did you?" He clasped his arms across his chest, his glare on her meant to intimidate.

Her eyes closed, her head shaking. "You let me escape?" A rasping scratch still hung in her voice. "You let me escape so you could follow me?"

Astute. He nodded. "Where's the key?"

She looked up at him, her eyes going to slits.

"I know you have a skeleton key. I know that's how you got out of here. Where is it?"

Her shoulders lifted.

The casual motion of it sent a spike of fury down his spine and he closed the space between them, jamming his knuckles down onto the bed on either side of her thighs, his face only a breath away from hers. "I will strip you down until you are bare naked to find that key if I need to."

She leaned back, her body trying to avoid him even as she held his stare. "It's in the purse strapped to my leg. If you would be so kind as to move, I will fetch it for you."

He shook his head. "I don't think so. For I'm guessing you mean it's tucked in along next to that dagger I felt strapped to your thigh. I trust you not even a sliver, so forgive me if I'm not about to let you pull a blade on me."

He dropped down to balance on his heels and he caught her right calf with his left hand before she could scurry across the bed away from him.

At his hands on her leg, she froze, her fingers digging into the blue velvet coverlet on the bed.

His left hand clamped hard around the slim part of her calf, holding her in place. He looked up, watching her, waiting for her to make a move as his right hand slithered up along her leg. Stockings. Ties just above the knee. Skin.

Damn. Smooth bare skin. Her inner thigh.

Farther up.

There. Leather strapped about her leg.

He plucked the leather bag from the strap, then grabbed the dagger in the sheath on the outside of her leg.

She glared at him, her green eyes simmering, defiant, like he was taking away a piece of her soul.

He pulled his hand out from under her skirts slowly, the back of his knuckles dragging against her thigh. Unnecessary, but he couldn't quite stop his hand from brushing against her.

At the touch, her bottom lip dropped, air wisping into her mouth. Her very full bottom lip, swollen as though she'd been gnawing at it for the last hour.

He released her calf and looked down at the dagger. Carved into a black onyx handle were bones. Bones connected, one after another, moving along the handle in a

spiral until the shapes bled onto the silver blade, the bones etched into the metal all the way to the tip. He'd never seen anything like it. He tucked the blade into the side of his boot.

Standing, he pulled the cord to open up the pouch. Coins. There. The key.

He plucked the silver skeleton key out of the bag.

She reached out for it. "No. You cannot—you cannot take my money. I need it."

He jerked it out of her grasp and he motioned around him. "Not here, you don't."

"No—I earned it—I need it."

His eyebrows slanted inward, challenging her. "For what?"

Her mouth clamped shut, her green eyes flipping from pleading to defiant in an instant.

"You can have your purse back once you tell me exactly what I need to know."

"I cannot tell you anything, for I don't know anything."

He barked out a hard, abrasive chuckle that shook his chest. "Don't insult me, Verity." He took a step closer. "You will tell me who you work for, exactly what you're doing here, and exactly what information you've gathered."

Her mouth slammed closed and her eyes dropped, staring at the floor.

"No answer?"

Silence.

He took another step forward, looming over her, his words seeping with disdain. "You think I won't hurt you? You think wrong. Any trust that I had in you is gone—

never to come back. At the moment, you are a liability to me—nothing more. I will spill your blood without thought or remorse."

Silence.

Silence that stretched onward.

He grunted. "You seem ready to bleed, but are you ready for me to strip you down and let my men take turns with you? Would that make you turn? You've done an admirable job of covering every asset you own for the last two years, but now I can see every last inch of it." He reached down, grabbing a lock of her hair and twisting it through his fingertips. "I see everything you've tried to hide."

She looked up at him, the glare in her eyes making her green irises come alive, like a field of spring whey twisting in a storm. Yet her lips remained a stubborn line across her face.

Cursed woman.

He'd never do it—let anyone touch her without her approval—there were some lines he wasn't willing to cross when meting out justice. But he hoped the threat might nudge her in the right direction—to be more agreeable.

Yet, nothing.

Her body and what it suffered in order to keep her secrets was of no concern to her.

So what was?

A smile curled onto his face as he looked down at her, his fingers still entwined in her hair. "Who was the boy at Harrow?"

She jerked her head back, slapping his hand away from her hair. "No one."

This was the spot to dig in and scratch. Scratch until the spot was bloody and words flowed from her—every last secret she was keeping in that wicked brain.

He clasped his hands behind his back. "Verity, you know no one in London other than the people you've worked with here at the Alabaster. You live alone. Don't tell me the boy is no one."

"He is no one."

"Then you won't mind if I go visit the school tomorrow? I did get a good look at him, so he shouldn't be too hard to identify. About this tall." His hand motioned at the height of his mid-chest. "Sandy blond hair. Skin and bones. I'm sure I could identify him."

She jumped to her feet in the sliver of space in front of him, her hands curled into fists, but she didn't come at him. "You cannot—you cannot approach him."

"I can do whatever I damn well please. And I'll do whatever I damn well please to the boy if I don't get answers from you." He moved toward the door.

She looked ready to charge him, her words seething. "Don't make me hate you, Declan."

He paused, his head tilting to the side as he looked her up and down. "Don't make me kill you, Verity."

Her chest lifted in a ragged gasp she tried to hide, her mouth twisting to a hard line.

"Guards are outside the room. Don't even think about escaping again."

He left her to stew in her lies.

She would tell him what he needed to know.
One way or another.

{ Chapter 9 }

Two days.

Two days he kept her in that room.

Threatening her—railing at her—every time he brought food into the room. And he was the only one to come and go from the room. Food and coal in. Chamber pot out. That was it.

He wasn't going to let her go.

But never once did he lay a hand on her. Not like he threatened to do.

He didn't leave the Alabaster long enough to go to Ned's school—not that he couldn't have sent one of his men for the job. But he hadn't mentioned her brother again, which meant Ned was safe—for the moment.

She was walking a fine line with Declan, and she could tell he was at the end of his patience with her.

Threats were about to become reality.

For the odd code of honor that she knew Declan lived under—don't hurt women, children—she could see that he was about to break that code.

She'd held her silence as she'd held onto that hope—that his instinct was to not hurt her.

But it was clear he wasn't going to release her—wasn't going to let her go anywhere. And things were only going to get worse for her locked in this room at the Alabaster.

Declan wasn't going to hurt her, but he had plenty of men that would do the job.

It was an impasse she couldn't live with—couldn't live beyond—if she let it continue.

She would just have to set her faith in that honor that she'd always recognized in Declan. Honor that had no right to exist in a cold ruler of the rookeries.

The key clinked into the lock of the door and Verity jumped to her feet, leaving the wingback chair by the fireplace. She swiped her fingers across her eyes, tucked a few loose strands of her hair under her black cap, then smoothed down the front of her black dress.

She was still in her maid's clothes—no one would care if her dress was wrinkled and rumpled, but the habit from her youth of smoothing her clothing had never quite disappeared during the last two years.

Balancing dinner and a tea pot on a silver platter atop his left forearm, Declan moved into the room, then turned to close and lock the door with his right hand.

"Take that cap off." He gave her one quick glance before moving to the small round rosewood table by the window and setting the tray down.

Her hand went up to the cap, feeling the thick of her hair underneath the thin black fabric. "No. Why?" She always had it covered. She *needed* it covered.

"Why?" He shot her a look over his shoulder as he removed the dinner plate and fresh tea, then gathered the dirty plate and cup from earlier in the day onto the tray. "Because you're not a maid at the Alabaster anymore. You're keeping up a pretense that has nothing to do with the reality of who you are and it is grating on my nerves."

She puffed out a breath, not ready for his instant ire. Not when she was finally ready to tell him what she could.

Not that he knew her intention.

"I am ready."

His hands paused and he turned around to her. "Ready for what?" His finger flicked up to point at her head. "And I said to take that blasted thing off your head."

He was in no mood to listen to her, yet she had to make him. Her fingers twitched. It was just a simple cap.

She reached up, dragging the black cap off her head. Her fingers dug into her head, scratching at the hair that had been matted to her head under the cap, suddenly anxious about how her hair must look. A mess of a nest— she hadn't properly combed it in days.

His arms folded over his chest and he leaned back against the edge of the table, studying the top of her head for a long moment. Too long.

She really must look a disaster.

Her fingers went into the thick of her hair, trying to smooth and straighten all the errant locks that couldn't be wrangled. "I need to tell you things."

He nodded, slow, his eyes eating into her, dissecting every word she uttered.

Not that she could blame him. It was odd enough for her to talk in front of him—it must be even more disorientating for him to hear her speak.

"You are ready to talk?"

"I am."

"What exactly, do you think you need to tell me?"

"The truth."

He scoffed a chuckle. "You think I'm going to believe a word that comes out of your mouth?"

Ire set into the breath she seethed inward. "Why have you been demanding the truth from me if you didn't want it? When you never intended to actually listen to it?"

His hand flipped up from his elbow and he gestured with his fingers toward her. "Speak then. I'm waiting."

Her hands clasped in front of her belly, the knuckle of her thumb pressing into her bottom right rib. "Before I tell you…I need assurances. You cannot breathe a word of this to anyone."

His right eyebrow cocked. "You're not in the position to be making demands."

"No. No, I'm not." The words came out defeated and her look dropped to the floor between them. If she told him this, then she would be at his mercy, her life held dangling from a thread he could clip at any instant.

"Tell me. Then I'll decide if I can keep my mouth shut."

She looked up at him. At his black hair and grey eyes, as though the rainbow had hidden the day he was born. She'd always liked that about him. His lack of color. Color tended to draw attention to the fanciful, the foppery, when it truly only existed to conceal ugly truths beneath.

But not Declan. He was forthright—there was no guessing with him. No games she didn't know how to play. No innuendos or second-guessing or tiptoeing around him. He thought what he thought and to hell with anyone that didn't agree with him. To hell with trying to hide anything.

His partner, Talen Blackstone, had always set her on edge—danger oozed from his pores. Declan, by contrast, was easier—just as deadly—but he was always one to watch, wait, listen. Study everything around him before he made a move.

Talen had been absent for months from the business and the Alabaster, his life taking a new turn, and the weight of all they had built together had been heavy on Declan's shoulders. She'd watched Declan, day after day, his shoulders drooping more than usual, the dark circles under his eyes etching permanence. He was bearing the heft of their entire empire on his back, and she was currently doing nothing but adding to that weight.

Yet in this room, Declan looked so big, as if he was about to snap the table behind him in two just by leaning on it. He stood so casually, like this was all sport to him. Maybe it was. He didn't know anything of her life, and she'd never imagined she would be in the position where she would have to trust him with her secrets.

But she had to chance this.

She cleared her throat, her spine going straight and she met his stare. "I was hired. Hired to protect you."

He coughed out a laugh. "What?"

"I was hired to protect you." She lifted her hand to him to stop him before his laughter interrupted her again. "I know. It is silly. Me. Half your size. But I was hired to protect you. To be the eyes in the back of your head."

His fingers curled in front of his mouth to hide his laughter. "Let me make sure I'm understanding this correctly—you were hired to protect me and that is how you ended up at the Alabaster two years ago? It wasn't because you needed a job? It was to protect me?"

"Yes. And my job as a maid was part of the plan. I would always be close, always be available. No one notices a maid."

He stilled, his look running up and down her body. "Especially not one completely in black from head to toe, with not a wisp of your hair showing. Nothing of your body showing."

"That was by design, yes." She nodded. "Any undue attention and I cannot perform my job."

His head shook and he looked to the ceiling for a long moment, then shrugged to himself and pinned his gaze on her. "Let us presume, for a short—very short—second, that I am considering believing you. What of your muteness? You didn't say a word to me—to anyone—in two damn years."

She sighed. Here was the crux of it. The lie that clearly ate away at him more than anything. "No. No, I did not."

His eyes narrowed at her, his words pointed. "No, you did not."

"Did you pay less attention to me because I didn't talk? Did everyone pay less attention to me? Did I seem weak? Unthreatening? Did I appear like I would never spill any of the secrets of the Alabaster, because I couldn't? Couldn't talk, couldn't write? Do most, maybe you even, think I am addled—dumb?"

His mouth pulled to a thin line, his words seething. "I think you are the furthest thing from dumb at the moment."

"But you did. And I did my job well. A job I no longer have. But yes, I can talk. Yes, I can read and write."

His head tilted back, his glare still slicing her in two. "I'm still having a hard time listening to you now, Verity. I'm having a hard time not flipping over that bed expecting to find someone else talking and you just miming the words."

Her shoulders lifted as her lips pursed. "It is what it is. You know the truth of me now."

His grey eyes narrowed at her. "No, what I know is that this is a tale, and a wild tale at that. One with little merit at its core, as I don't need to be protected. Never did."

She scoffed an exhale. "Believe me. You do."

Both of his eyebrows lifted.

"Truly, have I spilled any secrets of the Alabaster or any of your other businesses? Think of all I've been privy to. I have access to your office, to Talen's office, any time I want. And have I imploded the Alabaster? Have I taken down any of your other establishments? I've been here more than two years and none of that has happened. Do you think if someone that wants to see you toppled sent me here on that mission, it wouldn't have happened already? For the things I know, I could have taken down this place and its patrons a hundred times over. I could have taken down you. Taken down Talen." Her voice steeled, her gaze digging into his glare. "But nothing has happened. Nothing. Nothing because I am not here to cause your fall. I'm here to keep you upright."

His stare probed into her, the storm clouds in his eyes that had been rumbling with wicked thunder minutes ago now parting, calming.

His hand flicked up into the air. "Fine, then who in the hell hired you to come in here?"

"Honestly, I don't know. All I know is that my employer was hired to provide protection for you. He hired me for the job. I don't know who hired him—who it is that knows you and wants to keep you safe. All I know is that it isn't an inexpensive prospect to hire our firm."

He stood straight, taking a step toward her. "Then who is your employer?"

Her mouth snapped shut, teeth banging teeth as her arms folded over her middle. "I cannot tell you that. For what we do, too many lives are at stake, and I cannot risk them. You aren't the only one protected by us."

A demented chuckle rumbled through his throat. "No. Of course not. Of course you cannot tell me." He took another step forward, his stare stalking her. "Which is where the folly in this whole story lies. Who in their right mind would hire *you* to protect me?"

She held in a sigh. He saw her as weak, incapable. That was the persona that she had cultivated for the last two years, so why not?

She met his stare. "Someone that noticed my skill with a blade and saw that I don't blink when death is upon me. Someone who was willing to train me to be a protector."

"Why in the world do you think I would believe this dung heap of lies?"

"Why would I bother to concoct this ridiculous story, of all things?" Her hands flew up at her sides. "If I truly wanted to lie to you, I would have at least attempted to manifest a story that was plausible. That I was scared to talk to anyone, so I pretended to be mute. That some other titan of the underworld really did send me—that would make the most sense, wouldn't it? If Bloodwater sent me? And then you would let me go and I could just disappear into the night never to be seen of again. But those would be lies. And the truth is the truth. The truth is what you wanted. The truth is what I'm telling you."

He shook his head.

She unthreaded her arms, letting them hang at her sides and her chin tilted up. "Come at me. Charge me."

{ CHAPTER 10 }

"What?"

"Come at me. Try and pin me down."

She thought Declan would pause, try to talk her out of it, but he charged, a bull let out of a pen.

He was to her in two strides, and she ducked just below his arm as it swung to trap her against her chest and fling her back onto the bed. She rolled on the floor, springing up onto her feet behind him before he spun around.

He came at her again and she scooted backward. Just as he trapped her in a corner, she slid her right calf out and around his legs, yanking in with her heel on the back of his knee. His weight unhinged, he shifted forward and had to catch himself on the wall as she slipped out past him.

Skirting by the desk, she picked up the quill that was lying atop and raced to the other side of the room. Fast, but not fast enough. He caught her right wrist and her body swung out wide, slamming into the wall.

In an instant, he pinned her hand up high against the wall and his right fingers wrapped around her neck, shoving her body against the wainscoting.

The opening she needed.

She swung her left hand up, pressing the sharp tip of the quill into the soft flesh in the middle of his throat.

Not enough to draw blood. But close.

He stilled.

Her head pinned in place by his hand on her throat, she looked up at him the best she could for his height over her, their air mingling in heaving breaths, their eyes locked.

The grey in his eyes was alive, sparking in a way she'd never seen it, little bursts of silver exploding, making them shine.

Her heartbeat galloped out of control, even as one word echoed in her mind.

Settle.

Settle.

Settle.

The one word drilled into her every day by Hector. The one thing he needed her to do when she was in the midst of danger.

Settle.

Settled minds made the right decisions. Settled minds came out alive.

Except she wasn't in danger. She knew that in her bones. Declan was never going to hurt her. Her heartbeat wasn't out of control because she knew death was looming.

Too close. She was too close to him.

Too *intimately* close to him.

This was something she didn't admit to anyone. Not to Hector. Not to Jack. And above everyone else, not to herself.

She liked Declan. Not as an employer. Not as a job for her to do. She liked the *man*. A little too much. Liked watching him. Liked listening to him. Liked when he would spar with the rough young boys at the corner and make them laugh and they would look at him like he was

an Olympian god come to walk the streets. Liked staring at
his mouth when he didn't know she was in the room, which
was most of the time. Liked him late at night after the
gaming had ended and there was a dark shadow of stubble
across his jawline. Liked his eyes. Liked his eyes the best,
how astute they were, holding worlds of wonder in them.

Settle.

He was a job. That was it. That was all he could ever
be.

Words squeaked out through the tightness around her
neck, his grip iron, but not painful. "I don't know if you
would kill me before I kill you, but I'd have a solid chance
on it."

He blinked, his head shaking slightly as though he'd
been sucked into a trance, and his fingers around her throat
eased, his hand dropping away from her neck. "That was
efficient, I give you that."

He took a step backward but realized he still had her
arm clamped high above her head. He shook his fingers free
from her wrist. Clearing his throat, he turned half away,
staring at the table with the now-cold food on it for three
full seconds. His head turned, his gaze finding her. "So, let
us pretend, for one moment, your story is the truth."

"Yes, let us pretend the truth is the truth."

His eyebrow lifted. Not expecting sarcasm from her,
then.

"While you are fast and I can imagine a blade doing
well in your hand, you are not around me all the time. That
seems like an oversight if you truly think you're protecting
me."

Her head clunked back against the wall with a sigh. She didn't want to tell him this—couldn't tell him this, but her mouth opened just the same. "There is another that is in place just like me."

"What? Who?"

She shook her head. "I cannot tell you."

"We are back to more secrets? Just when I was thinking I might believe you."

Her lips pursed. "I cannot tell you. But if you think—truly think on it—besides me, who is the other person almost always lurking about, always five steps behind you if I am not?"

His look shifted off of her to the fire. Thinking. Thinking.

His eyes widened and his gaze flashed to her. "Jack."

She held the countenance of her face neutral. "I am neither denying nor confirming it. But let me say, you can never—ever—let it be known that you suspect anything of anyone here."

His hand ran through his dark hair, his head shaking. "Why not? Why do I not clear out the whole lot of you?"

"Because we've saved your life more times than you'd care to know about."

"You what?"

"Saved your life. The skirmish at the docks a year and a half ago—how many men had surrounded you?"

"I don't know, it was dark."

"Think."

"Five—maybe six."

"Eight."

"Eight? No."

"They were two deep on the wharf side—you think you took them all down yourself?"

"I…it was a blur. And dark." His words hesitant, as though he was remembering that scene differently than he ever had.

She took a step away from the wall, setting her feet directly in front of him. "You're deadly, Declan. I am well aware of that. As are the men that have been sent to attack you. And they cannot figure out why it is never enough— never enough men trying to take you down in a dark alley." Her gaze set hard onto his, for she needed him to understand this. "You are deadly—I trust in that—trust that you can handle far more than a normal amount of danger. But when it is too much, when a blade slips unexpectedly, when there are more cutthroats than one man should rightly be able to handle, I—we—are at the periphery."

His lips pulled into a tight line. "That was why you were in the alley the other night?"

"We don't let you walk down alleyways alone. Even though you have a penchant for it. It has turned out poorly more times than it should."

He exhaled a long sigh with a slight shake of his head.

She took a step forward, wanting to reach out and grab his arm, but she kept her hands locked to her sides. "I know I am done here, will never be allowed near you again, but before that happens, you need to know something."

"What?"

"Someone is after you—truly after your demise. It isn't random—it isn't you being in the wrong place at the

wrong time. There have been too many attacks over the last month."

"I've only been in two street skirmishes as of late."

"There were three other incidents that happened that never got to you. One in the mews behind your house. Two others in alleyways. Jack or I stopped them. Someone wants you dead and we don't know who it is. The threat is specific and direct. I had hoped to grab that one man you felled the other night in the alleyway and have him interrogated for information. But then…"

His gaze drifted to the side. "But then you were knocked into darkness."

She nodded. "That was my best chance for information and I failed."

He looked back to her. "I'm alive. It seems you didn't completely fail."

Her right cheek lifted in a half smile. "I am out of a job, so yes, I did fail."

He stared at her for a long breath, his grey eyes cut off to her where she couldn't tell what he was thinking.

Then he suddenly jerked backward, stepping away from her and toward the door. "You're staying in here."

Before she could answer, he opened the door and walked out.

The key setting the lock in place.

{ CHAPTER 11 }

Betrayed.

Aside from Talen, the two people he trusted most were lies.

Lies from the very first day they'd stepped into his life, and he'd never suspected a thing.

Sitting in his office, Declan stared at the amber liquid in his tumbler, the light of the fire reflecting sparks through the brandy.

Bloody poor ruler of the underground he was turning out to be.

Everything he'd built with Talen at risk—at risk this whole time.

And he still had a thousand questions—questions in a limitless barrel that he hadn't even started to truly probe into. What was this ridiculous protection firm Verity worked for? Clearly outside the law and clearly with ample amounts of money flowing into it. It would have to be, to be paying two spies to be watching over him for the last two years.

Who would pay for that? And why? Who would want to keep him alive so badly that they would go to such extremes?

Talen wanted him alive—but Talen also would never betray him like that. Talen would be loud and obnoxious and needling about setting guards around Declan for his

own good. And then Declan would instantly fire said guards.

This wasn't by Talen's hand, so then, who? There was no one. He had no family, no close friends aside from Talen.

It had to be someone who knew death was coming for him, which, according to the lying minx in the room above his office, was imminent.

Verity's footsteps echoed downward through the floorboards. She'd been pacing the entire last hour since he'd left her in the room.

Truly, she'd been pacing off and on during the last two days. A wildcat trapped in a cage. Not the fragile little finch he'd always thought her.

A little finch that turned out to have talons able to rip him to shreds.

His eyes closed as he lifted the tumbler to his lips and took a slow swallow.

Her damn red hair.

He couldn't think of anything else. One image every time he closed his eyes for too many damn days now. Her blasted red hair, the color so rich and moody and slipping into dark depths, he could think of little else other than sinking his hands into it.

How had he not known?

Never bothered to look at who she truly was?

Because she'd painted herself not to be seen.

So he hadn't looked.

Duped. Betrayed. And he'd gone along willingly, trusting too easily. Talen had always said that about him. He trusted too easily.

Yet Talen had been gulled by her just the same. His partner regarded Verity with just as much respect as Declan did—had.

Had respected.

Didn't currently respect.

Except for her unnerving knack for escaping his grasp, as she did an hour ago in that bedroom. That, he had to respect. She was quick and agile and slippery. And her hands held admirable skill with how quickly she had the spear of that quill at his neck.

But that was it.

Except that she wasn't willing to set others in danger when he demanded to know who her employer was. There was integrity in that. He respected integrity.

But that was it.

Except for the look in her eyes when he had her pinned to the wall. When had the green of her irises become so vibrant, like spring had exploded in her eyes? When had her lashes turned so dark, framing those eyes as she looked up at him, challenging?

Her eyes…her eyes were nice. Unsettling. Just like her hair. But warm. Genuine.

He shook his head, taking another swallow of the brandy. He damn well respected beauty when it was in front of him.

But that was it.

Other than those few things, she was dead to him. She could go back to her employer and if he never saw her again, he would be a happy man.

Except that he still needed her.

Apparently, she knew more about the threats on his life than he did, and it would be stupid to not use her to help root out the person behind the threats.

Downing the rest of his brandy, Declan stood, ready to face her traitorous face once more.

Minutes later, he opened the door to her chamber without knocking and he found her standing in the middle of the room by the foot of the bed, her hands at her sides curled, like she was ready to dart past him out into the hallway.

He stepped fully into the room, closing the door behind him.

"What do you think to do with me?" She blurted the words out before he could set his look on her.

He paused, taking her in for three long breaths. She'd pulled the pins from her hair at some point to let the waves fall downward, and then weaved her thick hair into a braid that hung down her back. Her green eyes held barely concealed panic.

Still trying to hide herself.

He took one more step toward her, stopping an arm's length away. "I think to use you."

"Use me?" Her head snapped back. "For what?"

"You are going to help me discover who is trying to harm me. You said it is specific, direct."

"It is."

"Then you're going to help me."

"I—"

"You know everything about me, Verity. And I—apparently—know nothing about you. But I find I am

in need of you, at least for the time being. So I have a
proposition."

"What do you propose?"

"You get to keep your job here. I don't breathe a word
of this to Jack. I don't keep you locked up in here."

"And in return?"

"In return, you help me find out who wants me dead."

"I can do that." Hope flashed in her eyes. She thought
she could keep the farce of her business here intact without
consequence.

He wasn't about to gift her with that.

He held his hand up. "Before you get excited, this will
involve a trade—a course correction, so to speak. I don't
trust you, so I will need something of value from you that I
can trust."

"What do you want?"

"I need a secret from you."

Her jaw dropped, fear instant in her eyes. Of course,
she had secrets. Lots of them. He already knew that. Her
eyes alone, now that they had lifted to look directly at him,
told him she had layers and layers and layers of secrets. And
he planned on peeling them away from her one at a time.

Her lips pulled inward for long second. "A secret? What
is it you want to know?"

"Who is the boy at Harrow?"

Her head shook. "No."

"Yes." His arms clasped over his chest. "That is the
trade. You want me to trust you, I need to know something
real about you. Something you hold very dear to you. And
it was clear you hold that boy dear to you."

"I…" Her voice trailed off, her look dipping to the corner of the room.

Declan waited. Silent. Her options were limited at this point, she had to recognize that.

It took longer than he expected, her defiance. Her choices were, at most, one, and they both knew it.

Her green eyes finally lifted to him, her voice small. "He is my brother."

"Your brother? Where are your parents?"

Her eyes flickered into alarm for half of a second. A look he would have missed if he wasn't watching her so closely.

"Dead."

"Do you have other family?"

"No."

"Is Verity Jones even your true name?"

"Verity is."

Short answers. Which meant more secrets, just as suspected.

Secrets he would squeeze from her when she was at her most vulnerable.

He just had to be patient.

{ CHAPTER 12 }

Her boot sank into a puddle and Verity grimaced, lifting her foot as silently as she could.

The leather of her boots was already soaked and now the muck of the mud would make them even harder to dry out.

This was stupid.

The best way to avoid danger was to not be in it in the first place.

Not seek it out, night after night, dark alley after dark alley.

Four nights out and no attacks.

Jack had been in their vicinity each of the past four nights, and there hadn't been the slightest whiff of any danger around Declan, even though he was visiting some of the most wretched corners of the rookeries.

It had been awkward for her, watching Jack machinate reasons to be out on the streets with Declan. He had no clue Declan knew about him, and Verity couldn't very well tell him.

She couldn't talk to him at all, for that matter, as she was well immersed back into her mute maid façade.

Jack was one of Hector's best guardians—strong and cunning and actually quite handsome when he didn't have coal dust covering most of his face. His teeth were white and straight and they gave him away as much more than a coach driver if one was to look close enough.

Good thing people didn't study the laborers around them.

Jack was the exact type of man she would have fantasized about when she was young and naïve. For now, Jack's job required him to be dirty. Unkempt. Goofy. That was the part he'd been playing at the Alabaster ever since Declan had hired him as his driver and general errand runner.

Having Jack out and about the rookeries with her at Declan's back settled her mind slightly, especially for how determined Declan was to put himself in the position to be attacked. Jack would handle any major threats. She would handle the rest.

So when Declan had declared to her they were going out without Jack that night—that he had set Jack onto an errand into the west end—she'd had a stone of dread rolling about in her belly for the last three hours.

It was misting, the heavy rain from earlier clearing enough that the streets were alive once more with all the debauchery that came with the deepest part of the night.

Declan had gone to and from three of the other five gaming establishments he owned with Talen, then stopped off at three of the boarding houses his men protected.

He took alleyways whenever he could.

Lane after lane of dark shadows, all perfect places to be attacked.

Yet nothing, not the slightest inkling of danger.

Verity stepped to her left of the walkway, dodging a heavyset drunk that blocked her view of Declan a third of a furlong ahead of her. With the motion, she almost missed

Declan veering left into an alley that ran between two tenement houses.

She scanned the shadows on either side of the alleyway entrance. No one moved to follow him.

But then, there, from across the street. Four brutes spilling out from a tavern, swiftly slipping past horses and carriages as they crossed the road.

Her feet sped, her head down, but her eyes trained on the four men. Then two more walked toward the alleyway from the next street ahead of her. All looking to converge.

One of the original four brutes peeled away from the line headed toward the alley and moved toward the other two men, talking and pointing.

The two rogue brutes turned around and went back in the direction they came from.

What was that about?

Oooofff.

The grunt echoed out of the alley Declan had disappeared into. It wasn't his voice, but that meant the first three brutes had already reached him.

The fourth cutthroat ducked into the alleyway in front of her, and Verity was able to run without notice, rushing into the lane behind the last one.

Her hand went down into her open-bottomed pocket and she drew free her dagger from the sheath around her thigh. A mercy that Declan had given it back to her, along with her purse—the blade was weighed specifically for her hand.

Ahead of her, scant shards of light from windows above flickered down, illuminating the fact that Declan

was already engaged with the second brute. One cutthroat was already lying on the ground behind his feet. The silver of blades flashed again and again between the two, one lunging, one jumping out of the way.

Yet, no pistol—for how many men had been sent after Declan—they never used a pistol. They wanted this to look like a robbery—nothing more. Either that, or they were the cheapest ruffians that could be bought and they didn't have access to a pistol—at least one that shot straight.

Silently, her hand steady, Verity sprang forward and jumped onto the back of the last brute, her blade slicing across his throat. She dropped off from him before he staggered down to his knees, then landed face down in the muck.

Not fair. But then, she wasn't paid to be fair. She was paid to keep Declan alive.

At the thud behind him, the third brute turned around and looked down. At the sight of his cohort, his head flew up, his eyes searching the alleyway.

She'd shifted to the side with her back pressed against the soot-stained brick wall and deep in the shadows. It wasn't enough. He spotted her and charged.

Blast.

She hated this. Head-on.

Blood started to pound in her ears, taking away all sound except for her own heartbeat.

And he was to her, the short blade he had swinging in the air at her head.

She ducked at the last second, sending his blade clanging into the brick an inch above her cap.

Up close, she saw the blade was a cutlass—not a long one, but still too big to wield properly in the thin space between the buildings.

Her advantage, thank the heavens. She shoved off the brick wall behind her to land on the opposite wall, his blade chasing her the entire way. Bouncing off the second wall, she curled down into a ball and rammed into the front of his knees.

He didn't expect it, couldn't avoid it, and the blow sent his legs out from under him and the top half of his body barreled forward, his head and blade hand smashing into the wall.

Verity rolled, springing to her feet with her dagger ready just as Declan jumped past her and grabbed the man by the back of the head. He slammed the cutthroat's forehead into the brick wall and the man crumpled to the squish of the ground. Declan ripped the cutlass out of his hand and then set the heel of his boot on the brute's neck.

He looked up to her. "Didn't mean to interrupt. We just need this one alive." He pointed over her shoulder. "I was a bit too rough with those two."

Verity glanced over her shoulder to see two bodies slumped in the shadows, motionless. Dead.

It was always this—kill or be killed—and she was getting tired of the whole of it.

Until she turned around and saw a fifth cutthroat snaking into the alleyway behind Declan, his blade already high and poised and swinging at Declan's neck.

In that instant, she wasn't tired—not tired at all.

She was ready to kill.

{ CHAPTER 13 }

Verity looked back to him, her look anguished. Even in the shadows, Declan could see the toll that killing anyone was taking on her. But then the anguish vanished, replaced by ferocity as her eyes flew wide and she lunged past him, shoving him to the side as her dagger swung.

The tiniest screech left her lips as she drove her blade into the belly of the brute with a short blade only an inch away from Declan's neck.

The man didn't go down immediately. No. He attacked. Like a cornered rat, he lunged, rabid, his blade swinging wildly at Verity. The sword sliced across her right arm and she yelped, but her hand didn't leave the handle of her dagger buried in his gut. She yanked it upward, tearing flesh, then ducked and kicked him in the belly just below her dagger. He sputtered backward, dropping his sword as he held his gut, until his shoulder hit the brick and he slid down the wall.

Bloody hell, the minx *did* know how to save him.

Worse, even in the dim light from the windows above, he could see the white of her arm through the tear in her black dress.

White that was quickly disappearing out of view from the blood seeping onto her skin.

Switching her dagger into her left hand, she looked back to him. "Behind you."

Declan ducked, spinning low just as another brute came at him with a pistol in one hand, a blade in the other.

Pistol first. Declan swung, driving his blade through the man's right forearm until it clanked into the wall. The pistol dropped out of his fingers without firing.

Lucky.

Roaring, the cutthroat swung his meaty fist and the too-small dagger in it at Declan's head. The tip of the blade nicked Declan's forehead and he used the man's wasted momentum to tackle him to the ground. Finding the handle of his dagger still embedded in the man's forearm, Declan ripped it free and sent it straight into the man's throat.

Hovering over the ruffian, Declan heaved several breaths, waiting for the man to twitch, to move.

Stillness. Stillness all around them.

Wrapping his fingers around his dagger, Declan pulled it free from flesh and jumped to his feet, moving over to the man that he had felled earlier.

Verity pointed to the man still unconscious in the thick muck of the alley. "That one still alive?"

Declan looked down at him. Not enough light. He leaned down, setting the back of his hand in front of the man's nostrils. Breath. "Yes."

"I will go and get Jack." She squeezed past him in the tight space between the two buildings.

He grabbed her arm. "No, you cannot go alone."

Her forehead scrunched as she looked up at him, the black coal dust she'd layered onto her face creasing so hard white lines of her skin appeared. "I walk these streets all the time by myself."

"Not anymore."

Her head snapped back as though he'd struck her. "Whatever you are thinking, Declan, rethink it." Her words hissed. "I'm going to get Jack, and I'm going to take the main roadways because I'm not prone to alleyways like you are. Jack is going to drag this brute back to the Alabaster. Then you two can do whatever you feel necessary to unearth who is behind the threat. I am done."

She spun, running down the alley and leaving him with his jaw agape.

For a second, he considered running after her. But the man next to his boots groaned.

Getting this cutthroat back to the Alabaster was the most important thing at the moment.

He attempted not to count the seconds, the minutes Verity was gone, but it was bloody well hard to stop his infuriating mind. He'd meant what he'd said. He didn't want her anywhere near danger, and he certainly didn't want her walking the streets alone.

These last days, roaming the streets with her, her constant presence, the damn scent of her hitting his nostrils at unexpected moments, her green eyes flashing at him—the whole of it had unnerved him in ways he wasn't excited to explore. She wasn't anything he thought she was.

Too much more.

Too much more that needed to be protected from herself.

Barring locking her into a room at the Alabaster again, he'd determined the best course was to keep her close. At least he could keep an eye on her, rather than letting her continue on with this fool notion that he should be protected from afar. She was far more liable to get herself into trouble if he wasn't within arm's reach.

Or so he'd been telling himself.

Fifteen minutes later, Jack appeared with the old coach positioned at the end of the alleyway, Verity next to him on the driver's perch.

Their bodies close, too close on the small seat.

Necessary, for she would have had to direct him where to go. Still, it stung something deep in his gut, seeing her body pressed up against another man.

Declan watched Jack warily as he jumped from the carriage and moved into the alleyway, his look noting the bodies scattered down the length of it. "Run into a splatter of trouble, sir?"

"One might say that," Declan said. "This one is still alive. He needs to be brought back to the Alabaster for questioning. You know where to put him."

"Aye." Jack moved toward the head of the man and picked him up under his arms, dragging him backward toward the coach.

Declan followed and helped dump the man onto the floor of the coach. Jack snagged a length of rope and secured the man's legs and wrists together.

Declan looked up to the perch of the carriage, only to find Verity missing. "Where in the hell did Verity disappear to?"

Jack slammed the carriage door closed and they both moved around to the other side of the carriage to search the street.

"There." Jack pointed to his right.

Verity was walking away, her slight figure disappearing into the shadows of the buildings lining the street.

"What in the bloody hell?" Declan muttered under his breath. He glanced at Jack. "Can you get him into the Alabaster?"

"Aye—I'll get Shamus or Freddy to help." His mouth pinching to the side, Jack looked over his shoulder to Verity. "Do you want help with her, sir?"

"No. Just bring that cutthroat back to the Alabaster before someone stumbles upon these bodies. Keep him bound. I'll handle Verity."

"Aye." Jack scrambled up to the driver's perch, his lithe movements not characteristic of a man his size. Sturdy and strong. The perfect build for a guard. Whoever had hired Jack knew what they were doing.

Whoever had hired Verity was going to be strangled by Declan's bare hands.

He started down the street after her, his gait quick, and he caught up to Verity just as she stumbled a step and fell against the corner of a soot-stained brick building.

His hand instantly went to her shoulder, steadying her.

She jumped at the touch, the fear in her eyes immediately dissipating when she saw it was him.

His eyes searched her soot-stained face. "Why did you just stumble?"

She shook her head, her lips remaining tightly locked.

"Jack is gone. You can talk. Why the stumble?"

She pushed herself away from the building to step beyond him and looked back toward the coach that was already moving away.

Her lips parted, a slight exhale leaving her. Her stare remained on the retreating carriage. "It was nothing." Her voice was scratchy with lack of use, but also warbling as if she was woozy.

"It's bloody well something." He moved in front of her. "You're more sure-footed than a mountain goat."

Her hand went to her forehead. "I…I don't know. I am just dizzy. I am positive it will pass. Go back to the Alabaster and learn what you can of that brute. I was on my way to the boarding house."

"No. Jack is taking care of the man. Why are you dizzy?"

Her shoulders lifted. "It's the cut and the blood, and then I ran back to the Alabaster to get Jack, and I haven't had much to eat and…"

"The cut, is it deep?" He caught her elbow and lifted her upper arm into the light from a lantern outside a tavern across the lane.

She looked down at the tear in the dress along her arm. "I don't think. I was going to check on it."

He dropped her arm. He couldn't see much of anything in this poor light and his stare settled back on her face. "And what else?"

She looked up at him. "What do you mean?"

"You listed off one more 'and' but didn't finish what you were about to say."

Her mouth closed and she looked away from him. "And?"

Her gaze shifted back to him, a glare entering her eyes. "And the killing. Death." She exhaled a shaky breath. "I do what I must, but it is…it is a lot…sometimes."

Raw vulnerability—something he'd never seen in her before. She'd been spitting arrows at him with her eyes ever since he discovered her secret days ago. Anger, defiance, but vulnerability…that was new.

And it made him want to wrap his arms around her and drag her into his chest.

Just as he lifted a hand to set it along her neck, her eyes flickered back up into her head and she fell backward, her shoulders hitting the exterior of the building before she caught herself, her eyes popping wide open.

He grabbed her by the shoulders. "I'm taking you back to the Alabaster."

"I am fine, Declan. Fine. I just need to get back to my room and sit. Be still."

"You can sit and be still in my office. I'm taking you back to the Alabaster."

Her mouth opened as though she was going to fight him on it, but then he turned her, wrapping his arm along the back of her shoulders and started propelling her toward the Alabaster before she could protest.

Even if her mind was telling her differently, her feet shuffled along as directed, letting him manhandle her.

Ten minutes later, he had her in his office, sitting on one of the wingback chairs by the fireplace. She'd insisted on washing the coal off her face the moment she entered the

room, mumbling something about how the dust made her skin itch if she left it on too long.

With her boots and stockings off and drying by the fire, her backside finally hit the cushions, and she curled back into the chair, her eyes closing, her lips parted as she drew in deep breaths.

She was fighting fainting.

He walked across the room to the washbasin and pushed the dirty washcloth aside, then lifted out the water bowl, and grabbed the pitcher and a clean washcloth and brought them over to the chair.

"I need to look at the cut."

Her eyes remained closed, her breathing labored, but she nodded and lifted her upper arm to him, propping her elbow on the side of the chair.

It was in that moment that he realized that the tear in the fabric wasn't just on her upper arm. The fabric just behind her arm onto her back had torn as well. Blood just the same soaking into the fabric around it.

"Hell, Verity, the cut goes along your back."

"That seems right." Not surprised, her voice came out soft, resigned.

She knew? Knew she had another cut along her back and never thought to mention it?

Teeth gritting, he walked away from her to the sideboard and poured himself a dram of brandy, downed it. Poured another. Downed it.

He stripped off his coat and waistcoat, tossing them over the back of a chair by the small table next to the sideboard, then rolled up the sleeves of his lawn shirt.

One more generous pour into the glass and he moved to her and handed her the tumbler. "Drink it."

Her eyes lifted to him, wary. "Are you trying to get me foxed?"

It was a healthy amount for her small frame, but he pressed it into her hand. "I'm trying to dull the pain you're attempting to keep from me."

Her lips pursed, but she took the tumbler, then tilted the glass back, swallowing the brandy in one motion. At least she didn't argue the point with him. Though she could have sipped the brandy. That probably would have done her better.

He took the glass from her hand and set it on the floor. "Now, I need the top of your dress off."

Her eyes flew open, her look pinning him. "What?"

He motioned for her to spin away from him. "I need your back. I have to look at the wounds to see if I need to call the surgeon."

"You don't need to call the surgeon."

"I will be the judge of that. I'll not have you bleeding to death under my watch."

"Except I'm not under your watch. You're under mine."

A hard chuckle slipped out of his mouth instead of the aggravated growl he held back. "Turn."

Pink flooding her cheeks, she twisted on the chair to set her back to him.

His forefinger drifted over the tear in the black fabric where the blade had sliced. Bloody bastards. He quickly worked down the row of black buttons along her spine. "This has been happening too often lately."

"You almost getting killed?" She looked over her shoulder at him with an errant twinkle in her green eyes. Unexpected and irritatingly beguiling. Especially as she pulled free one arm from her dress, then the other as she clutched the bodice to her chest.

"No. You getting injured on my behalf. I am finding that I don't like blood on you because of me."

The cut across her upper right arm was hard to gauge—blood so smeared and crusty it was difficult to distinguish where exactly the cut started and ended.

She turned away from him. "It's my job. You never knew about the blood on me before, so I don't see why it should concern you now."

Why it should concern him now? A poignant point. He had plenty of men working for him that were bloodied all the time and he didn't blink at it. She chose this. Chose this life. Chose to take him on as a job.

So why did it matter now?

He wasn't sure he was ready to answer that question.

He cleared his throat. "I didn't know about it before. Now I do."

She nodded, her fingers clutching into the front of her black dress covering her chest.

His look dropped down to her back, only to be met with not a shift, but long strips of linen tightly wound around her chest. "You bind your breasts."

Her spine stiffened and she refused to look back at him. "I do."

"Why?"

"If I don't, my chest draws attention."

It sure as hell did. He gave her breasts far too much attention the other day when they were unbound and straining against the tight fabric of her maid's dress.

Focus. *Focus.*

He blinked, studying the long white strips of linen wrapped several times around her chest, not sure how to unfurl the binding.

"Where do you tie it off?"

"You cannot look at the cut with the binding in place?"

"No. The rip is half through the binding as is."

"I…I tie it off in the front."

In the front, between her breasts. His cock twitched. Heaven to hell, all he needed was an invitation to set his fingers between her breasts.

He clamped down on the surge of hunger flowing through his veins. "I can untie the binding, or I can cut it free."

"Cut it."

Her answer so quick, it took him aback. He studied her face for a long moment, the pink into her cheeks turning redder by the second. She'd rather have steel next to her skin than his hand between her breasts.

In her line of work, he assumed that she wouldn't be blushing like a young chit fresh from the schoolroom. That she would be comfortable with her body. Comfortable with it being seen. Hell, for all she'd surely seen and heard in the upper rooms of the Alabaster alone, she shouldn't have the slightest modicum of propriety left in her. Yet he was quickly learning everything he assumed about Verity was far off the mark.

His lips pulled to a tight line as he pulled free his dagger from the outside of his boot and slid it between the linen strips and her chemise. One quick tug, and the bindings fell loose about her torso.

"And I need your shift down."

She drew in an embarrassed breath, but she didn't argue. Instead, she dropped her right shoulder, slipping the white fabric downward until she freed one arm. She let it slip off her left shoulder and the shift dropped down to pool about her waist.

Her back. An expanse of creamy smooth skin marred with an ugly gash along her ribcage. The blood had dripped and smeared and crusted so thickly to her skin he almost gagged at the sight.

He didn't gag at blood. Ever.

But he was close at the moment.

Dropping to his knees, he reached down and dunked the washcloth into the bowl of water, wrung out the excess liquid, then started to dab away the crusted blood from her skin.

She flinched when he got close to dragging the cloth near the open wound.

"How many men have you killed for me?" he asked, mostly to take her mind off the stinging pain, but also because he'd come to the realization that the world he'd been living in for the last two years was not always one of his own making.

She shook her head. "It doesn't matter."

"Except it does." One long swipe of the washcloth and he could see the edges of the cut along her back. Not too deep, it wouldn't need stitches, but it would ache for quite some time.

"Eight." The one word came as a raw whisper, a confession he doubted she'd ever spoken out loud.

His look snapped up only to see her head had turned away from him.

Eight.

Eight was too many. One was too many.

What in her life had driven her to this monstrosity of a job?

On his knees, he shifted to the right so he could see her profile. She'd remained stubbornly turned away from him ever since her shift fell to her lap, clutching her black dress to her breasts. "I saw your face in the alleyway, Verity. Even in those shadows, you couldn't hide it, the toll this takes upon you. This business—it isn't you. You don't kill indiscriminately."

Her shoulders lifted, her stare trained on the fire. "Except I do. I do kill. I kill without thought. Without mercy. It didn't start like that…but it has just…sunk into this. I'm so…immune to death at this point."

"Verity—"

Her head shook, her shoulders drooping. "I know it is not normal, not right that I am like this. I know that. With what I've done, with what I do, I have placed myself onto the fringe of humanity, and now I'm just desperately trying to hold onto the last shreds of decency that I still possess."

He nodded to himself, for he recognized the jading of a soul when he saw it. Recognized it because his life had taken much the same path.

Where he had started. What he had turned into.

But on her—on her this was wrong. Intrinsically wrong. Even with her lies, even with what she had kept from him, he recognized the inherent kindness in her. How she took care of the other staff, the people that moved in and out of the Alabaster—and how she took care of *him*. She was kind, when kindness was a foolish commodity quickly stamped out in the rookeries.

Except…except he wanted her to latch onto that kindness, to not lose it even as her world burned down around her.

He cleared his throat. "Yet have you ever killed innocents—women and children?"

"What?" Her look swung to him. "No. Heavens no. Only the cutthroats that are after you."

His look locked with hers and he lifted his left hand, wrapping it around the back of her neck, his voice vehement. "Then you haven't lost your humanity. You've only lost the privilege of making the humane choice. Don't mistake what you do in a dark alleyway for what you are as a person. Everyone has valor and honor and mercy until their own life is at stake. Those are luxuries for people that live in a different world than we do."

Her jaw dropped slightly as she gasped the tiniest breath. She exhaled slowly. "Then I don't always understand this world."

"Understand that we live hard choices every day. We live in a world that forces us to survive." His fingers along her neck stretched upward, grabbing the back edge of her cap and he pulled it down, freeing her hair to the world.

Damn, he loved her hair. "We live with blades and blood and loyalty. And we live in a world that insists we take what is in front of us when it is offered, for tomorrow it could be gone."

The green in her eyes started undulating, pulsating in accord with every beat of her heart he could feel along her neck under his palm. She didn't look away, didn't cower at his words.

The tip of her tongue stretched out, wetting her lips and it nearly undid him.

Hell.

This was why it was so unsettling—everything about her. Her hair. Her eyes on him. Her damn voice.

He wanted to devour her.

Like a madman, the guttural urge ripped through him, wanting to strip off the rest of her clothes and throw her to the floor and pound so deeply into her, her gasps would turn into begging which would turn into screaming his name as she came. And then he wanted to pick her up and slam her against the wall and drive into her until she came again.

He wanted everything. The whole of her body pressed against his. All of her skin. All of her words. All of her thoughts. All of her breath.

And he wanted it to start now.

His fingers curled into the base of her hair and he dove forward, his lips finding hers. Devil take it. Lips so damn soft. Lips that parted to him without hesitation and he pressed forth with his tongue, tasting, exploring, ravaging.

She didn't fight it, falling into the kiss, responding with her own lips, her tongue, her fingers lifting to grip onto the back of his neck like he was the only scrap of wood keeping her afloat far out at sea.

And then, the softest mewl from her throat. More sound where there had been none for the past two damn years.

It was the most glorious thing he'd ever heard.

And he only wanted more.

{ CHAPTER 14 }

The kiss tunneled down deep into her gut, twisting her insides until she couldn't breathe. Couldn't think. The pounding of blood between her legs angry, demanding.

Declan's lips on hers, his tongue slipped in to devour her, as though he was trying to steal her very soul from her body.

He could have it.

She was so far lost in the kiss, lost in him, it didn't matter what he stole from her.

His right hand stayed latched to the back of her neck, holding her to the crushing kiss as his left hand dropped, his palm rough but the pads of his fingers soft as he shoved down the fabric of her dress and fully cupped her right breast. His fingers teasing her hard nipple, rolling it as he played with the heft.

A carnal growl rumbled through his throat, but he didn't pull away from the kiss. Wouldn't, until his mouth drifted downward to her chin, her neck, her chest, and then his lips dove to her breast.

Great Zeus.

Her body shuddered. This was what it was to have a man's mouth on her breast. *Declan's* mouth on her breast.

Whatever sorcery he was doing to her, it made her want to strip off the rest of her clothes and crawl onto his lap, giving his tongue free rein on every part of her skin.

Her hips wiggled, making the dress and shift fall lower on her hips.

At the motion, he grumbled a laugh, his hand on her neck sliding down to explore her skin, and his fingers ran along the wound on her back.

Instantly, he froze, his head pulling away from her body. "Hell, Verity—you're hurt. I'm sorry, I need to finish with your wounds. I don't know what I was think—"

"I'm not in pain." She grabbed the front of his shirt before he could retreat.

She'd made up her mind on this score the second his lips touched hers. She would never—could never—have a real relationship with a man. A marriage, a family, those things would never be hers. So why would she hold fast against this?

This. Declan touching her. More.

She'd never thought it could be hers, even for one fleeting moment. Her heart was already entangled into everything about him, so what could this hurt? Taking this one little piece of life for herself?

No promises. No future. This moment to just enjoy. To take and hold tight to her heart for whatever days she had left.

Against her clutching hands, he managed to pull away from her, his face pained like he'd grievously wounded her himself. She set her eyes directly on his.

"I'm not in pain, Dec. Not anymore. I'm in the exact opposite of pain at the moment."

He held her stare, the grey of his eyes brewing a fierce storm. "Verity…"

"I'm not lying." Her hands went up to clasp either side of his face. "I'm not lying."

An agonized rumble lifted from his chest and he crashed into her, his arms enveloping her. Moving to his feet, he lifted her with his mouth on hers, hungry. Carrying her, he stalked across his office and into his adjoining bedroom.

Her dress and shift fell down her body on the way— she wasn't sure if she pushed all the fabric out of the way or he did. All she knew was that, by the time her backside hit the coverlet of his bed, she was bare to the world. Bare to him.

After setting her on the bed, he drew back for a second, ripped his shirt off even as his gaze raked her over from head to toe. Each part of her body his look touched heated, pulsated under his scrutiny.

A wicked smile curved onto his lips as he drank her in.

"Blast it, Verity, you're beautiful. Why in the hell are you doing this to me?"

"Doing what?"

"Everything I uncover about you, everything you've shrouded from me, is bloody gorgeous. And it's infuriating you've hidden all of who you are from me for so long."

"You were never supposed to see me. Never."

"Well, I sure as hell see you now."

He charged forth, as though he couldn't hold himself back from touching her a moment longer. His hands seemingly stroking everywhere on her body at once.

Where she should pause—be nervous or at least let propriety rear—she refused the notion, leaning into every

press of his fingers against her flesh, of his hard chest brushing against her breasts, of his tongue tangling with hers.

Until her body could no longer take the frenzy firing through her nerves and she slipped her hands down, unbuttoning the front fall of his trousers.

His hand slipped between them, finding her folds, and he stroked a finger down the length of her.

Her body jerked at the touch, fire scorching her veins. He parted her folds, finding her nubbin and she gasped, a scream at her lips quick to follow.

Heaven to hell.

Again and again he rolled his fingers through her core, until her hips were grinding against him on their own accord, her body losing all ability to control itself. Mewls mixed with screams as her back arched, space and time getting lost around her until he slipped one finger into her, then a second, and she exploded into a wild darkness that splintered with bright specs of light.

Gasping, her body rode the release, tensing and pulsing with every stroke he drew out of her and making her limbs quiver. One of his hands left her, and then the tip of his member was at her entrance, pressing in, asking permission.

Through the haze engulfing her, she looked up at him, nodding as she reached up for his neck, pulling him into her. She wanted this. Wanted it so badly it hurt, even through the ripples still vibrating through her body.

He slammed into her and instantly jerked still, his limbs shaking against the need to move within her. "Hell,

Verity—I didn't know. Hell." His hips twitched, like he was about to pull out. Abandon her.

He started to pull out.

"No." She grasped the sides of his hips through his trousers still loose around his body. Not that she could hold him in place, but she could damn well try. "No. Don't stop. Please. Don't stop." Her gaze locked onto him, her eyes desperate as she adjusted to the feel of his thickness deep in her body.

She may have been a virgin, but this felt painfully, oddly, curiously right. She could have told him. Should have told him. But she doubted she would be right where she was at the moment if she had. And this…this was everything.

There. The pain eased. She wiggled her hips slightly and titillating sensations spiked from her core outward to her limbs. "Does it get better?"

He chuckled, his body nearly collapsing as his forehead dipped down into her hair on the pillow next to her. His mouth turned to her, his low voice a whispered rumble. "By the graces, it does if I have any mettle in me at all."

"You have a spine built of solid mettle."

He pushed himself up, balancing above her. "Tell me more about my strengths and I just may prove how weak I am."

"Why?"

His mouth nuzzled into her neck. "Because I am near to bursting inside of you at the moment—your voice—every word you utter strikes something so carnal deep within me, you're strumming it like a tight violin string

ready to snap. Which is making me want to pound you so hard into the mattress that you'll barely be able to scream my name."

Her eyes went wide. "That—that does not sound bad." She gasped a heated breath. "It sounds good—the pain—it is nothing now."

"I don't think you can take that."

"We won't know unless we try."

He groaned, his patience near to snapping in the timbre of his voice. "Heaven help me."

"I'll help you." She flexed her hips backward, deep into the mattress and gained a sliver away from him. Just enough motion against his cock that he moaned.

"Do what you need to, Dec."

With that, he snapped, pulling fully from her and easing back down into her.

Three times more and she smiled, wrapping her hands around his neck. "I can take so much more."

A grimace hit his face and he withdrew, slamming back into her. He paused, his stare intent on her face, waiting for her to tell him to stop. She opened her mouth, licking her lips.

All the permission he needed.

He pulled out, thrusting into her again and again, driving her into the mattress until he was growling with each drive, holding hard against his finish.

His thumb slipped between them, finding her nubbin, and he stroked it, sending her over the edge. Splintering. Screaming. Again.

At the spasms rocking her body, he sank into her one last time, his body shaking with force as he pulled from her to come across her belly. The warm of the liquid against her skin churning something guttural deep in her soul.

No children. There could never be any children.

He knew it as intrinsically as she did.

They just had different reasons.

{ CHAPTER 15 }

His hand wrapped a long strand of her hair around his palm, spinning it, letting the silk run across the rough of his knuckles.

Declan still had to finish cleaning Verity's wounds, but the cuts didn't need to be stitched closed, so he just may make her stay draped on top of him for the next day—hell, he'd take a month, if he thought he could get away with it.

If he was honest with himself, he'd wanted to devour Verity for days—a passing obsession that he thought, once sated, he could move past.

But that—what had just happened between them. His cock deep in her tightness. He'd never felt anything quite like it. Never felt anything quite like her body pressed against his, wanting—demanding everything he was.

She wanted his soul.

In this moment, he wanted hers.

He wasn't exactly sure what this was between them, all he knew was that he'd had the guttural urge before sinking into her that he wanted to possess her from the inside out, from her toes up to the red of her hair.

And now, that compulsion paled to how much he wanted to curl her into his chest and never let her go. How he wanted to set his mouth to every inch of her body, inhale every thought in her mind, feast upon every feeling in her soul.

From the second she had first spoken actual words to him, she'd become an obsession that was expanding instead of contracting.

He didn't want this, didn't need this. His life wasn't permanent. Wasn't safe and secure. His time in London had given him the closest thing that he'd ever had to a home, and it was weak at best. A townhouse he rarely slept in. A bed above a gaming house he collapsed into.

He'd never known a home—a real home—and the thought of it made the nerves under his skin itch.

Not to mention that, foolish man that he was, he still didn't know anything about Verity's life. Who she was. Where she came from. How long she had survived with just her and her brother. Why in the world she would fall into a profession such as hers.

So many damn questions. So few answers.

He restrained himself, letting just one simple question slip through his lips so as to not overwhelm her.

"Who taught you to wield a blade like that?"

Her head shifted on his chest, her chin settling onto his breastbone as her left hand went onto his skin in front of her chin, drifting tiny circles across the surface. "The blacksmith's daughter. Her father was a spy during the war on the continent. He taught her how to properly use all manner of steel, and she taught me everything she learned because she needed a practice partner. And the baker's boy—when his father didn't need him in the shop, he liked to fence, and he liked me as a sparring partner because I was usually available. He was good, but I was middling at best."

"This was in the countryside?"

"It was."

"It is a mighty leap from playing with blades in the countryside to slicing into men in the dark alleys of the rookeries."

She fell silent, closing off from him. He could feel it in how her muscles tensed on top of him, her skin tightening. Her head turned, her cheek landing on his chest without answering.

The question too probing, too soon.

This woman locked her secrets away more securely than the crown jewels.

Her fingers tapped against his chest. "We need to find out who is after you. Do you think the man in the cellars will be a help with that?"

She wanted to talk business. Fine. If it would keep her talking.

"Possibly, though the man strikes me as just another poor-quality thug hired on the cheap to do the dirty business. I doubt he'll know much, but he may give us a lead or two."

His jaw shifted to the side, his mind wanting to go back to questioning her about her life before the Alabaster, but there would be time for that in the future. He would make sure of it. And he would sneak away with every one of her secrets so he could hold them as his own.

His fingers ran up along her spine. "The man in the cellars is a start, but I also think we need to go about this in a different way."

"What way?"

"Who hired you to keep me safe? You were lying before—you know, don't you?"

"I told you, I don't know."

"Verity—"

She pushed herself up off his chest, her look intense on him. "I wasn't lying. Why do you think being mute suited me so well?"

"So people—men in particular—wouldn't bother you?" he hedged, trying not to let his eyes dip down to her bare chest. Damn, but she was gorgeous, her skin ripe for licking, her nipples begging to be sucked.

"Yes." Her head cocked to the side. "But also, I'm a terrible liar if I have to open my mouth. I think you've already seen that."

True.

Once he knew she could talk, it was rather easy to tell when she was holding words back or trying to misdirect him.

Her look met his in earnest. "I don't know who hired my boss. I only suspect that it is someone powerful—it would have to be, for the cost of it." Her lips pursed for a lone moment. "You don't have any ideas who would have hired him?"

Declan shook his head. "No."

She exhaled a sigh, her shoulders falling with her gaze. "I assumed you must know who it was, or at least have a guess." Her look snapped back up to his face. "Some relative you never talk about? An old friend repaying a debt?"

His mouth pulled to a tight line. This answer was easy. "I have no family and I have no old friends other than Talen."

Her forehead wrinkled. "No one? I find that hard to believe. No one? No one in your past?"

"No."

"But how could you have no people aside from Talen?"

His eyes narrowed at her. "As you don't appear to have anyone?"

That made her mouth shut, her green eyes flinching, wounded. Whereas he truly had no one, he could tell that she did—or had—at some point.

He sighed. "Verity, I am not hiding anything on this score. There truly is no one that values me enough to do this, other than Talen. But Talen would tell me outright if he hired someone to protect me. And he most certainly wouldn't hire a wee hurricane for the job."

The ache in her eyes softened. "But why is this so important—finding out who hired my employer?"

"Because if I know who hired you and Jack to protect me, there might be a trail directly to the person trying to harm me. Whoever is paying your salary knows there's a threat on my life, and they know where that threat is coming from."

She stared at him for a long moment, weighing his words, then nodded. "We are paid to not ask questions, to follow orders blindly. But maybe I can find out without anyone knowing. I will need to get into my employer's files. I am sure, somewhere, there is record of who hired us. It

will have to be at night, though, and I will have to break into the office."

"I will come with you."

Her hand flew up between them. "No. We have to function as we normally do. Everything must remain the same, just as it has for the last four days. I cannot have Jack suspecting anything."

He captured her hand hanging in the air between them, curling his fingers around her palm. "Except it's not the same."

He wasn't going to chance her body and limb ever again. Why he thought he'd ever put her safety at risk to help him was idiocy beyond belief. Locking her into the Alabaster would have to do.

"It has to be the same," she grumbled. "What do you think would happen if it is discovered that you know about me?"

He shrugged. "I don't rightly care."

"Well, I do. If it was discovered you knew what I was, then it will be presumed that you also know about Jack. My employer will find new people to infiltrate your life—and I don't trust new people with you. I trust me. I trust Jack. Please, Declan, just let it be—at least until we can discover where this threat against you originates from."

He dropped her hand and set his fingers under her hair along the back of her neck, his thumb tracing the line of her jaw. "I'll not have you in danger. Not anymore—not ever. I never should have let you come out with me these past nights. Never."

Her brows lifted. "Just as I won't have you in danger?" She shook her head. "If I am pulled from this job, then I am not employed until a new one appears. That is, if any new jobs actually appear for me, especially after I have failed."

"You haven't failed anything."

Her mouth quirked to the side. "Falling into bed with the man you've been tasked to protect is a failure."

"There are specific rules against it?"

She paused, the question flustering her. "It is implied. Enthusiastically implied. While I was never specifically told not to couple with you, I am also intelligent enough to figure that rule out on my own." She exhaled a sigh. "Regardless, I cannot afford to lose this post. Neither can Jack."

"Then I will pay you."

"Pay me for what?" The look she gave him curdled his tongue. "I'm not a whore, Declan, and that is what you would be paying me for."

"Verity, you—"

She held up her hand as her eyes closed for a long second. "But most importantly, I will not have access to your case if I am dismissed. Helpful developments would be missed." Her eyes opened to him. "And that is the most important thing at the moment—we need to find out who is after you. Who hired my employer. Things must remain the same."

Uncharacteristically, he let her finish before jumping on what he was about to say. "You're not a whore, Verity."

Her green eyes narrowed at him. "Then don't make me into one, Declan."

He bit his tongue.

For now.

For now, he'd let her play the spy, but as soon as they discovered where the threat on his life was coming from, there were going to be changes coming her way.

Big ones.

Whether she wanted them or not.

{ CHAPTER 16 }

On her hands and knees, Verity scooted along the floor of the hallway that passed by the front receiving room, balancing a small lantern with a rounded copper top that directed most of the light emanating from the enclosed candle downward. Light bobbing along inside the main office in the dark could easily be seen from outside on the street and she couldn't afford that.

Best to stay low and fast. Once she was in Hector's office, she could shut the door and stand.

Keeping watch, Declan waited outside for her, poised deep along the shadow of the wide marble staircase that led up into the building.

She would have preferred to come to the offices alone—she knew well how to move about the shadows of the night, but now she had a man almost double her size lurking about. Subterfuge was not Declan's forte. He went where he wanted, when he wanted, and no one questioned it.

Unfortunately for her, he wasn't about to let her come on this mission alone, drat the man.

Though his strength had been helpful in popping open the old iron grate that lined the beer cellar below street level and led into the servants' hall. It saved her from having to find another way into the building, as picking the lock of the front door in plain sight of the street was not an option—especially because she was terrible at picking locks.

She had to be quick, for Declan had already told her if anyone so much as looked at the front door of the building, he was breaking glass to get in and get her out of there.

Not subtle, that one.

Reaching Hector's office, she reached up and jiggled the handle. Locked, of course. From the side of her boot she pulled free lever wires, then set the lantern on the floor and stuck the wires into the lock, searching for the pins. It took longer than her usual awful attempts—she didn't remember the last time she had been forced to pick a lock, but it was just one of the skills Hector had made sure she learned.

Click.

She was in.

She attempted to stuff down the uneasiness in her chest. Sneaking around like this, breaking into Hector's office—it went against her nature. She wasn't a spy. Wasn't out to uncover secrets that she had no business knowing.

She was a guardian. Nothing more.

But being a guardian, in this instance, meant breaking into this office in order to protect her charge.

She imagined she would be in this very same place, doing this very same thing even if she was no longer a guardian, for she was quickly realizing rational thought left her when it came to Declan.

She nudged Hector's office door open, peeking into the room just to make certain there was no one in the office. Hector may very well sleep in his office, for all she knew of the man.

Nudging the light forward, she checked over the chairs and the settee along the far side of the wall.

Empty.

She crept into the room, closing the door behind her as she got to her feet. Quick to the cabinet that spanned the wall beside the door, she opened one cabinet door after another, looking for the case files. She'd seen several of them since Hector had hired her, and the notes that he kept in the files were detailed.

The answers had to be inside this room.

There. Rows and rows of files, each one bound by its own thin leather portfolio.

She riffled through them—four rows of them—without luck. Not finding one that mentioned Declan's name.

She was running out of time.

Declan had also mentioned if she wasn't back out to him within a half hour, that would be cause to hurl a brick through a window to get in and drag her out.

The fifth row, down by her feet. The files down here were fatter. Far fatter than the portfolios above, with small brass nameplates affixed to the top right corner.

She dropped to her knees, setting the lantern on the cabinet ledge just above the row.

Simpson. Handover. Jones & Wallis. Casson-Rudderton.

Rudderton.

Her heart stilled.

Rudderton. Her fingers ran across the names etched into the brass plate. But who was Casson?

Spreading her fingers wide, she grabbed the thick file—the thickest one in the cabinet—and pulled it free.

Unwrapping the thin tie, she flipped open the leather flaps to free the stack of papers inside.

Her fingers quick, she flipped downward from the top.

Sheet after sheet of reports from the last two years from both her and Jack. Each of them noting anything unusual. The attacks in the alleyways. The attack the previous year at the docks.

Incidents Jack had reported but never told her about. Nothing grievous.

But then the papers started to get older. More wrinkled, the vellum crisped under her fingers like it might disintegrate at touch.

Her fingers moved more gently through the stack.

Older reports. The years before she had been assigned to Declan. Two different men posting reports. Bernard and Lewis. Older. Two other men. Older. Before Declan landed in London. Posts from a ship. From a Jordan. Then from another. Murray. A ship—the *Firehawk*. Years and years back the reports went.

Her jaw dropped of its own accord as she skimmed through the depth of the stack.

How long had Declan been watched over?

She flipped down to what looked to be the first report posted. 1807.

How old was Declan?

Twenty-three when she first came to work for him. So twenty-five.

The math flew through her head. He'd been watched over since he was Five. Five. *Five.*

What in the bloody hades was going on?

She dumped the top of the stack onto the floor next to her, searching in the bottommost of the pile of papers.

Where was the initial assessment? In all the files she had ever seen, there was an initial assessment of the situation—the intake interview that Hector conducted that gave the client's information. Threats, dangers, people of interest to watch out for. The usual information.

She flipped through the last ten papers at the bottom of the pile, thinking it got misplaced.

Nothing.

No assessment. No intake.

The first report from a Royal Navy ship in 1807.

That was the start of Declan's file.

Breath she hadn't known she was holding exhaled.

It didn't make sense. The most vital piece of information was missing.

She glanced up, looking at the wall that faced the street, imagining Declan leaning against the side of the marble stairs, his feet twitching, getting impatient.

Desperate, she quickly flipped through the stack of reports once more, convinced she must have missed the initial assessment.

She hadn't.

And she needed to get out of there.

She thumbed through the remaining files on the bottom shelf, hopeful she had missed another file on Declan. Nothing.

Carefully putting the file back together and into the cabinet just as she had found it, she closed the doors behind her as she left Hector's office.

She didn't take a full breath until she cracked open the door of the servants' entrance and peered up at Declan still deep in the shadows and leaning against the stairs.

His eyes were locked on the street and he didn't look down at her as he whispered to her, "That took too long. You said you would be fast."

Angry then. She knew she took far too long.

Quick up the narrow staircase, she joined him in the shadows, her fingers unconsciously reaching out for his arm and settling on the back of his elbow.

He nodded with his head toward the street. "We need to get moving. A watchman has been by three times. One more pass and he might actually get up the courage to stop and ask me what I'm doing here versus just twitching glances at me, scared out of his mind at approaching me."

Verity held in a grin. This wealthy, but unexceptional neighborhood rarely saw the likes of anyone with less than the tallest top hats and gowns of silk moving through it.

Three streets over, Declan waved down a hack and ushered her into it.

"Bedford and Gower." He called out to the driver, then ducked into the coach, filling up the seat opposite her.

Her eyebrows lifted as she watched him settle. Not too many people knew about his residence in Bedford Square. Both he and Talen had made a fortune in London— probably before that, for how they had landed in port. And both men liked to keep the knowledge of their residences to a bare minimum.

He caught her eye. "This conversation isn't for the Alabaster."

She nodded, her head clunking backward against the worn wood of the carriage. Not able to look at him, she stared out the window at the buildings drifting by.

He would want to know everything she found.

She just didn't think she could give him that.

{ CHAPTER 17 }

He reached up to help Verity down from the hack.

Not that she wasn't sure-footed on her own. He liked that about her. But he also liked how she took his hand, her fingers instinctively seeking his out.

He liked that even more about her.

What he didn't like was how she had avoided eye contact with him the entire ride here to his Bedford Square residence.

He kept four guards at points along the perimeter. An overabundance of caution, as he was rarely at his townhouse. But he always took to the idea of being able to disappear somewhere without thought or worry about the next man looking to sink a dagger into his back.

Verity had been to his residence twice, both on missions to retrieve ledgers he'd forgotten to bring back with him to the Alabaster, so the front guards didn't blink as he let them into the front door of the home. It was so late into the night—only hours away from daybreak, and there was a ball being held several townhouses down at the marquess's home, so none of the people along the street paid them any mind.

He paused as he closed the door behind her. While he wanted to bring her directly up to his bedroom, strip her down, and toss her onto his bed, he tried to squelch the thought. He couldn't just assume that she wanted what happened between them to continue.

He exhaled a silent sigh. Upstairs would still be preferable. Just thinking of her skin, of the scent of her filling his sheets, he got hard. But no. There would be time for that later. Hopefully.

He ushered her past the front drawing room to the expansive library off the main hallway that he also used as his study. The only room on this floor that overlooked the garden, it was one of the few rooms he used in the home. His chambers and the library—that was the whole of his existence in this townhouse.

He went to the fireplace where his men always kept coals hot to start a fire. Other than the guards of the house, he kept a housekeeper that came every day to attend to the needs of the house and the guards, including meals for them.

The fire lit in short order, he stood and turned around to Verity, only to find her still standing near the doorway, watching him warily. He must not have hid the ravenous look in his eyes as they moved deeper into the house.

He went to the sideboard, grabbing two glasses and pouring a healthy amount of brandy into his glass, and a much more modest dram into her tumbler.

He needed the extra fortification after standing and waiting for her outside that office. Worried about her. He'd promised he wouldn't come in, but it had been torture, waiting outside and not being within an arm's length of her in case someone had been inside and there had been danger.

He took a long sip from his glass and then walked over to her, handing her the short tumbler of brandy. "What did you find? It had to have been something in order for it to take that long."

She sipped the tiniest drink of the brandy. "I found the file—your file."

A surge of trepidation ran through his gut. "What was in it—who hired your employer?"

She took another sip, not meeting his eyes for a long moment. "I've seen these files before. They always include an initial assessment of the situation." Her look lifted to him. "The assessment always included the person that has hired us. Your file was missing the assessment."

"Missing it? Then what was in the file?"

"Reports. Reports from me, from Jack. Some noting nothing unusual had happened. Longer reports detailing attacks on you."

"But there must have been something in there about how all this started."

"There wasn't. I looked—I flipped through the file again and again to make certain I didn't miss anything. And there was nothing."

His free hand folded into a fist and he had to fight the urge to turn and hurl his brandy at the fireplace. Instead, he brought the tumbler to his lips, tossing back the full of the glass.

Verity took a step forward, setting her hand along his forearm. "I know it must be frustrating—I thought there would be an answer—somewhere—in there."

He shook his head, his eyes closing as his head rolled back, his face to the ceiling. This had been it—the thing that festered underneath all his waking thoughts ever since

he'd discovered what role Verity played in his life. He'd been desperate to know who thought themselves important enough to play with his life—and why.

He heaved a sigh. "It is unnerving that someone is out there and knows everything about my life—everything— and is controlling things around me that I can't even begin to imagine, and I don't know who in the blasted hell they are."

"We will figure it out. We will."

His shoulders lifted and his eyes opened, his look dropping to her. "It's as though my life is not my own."

"But it is yours—so let us walk back through it. Maybe the answer is in the past somewhere and you don't realize it." She wrapped her fingers around his wrist and tugged him over to the settee that sat perpendicular to the fire and sat. It took an extra tug for him to sit down next to her. Her canny green eyes settled upon him. "Where did you grow up?"

His shoulders lifted. "I grew up on a ship."

"I know you lived most of your years before London on a ship—that I was told. But what about before that? You don't remember anything about a family?"

He shook his head. "I don't have a family. All I ever knew were the ships. That was where my memories started."

"Do you remember how old you were?"

"Can one truly remember how old they were during their first memories?" His look swept over her.

"Well, how old do you think you were?"

"I don't know, five, six, I would guess. That seems right." His head tilted to the side. "Why are you asking me this?"

Her lips pulled tight for a long moment. "I am just trying to figure out who could have hired my employer. I think it has to be family that you don't know of—if what you've said about currently knowing no one with enough funds or wherewithal to hire us holds true."

"I did not hold back on that score. I haven't had time to endear myself to anyone since Talen and I moved into London. And I don't have any family."

"So you just appeared one day at five years old on a ship? You had to have been born somewhere. Somehow you made your way onto the ship."

Why did she keep going around this, again and again? "My first memories consist of the handle of a mop in my hands and a bucket by my feet on a Royal Navy ship. Bare feet. Clothes that itched with whatever vermin were in the hay in the sleeping quarters. I remember lots of crusty old sailors yelling at me and ordering me about from sun up to sun down. That is where I came from. Those sailors were as close as it came to having a family."

Her shoulders slumped. "No mother? No father?"

"No." He couldn't keep the clip out of his voice. "I could have been born on a ship and lived there my whole life for all I know. I cannot fill in blanks I don't have— those are just my early memories and I doubt they're much different from anyone else's."

"But you must have come from somewhere. Have you never questioned it?"

"I always assumed I was an orphan. One that was born either on a ship or near a port and that I was set on board before I could even make memories."

"You didn't find it peculiar that no one ever made mention of your parents?"

"No." His gaze cut into her. "You know more, don't you? What are you not telling me?"

Her hand snapped away from his arm. "Nothing."

He leaned forward, his stare pinning her. "It's something. Don't make me drag it out of you. You saw something in that file that is prompting all these questions."

Her jaw shifted to the side. Her mind churning through options on how to proceed. He scooted closer on the settee, his glare meant to make her cower—even if she wouldn't. She knew by now his ability to punish her for disobedience was lacking, at best.

Her hands threw upward. "Fine. I did see something more in the file, but it isn't an answer, it is only more questions. And it is going to upset you."

He stilled. "Upset me how?"

She paused, looking away from him as she sipped down the last of her brandy, stalling.

"Verity." He let the threat of looming danger lace his voice.

She turned to place the tumbler on the side table next to the settee and then shifted so she could look directly at him. "I wasn't lying—there were no records in the file that speak of the person that hired us. But there were the reports of the past guardians hired to keep you safe."

"There were more of you?" His words crept out.

She nodded slowly. "Lots of reports. Lots and lots of them."

His brow crinkled. "Lots? How many of them?"

"The file was thick. The reports go back to 1807."

1807?

His head snapped back, stunned.

In 1807 he was…five? Six? He'd always just assumed that he was the same age as Talen because they were of similar size and grew at the same pace, and Talen was born in 1802.

Her bottom lip jutted up, halting sympathy on her face. "If you are twenty-five now, you would have been—"

"Five in 1807," he said, his words wooden. "Or I could have been younger. I don't know my birthday."

Her eyes went wide, sadness etched into the green depths. "You—you don't know when you were born?"

He didn't need pity on this score. Plenty didn't know their birth date. Plenty didn't know where they were from. Plenty were orphans. He was just one of many.

He shrugged. "It is no matter."

"Except it does matter." She reached out and grabbed his forearm. "You have been watched over since you were a little boy—"

"Not to my knowledge."

"Except you were—I saw the reports of it on the opposite end of the pile from my and Jack's reports. Someone was there, always watching over you. Do you recall, was there a Percy on your ship? That was who signed the oldest reports."

With a sharp intake of breath, he ran his hand through his hair, pulling at the strands. "Hell. Cook—Cook's name was Percy."

She fell silent for a long breath, her head nodding. "Which must mean that you have family—or someone with an interest in your well-being—somewhere here in England, Declan." Her fingers around his forearm tightened in excitement. "Someone has paid for your protection since you were young, and has done so for twenty years. That someone must have unmeasured funds in order to afford this."

"And to what end? Why would anyone bother with me?" he growled.

All air seemed to whoosh out of her body. "You aren't excited?"

"Should I be?"

"Yes?" The word came out slow, half statement, half question.

"Because why? You're telling me that I have family—or someone that cares whether I live or die. When I've had no one my entire life? Talen. That is it. And that was begrudging at times—but we only had each other. And now you're telling me that for twenty years, I had a different life or different people that I should have known, should have depended upon."

"Maybe, yes…"

His arm jerked away from her grip and he stood. "They knew where I was, Verity. Someone *knew,* and they never came for me. Why would I want to know more? About them? About a life I was denied?"

"Declan, I know how you must feel, the loss—"

"No, you don't know anything about how I feel. I was abandoned for my whole life—which was fine—I was fine with that. But to learn there was someone—someone all along…" His voice trailed off, his head shaking as his lip snarled. "You don't know a damn thing about what I feel."

She stood, the entirety of her body turning frigidly still. "You are correct. I do not know."

He exhaled a seething breath. "We need to leave here."

He grabbed her at the back of her elbow and dragged her through the house and out into the street. The party three houses down was coming to a close and revelers bled out from the townhouse and weaved in amongst the numerous carriages jockeying for position on the street. His grip on her not loosening, he walked them down to a side street and waved down a hack, then handed her up into it after it stopped.

She paused, stooped over in the carriage as she looked down to him. "You are not getting in?"

"No. I'm finding out my own damn answers. To hell with the past and whoever thinks they can manipulate my life like they have." He paused, the smallest part of him railing against his tone. This wasn't Verity's fault—she was hired for this job. She didn't deserve his fury.

Yet in that moment she represented everything that was wrong in his life.

He managed to only slightly curb the ire in his voice. "I'm sending you back to the Alabaster."

"But what are you going to do?"

"Visit people that need visiting and then I'm going to interrogate that cutthroat."

"But—"

"Just go back to the Alabaster, Verity. Do your damn job."

Her mouth clamped shut and she sat down onto the edge of the cushions, her back rigid and her mouth pulled to a tight line.

He slammed the door of the carriage closed without another word to her. He went to the driver, handed him up a few coins and told him the address.

For as angry as he was at the moment, he stood on the edge of the street, motionless, watching the hack roll away.

Hell, maybe she did know what he was feeling—for what did he know about her?

About her real life?

Damn, that he'd never bothered to ask long ago. Never bothered to think about her as a person existing before she arrived at the Alabaster.

That was his own oversight.

For a long moment, his toes shifted back and forth on the cobblestones, and he almost ran after the hack.

But then he stilled himself.

He had a cutthroat to interrogate.

{ CHAPTER 18 }

There. Jack.

Verity looked both ways on the busy street by the wharf, picking her spot to cross the street. Cart, horse, phaeton—her feet sprung her forward and she scurried across the muck of the street, only slipping once and just by luck and a whisker avoiding being trampled by a horse pulling a hack.

Only three streets away from where he had left Declan's carriage, Jack stood in the shadows alongside a brick warehouse, his gaze focused out onto the nearest pier.

Since the previous night, she hadn't seen Declan all day and well into the evening, and when she poked Igor, one of the Alabaster's guards, and motioned for Declan, he told her that Declan and Jack had gone down to the docks.

That had been hours ago, and they hadn't returned. The shiver that had initially skittered down her spine at Igor's report hadn't eased—it had only grown icier, making her back hurt with worry every passing moment, until she set out from the Alabaster, determined to find them.

Her steps light, she reached out to squeeze Jack's upper arm and he instantly swung his fist out, ready to crush whoever was attacking him.

Good thing she barely reached his chest, for he would have cracked her jaw open had he made contact.

His gaze found her and relief flickered across his features, barely perceivable for the rage that had set hard

lines into his face. "Verity—what in the hell are you doing down here at the docks? This is no place for you—I've told Hector a hundred times that you keep putting yourself in dangerous positions, yet both he and you refuse to take heed."

Was Jack actually mad at her for doing her job? She didn't have time for this. She motioned with her palm up, which Jack knew full well was a question for where Declan was.

Jack shook his head, his attention going back to the docks and the inky waters. There were four ships moored along the pier in front of them. "Declan was taken—crimped. We came to introduce ourselves to the man that hired that cutthroat from the alleyway, but it was a set-up." He nodded with his head toward the second ship on the right. "The *Rhianna Wind*. That's the ship they shoved him on. It's due out of port on the next tide."

"Shit."

Jack's head snapped back, his look crawling to her. "Verity—I—I haven't heard you utter a word…ever. I mean I knew you could—Hector told me you spoke, but I never…"

She held up her hand. "Now is not the time to discuss my voice, Jack. Where is Declan in the ship?"

"They took him below deck—I imagine into the hold somewhere. They probably have a cell down there. It took five men to carry him on board, for how he fought it. They wouldn't have just thrown him in a hammock. If I can get on board, I won't draw notice, as they'll think I'm a new sailor aboard, and I imagine I can get him out. But the three guards at the gangplank haven't moved an inch in the last hour."

Verity exhaled a glut of panic stuck in her chest, staring at the three rough-looking men standing guard in front of the gangplank. "How did they get him?"

"I was betrayed." His words ground out, disgusted, his glare on the ship.

He didn't expand on the explanation and her look shifted to Jack. No wonder his face looked like he was ready to crush boulders. Jack took great pride in his network of people in all levels of society—informants from the simplest chimney sweep to men with such power and wealth they had no right talking to Jack. But they did. All of them.

If one of them betrayed him, Jack would be out for blood.

Yet there wasn't time for that either at the moment.

Verity tugged the black cap off her head and quickly pulled free the pins and weaves that held her hair tight to her scalp. Letting her hair down, she fluffed it until the waves were juicy and crowding her shoulders. Reaching down, she pulled free the dagger alongside her boot and slid the blade between her skin and the bodice of her dress. She wedged the tip of the blade outward and ripped through the fabric of both her dress and the binding strips underneath it. Her lungs immediately expanded, as they did every time she freed herself from the bindings.

From the new slit in between her breasts, she cut away the black fabric along the swell of her chest until air hit her skin down to just above her nipples. She cupped the bottom

of her breasts, plumping the heft of them into place above the cut of her dress.

Not perfect, but it would have to do.

The night sky would hide the haphazardness of her hair and her dress.

Jack tore his glare away from the ship and he looked down at her, his eyes expanding to wide orbs as he stared at the flesh of her chest. "Verity, what are you doing?"

"Creating a distraction. Be ready." Her look blazed into him. "Forget you ever saw this, ever heard me utter a word. You understand?"

With a half smirk on his face, Jack nodded. "I am at your command, Miss Verity."

Her eyes rolling to the heavens, she moved past Jack. He didn't try to stop her, didn't tell her to be careful. She liked that about Jack. For the most part, he respected her abilities, even if he didn't like her putting herself in dangerous areas. He counted on her, just as much as she counted on him. He knew that there were places that were only accessible by her. And places that were only accessible by him. That made each of them invaluable.

Stepping onto the long wooden pier, Verity set a slow gait to her stride, one that swung her hips back and forth as she walked along the dock, pretending to search out the men that weren't busy carrying goods to and from the other ships opposite the one Declan was being held in.

By the time she stopped a short distance away from the three brutes standing watch over the gangplank, she'd had five offers for the night.

A sailor passed her, the crate he was carrying on his shoulder bumping into the side of her head, and she used the moment to stumble toward the brutes. She looked back over her shoulder at the man that had just bumped her, shaking her fist. "Ye bloody cur—watch where ye set those clodhopper feet of yers."

With a humph, she straightened, her gaze lifting as she sized up her targets. "Well, well, well, what 'ave we here? Three strappin' men, ready to take a go?"

Only one of the guards bothered to look her way, but once he saw her, his eyes stayed riveted on her. One down.

She moved directly in front of the other two, where it would be near impossible to ignore her, and set her hands under her breasts, heaving them upward.

"What say ye, mates?" She motioned toward the ship behind them. "Nothin' comin' or goin' from this ship at the moment. Ye settin' sail soon? That'll be a long time without flesh to press into." She trailed her middle finger along the slope of her breasts, drawing little circles onto her skin.

That got one. Then the other. Three sets of eyes locked onto her.

She looked directly at the shortest one, for his presence ate up the air around him. Definitely the leader of these three. "Ye have time for one more go-about, do ye?"

She stepped in, setting her fingers along the cut of the man's dirty shirt about his chest, playing with the fabric like it was spun with gold. "We can go behind those crates." She nodded with her head toward a stack of wooden crates twenty strides to her right. Far enough away for privacy, but with plenty of men still walking past where she could slip

into the chaos of the crowd of dockhands unloading ships. "It won't take much time, the way ye three are pantin' at me. Ye can keep an eye on the gangway."

Hesitation. The two taller men looked at the short one.

She glanced up at the taller one on her left, her smile coy. "Or if ye want to be quick 'bout it, I can do ye all at the same time. Three cocks, three holes."

That offer was the one.

All three mouths opened, near to salivating at the prospect. Good thing she had inadvertently walked in on that very scene once in an upper room at the Alabaster.

The short sailor pointed with his thumb over his shoulder. "Nah, let's have a go on the ship."

She took a step back, turning and starting toward the crates. "I never set foot onto a ship. Wouldn't want to curse a voyage, would I?" She motioned with her fingers for the men to follow.

Follow, they did. The tallest one quick to her backside, his hands wrapping around her from behind and grasping onto her breasts, squeezing them.

She choked back a gasp at the raw touch, and forced out a trilling laugh. "I like yer gumption, but we need to discuss payment first, ye whelp."

She brazenly looked over her shoulder at the sailor, and her gaze slipped past the three men to see Jack running up the gangplank.

Five more steps—plenty of time for Jack to get on board—and she stopped, turning around to face the three sailors before they reached the seclusion of the crates. Men like this didn't respect women and would rape an innocent in a second if given the opportunity. Oddly enough though, they usually respected a whore's right to a transaction for services.

Some bizarre moral code amongst cutthroats.

Her hands went onto her hips, her gaze scouring them up and down. "For a three shot, it'll be five pounds." So ridiculous, she knew they would never pay.

"Five? Yer mad, ye whore."

She fluffed her hair with an air of cockiness. "Not mad—I'm just a girl that knows me worth—and what I plan to do to each of ye will leave ye with enough visions in yer heads to last the next three voyages."

The tallest one of the three licked his lips, looking to the other two. "I say we go."

The shortest one sneered, his gaze rabid on her. "And I say we take what yer offerin' and pay ye what we think it's worth."

He advanced on her and she threw up her hands in between them. "It's not the deal, ye cur. Ye pay or I'll be getting me flash-man and his brutes down here to make ye pay."

He slapped her hands out of the air and reached for her waist with a laugh. "Won't matter if we're on the tide by the time he makes it to the docks."

These scrubs didn't adhere to the cur moral code. Sailors. Dubious bunch, the lot of them.

She glanced at the ship. No Jack. No Declan.

But she didn't have any more time.

She jumped to her left to avoid the brute's hands, but he managed to catch her halfway around the waist.

Verity spun, his grip tearing into her hip, but she found a step away from his grubby hands. She sprinted before the one on the left could snatch her and she aimed straight for a man balancing two crates—one on top of the other—on his shoulder. She rammed into him, sending the crates flying and blocking the path behind her. She hoped.

Weaving in and out of the carts and men moving goods and supplies on the dock, she could see solid ground in front of her, forty strides away. Her look bobbing around masses of men, she found a line toward a skinny alleyway between two warehouses that the sailors behind her would barely fit through—or they would at least have to follow her one-by-one.

Her best chance, for if she could get two streets away from the docks, they wouldn't follow her. The ship was set to sail too soon and they couldn't leave their post.

She made it ten more steps when two men in a brawl tumbled in front of her, arms swinging and curses filling the air.

Hell.

Just enough to slow her down, and a hand grabbed the back of her skirt, yanking on the fabric.

It stopped all her momentum and her hand went down instantly to the blade in her boot. She swung the dagger around behind her, hitting flesh before she could even see what she was aiming at. With a howl, the hand gripping her skirt loosened, but a fist was at the ready, coming at her temple.

It smacked her. Stars flashed in her eyes. Stars for too long. The hands reached her, the blade ripped out of her hand.

Grimy palms shoved her toward another wide pile of crates along the edge of the pier.

Hands, arms on her body, shoving her against the crates. A backhanded slap across her face, the metallic tinge of blood instant on her tongue.

Fingers everywhere. Hands pawing at her breasts, her neck. Skirt lifting, air hitting her legs. Her spine cracked into the stack of crates balanced along the dock's edge, the top one tumbling off and crashing into the water below.

The three of them blocking everything. Blocking her away from all light, all people.

There was only one way out.

Behind her.

{ CHAPTER 19 }

A hand went high up on her leg, grabbing the back of her thigh and lifting it. She'd have to use it.

Wedging her foot higher, she kicked off from the short man's belly with her right leg. The force sent her body crashing between the crates and over the edge of the dock.

The entire way down, weightless in the air, Verity prayed the water wasn't too shallow or too deep.

She hit the water on her side, the smell of the putrid, brackish river invading her lungs just before she went under the surface.

Cold. Freezing cold.

She knew it was cold, but this, this set her whole body to panic.

She needed out. Out.

Kicking, arms flailing, she fought the water for air before her skirts dragged her down.

Her face breached the surface for only a second, enough to gasp, to search. Hell—she'd thought there would be something to grab onto. The pilings of the pier. Crates or debris that had fallen into the water.

Nothing.

The blackness swallowed her downward, her hands frantic, splashing, touching air and then being devoured even as they searched for something to grab a hold of.

Swim. Swim. Swim.

She knew full well how to swim. Hector had made sure
of it. Just not in freezing water in a wool dress and a shift
and petticoat and boots.

Her arms tried to move her toward the riverbank,
even as her legs twisted in the heft of her dress, strangling
her from the ankles upward. The current of the water set
its tentacles upon her, pulling her out to the bowels of the
Thames.

Her hand hit flesh. Hard flesh.

Fingers wrapped around her wrist, pulling her upward
from the murky black depths. Higher. Higher.

Her mouth broke through the water's surface and she
gasped, sucking in air. Sucking more and more.

"Stop thrashing, Verity."

Declan—Declan's voice in her ear.

"You have her?" Jack's voice.

"Aye."

She could barely make out Declan's head bobbing
along in front of her for the darkness under the dock. But
her body began to move through the water, toward the
muck of the bank underneath the dock.

Her toe bumped along something solid. A rock. Then
the squish of the bed of the river. Declan shifted from
swimming to crawling along on his knees, struggling to find
solid purchase on the mud and rocks. Dragging her along
with him.

Her veins were turning to ice. Her body shaking so
fiercely it was a wonder she hadn't shaken clear of Declan's
grip on her wrist.

But that—that was solid. And warm. His fingers branding her wrist with heat.

He found rocks and solid ground along the bank and he hauled her up onto them.

"Can you stand?"

She tried to gain traction under her feet, but her boots slipped on the slime of the rocks, again and again. "C-c-c-c-a-a-n-n-n-n-o-o-o-t-t-t." The one word took forever to escape from her lips, her teeth clattering so hard.

Jack grabbed her from behind and lifted her to get her feet properly under her.

"You have her?" Declan asked.

"Aye." Jack's hands tightened around her waist.

Declan let go of her wrist and he pulled a blade from heaven knew where and slid it behind the front of her dress between her breasts.

With a quick downward slice that jerked her forward and would have had her stumbling to her knees if not for Jack's hands about her, the dress split wide open.

"Declan!" That word came out firm and strong.

"You'll freeze to death in this blasted thing." He ripped the dress away from her arms, pushing it and the petticoats down to her feet.

He was right. She was accustomed to a chill in her bones, but this, this was the torture of her bones splintering to icicles, tearing her up from the inside out.

"We move along the bank for a stretch before cutting up to the carriage."

Declan bent, picking her up and tossing her over his shoulder, her butt high in the air. And she was just in her wet shift. A shift one could now see quite clearly through.

"Dec—Declan—y-y-y-you—" The words rushed out, unable to finish as his shoulder dug into her gut.

His arm clamped about her legs tightened. "We won't move as fast along the shore waiting for you in your slippery boots and I can't carry you politely and see where I'm going. You want to land in the river again if I slip?"

Her mouth shut. No. That was the last thing she wanted.

Bumping along with her head upside down, she realized her hands were fisted, smacking against Declan's butt. Awkward. As cold as she was, she could still think straight enough to realize Jack was behind them, watching the show of all of this.

She tried to curl her hands upward closer to her head, to brace herself against the bumps. But her hands kept slipping.

Well then, Jack could just enjoy the show.

Declan turned inward away from the bank of the river and he stopped in the shadow of a building—a brothel, it appeared to be—and he set her down onto the ground. "You are steady enough to walk from here?"

"Yes."

He grabbed her hand, pulling her along behind him, Jack taking up the rear.

Within three minutes they were at the coach, Jack leaping up onto the driver's perch as Declan opened the door and lifted her into the carriage.

He vaulted in and slammed the door and the coach started rolling.

Declan didn't sit, instead, rummaging under the seat opposite her until he pulled free a wool blanket. Spinning around to her in the tight space, he unfurled the blanket and stretched it out over her, tucking it along the edges of her body.

She was getting the cushions of his carriage hopelessly soaked, but she didn't rightly care—as long as it wasn't freezing water or cold air swallowing her, she was grateful.

He puffed out an exhausted sigh and collapsed onto the bench opposite her. He was soaked to the bone as well, though just in a lawn shirt and trousers.

She looked down. "You don't have any shoes."

"No."

"Where are they?"

"I tossed them once I saw jumping was the only way off the ship."

"The cold water didn't slow you?"

"I've had to swim in colder—most of my life was on a ship if you recall." His words clipped, short.

Still irate with her. And exhausted, she imagined. Her body was still revolting from the icy waters and the phantom feel of those brutes touching her in all the wrong places—so she couldn't imagine how it was for him after having to pull her to safety and then carry her.

The stench of the brackish waters receded slightly as they moved away from the docks. She took stock of him in the flickers of the passing streetlights. He sat, the white of his lawn shirt splattered with blood and dirt the river didn't

wash out. Not that it would for the filth of it. But Declan was upright, moving, and she latched onto the relief that he was safe for the moment—the main thing she had focused on for the last two years. His safety.

His sleeves had been rolled up to his elbows and there was just enough passing light to see his knuckles were covered with blood. The fight onto the ship or the interrogation from earlier, she wasn't sure. Probably both.

He moved to the edge of the bench and reached across the carriage, his thumb streaking across her lower lip and onto her cheek. In the light flickering in and out of shadows, his eyes locked with hers.

"You're hurt." His words said so viciously, she blinked at the anger in them.

She lifted her hand between them, her fingertips running along the length of the cut across his cheekbone. His skin rough, still bloodied under her fingers. "You are too."

He reached up and caught the back of her hand, pulling her touch away from him. "Can you not just let me worry about you for once, Verity?" The words vibrated with simmering rage, even as his look sank into her, heating her to her core. "Blood is on you—blood because of me. I hate it and I never want to see it."

"Then look away."

"I think I'm long past that option." He paused, his breath heaving deep enough to swell his chest.

Three breaths they stared at each other. Three breaths too long. Three breaths where the world and what was right and wrong and possible and not possible shifted underneath them.

The carriage hit a rut, knocking him off balance and his hand snapped away from her. His look went out the window, and he settled back onto the opposite bench with a sigh.

It took several minutes before he looked to her again. "Thank you." The ire had all but disappeared from his voice. One second, he couldn't control it. The next, like it had never even existed.

But it was a thank you. Something to hold onto. "For what?"

"Saving me—I heard what you did in order to distract the men guarding the ship. I can only presume that is why we found you in the water?"

"It was the only way to get away."

Fury instantly flashed in his face. "They touched you?"

She should lie, should not provoke his anger anymore. But she was done lying to him. She'd done it for so long and she was exhausted by it. "They did. But I jumped off before anything too grievous occurred." The shortened truth. He didn't need to hear what exactly they touched or how just the thought of their greasy paws on her sent bile up her throat.

"That they laid one finger on you is grievous." The possessive growl in his voice reared, unmistakable and it made her start.

That was where the uncertainty between them hovered—what were they to each other at the moment? Still employer, employee? Still a guardian and her charge?

There hadn't been the slightest time to discuss anything. And maybe that was exactly how Declan liked it—she wasn't a commitment; she was an enjoyable perk to be had on the side when it suited him.

But yet, that possessive undertone in his voice told her things she wasn't sure she wanted to imagine. For they could never be together. Not with her past.

Maybe *he* was an enjoyable perk for *her* to have when it suited her.

Except…no.

She'd fallen in love with Declan a year and a half ago. That part she couldn't deny.

So here she would suffer, in the vast wasteland of ambiguity, always knowing that anything between the two of them could only be in passing.

Even if she wanted more—dreamed of more.

It was never to be.

Under the blanket, her arms latched across her chest tightened, her stare stubborn on the window. "It is my job." Her words were prickly, but she didn't have it in her to coddle to his possessiveness at the moment. Not after what those men had touched and groped.

She was just doing her job, just as he had requested of her when he'd left her the night before.

"And I'm sorry."

Her eyebrow quirked as she gave him a quick glance. "For what?"

"For how I treated you—sent you off in the carriage last night. I'm just coming to terms with who you are in my life, and why you're here. And how in the bloody hell I didn't know."

She flicked one finger out of the top fold of the blanket, pointing upward, her voice a whisper. "Jack can hear."

His stare sank into her, not a drop of emotion on his face. "I think Jack knows full well what the current situation is."

The air in her chest deflated. "He does?"

Declan nodded.

Her finger crawled back under the blanket. Not that it was warm in the cocoon of it, but she currently wanted to hide. Hide away from everything. "You think we played you the fool?"

"No more so than any of your other clients. I would be furious at you, at Jack, if I didn't know you were only looking to keep me alive. It is hard for me to fault you for that."

She nodded slowly, not quite trusting his words.

He looked down, his hand sliding along the wet thigh of his trousers. "You should know, Verity."

"Know what?"

"When we were at the office of your employer, I saw something."

She pushed herself up, her glare pinning him. "What did you see? You didn't tell me about seeing anything."

His look lifted to meet her eyes. "I wasn't sure you needed to know."

"Truly? I told you everything of what I'd found in your file, yet you decided you didn't need to give me that same courtesy?"

"I'm telling you now." His head tilted to the side. "I saw a nameplate across from one of the side windows by the front door." His stare focused on her, unflinching. "*Guardians of the Bones.* It was a small nameplate, but I could see the copper-pressed emblem on the wall opposite the door. That is who you are."

Hell. Panic seized her chest. If Declan knew exactly what they were—who they were—it would be no time before he discovered everything about Hector and the rest of the guardians. That put each and every one of them in danger. Her words came out cautiously. "You're going to discover everything you can about us, aren't you?"

"You haven't exactly been forthcoming about the organization. So I will do what I must."

"No—no—if they find out you are asking about us…I…it won't be good." The carriage slowed to a stop and her voice dipped to a low whisper. "If you have questions, ask me. I'll tell you what you need to know. Just promise me you will protect any information like your first-born."

"I don't have any children."

Her hand flew up from the blanket. "Then protect it like you protect the Alabaster—as I know there is nothing more precious to you."

His lips pursed for a second as the carriage shifted from Jack jumping off the driver's perch. "I will do so."

She looked out the window. They had stopped in the carriage lane behind the Alabaster. "This is awkward…but can I ask that Jack bring me back to my boarding house? I cannot rightly walk the streets in just my shift and this blanket."

"No."

"No?"

"You're coming inside for a proper bath. You smell like you just got dragged from the Thames."

She chuckled past her tongue that was suddenly very dry. "So do you."

Just where she would be bathing, he didn't say.

She wasn't sure if she was happy or not on that accord.

{ CHAPTER 20 }

He wasn't about to let her out of his sight again. Not after that debacle at the docks.

Left to her own devices, Verity was too predisposed to getting herself into mounds of trouble.

And also to saving his life.

He did have to give her that.

So she would just have to take a hot bath here, at the Alabaster.

Also, he was moving her here. No more boarding house for her, whether she wanted it or not. He just had to tiptoe into that demand a bit more slowly.

The two maids that had been hauling up buckets of hot water exited his bedroom adjacent to his office and he closed the door after them. While he had, in the past, used one of the larger suites on the floor above as his living quarters at the Alabaster, he'd had his bed moved into this room several months ago and put a connecting door in. The proximity to his office had only made sense, since he usually only gave up on work once he was blurry-eyed and his mind couldn't add one to two to come up with three. At that point, he hated walking up the stairs for sleep, so he would end up on his settee, night after night. Only so many nights could his neck handle falling asleep on the too-small-for-his-frame settee.

Standing at the door, it took him a long moment before he turned around to Verity. When he did, he found

her motionless in front of the fire, still wrapped in that blanket from the coach, and still shivering. The steaming hot bath sat several feet to her left, but she hadn't moved toward it.

"You haven't made it a step toward the bath."

She looked to the copper tub, then to him. "You aren't going to dip in first?"

"Why would I go before you?"

Her jaw went slack for breath, then pressed closed, and her green eyes drifted to the bath, lust in her eyes.

He'd rather have that lust directed at him, but if it would warm her bones, he'd let it slide for the moment.

"Would you rather I leave the room?" He choked out the suggestion. It didn't bode well for keeping her within his sight, but he was compelled to at least extend the offer.

A cringe creased the edges of her eyes. "Can I say no and not paint myself a trollop?"

He chuckled. "You can do whatever you want, finch."

She inched her way toward the bath.

Where he thought she would slowly strip and move into the bath, she didn't. The blanket dropped and she tore the clinging shift down her body, past her hips and jumped into the tub, the water sloshing with the momentum.

She sank low in the long copper tub, her body still shivering, and submerged herself fully underwater. Seconds passed, almost too many, before her face broke the surface and she stilled with only her nose, eyes, forehead, and lips above the water.

With her eyes closed, she let out a long sigh. It took several breaths before her eyelids opened and her look shifted to him. "Even the air in my lungs is cold."

"Stay in there as long as you need."

He walked over to the fire and tugged off his cold, sopping lawn shirt from his torso. It dropped with a wet thud onto the hearth and he could already feel the heat of the fire warming his skin.

He glanced at the copper tub. Verity was watching him over the edge, her stare raking over his bare chest. Hunger in the green of her eyes. And this time directed at him.

There was more than one way to warm up a body.

He moved toward the head of the tub and reached out to grab the bar of soap on the floor and the washcloth draped over the rolled copper edge of the tub.

After scrubbing the soap into the washcloth, he dipped his bare arm into the water, finding her shoulders and washing her skin, dipping in along her back.

Her body tensed and she pulled away from him, half turning in the tub as she reached to steal the washcloth from his hand. "I can do that."

He didn't let her take the washcloth from him, his look pinning her. "Why do you not want me to take care of you?"

Her head snapped back, her gaze flickering off of him, like she fully understood the question but didn't have a good answer for it. "I am just not accustomed to it." Her stare lifted from the water to his face, her look pausing on his lips before moving to his eyes. "I have been surviving on

my own, taking care of myself for a long time. Taking care of others for a long time."

He nodded, then motioned for her to turn her back to him. "And is it such a bad thing, letting someone take care of you?"

She stared at him for a long moment, then cautiously turned in the tub, curling her torso around her knees with her back to him. "It is only bad if I start to believe it is sustainable."

Sustainable? That was where her hesitancy lay?

In all fairness, why should it not? What had happened between them during the last fortnight had been fast and explosive and he had thought about little else in the last days other than his peculiar, crushing need for this woman in front of him.

But he hadn't moved into the future in his mind—he never did. *Never look ahead, for ahead was never promised.* It was the only way to live in the life he did.

Vexing thoughts filling his head, he silently draped the thick of her red hair over her right shoulder and set the washcloth along her spine, then dragged it back and forth, letting the beads of water roll down the smooth expanse of her back.

Damn, but she was a bloody goddess. How had he spent two years around her and never known? It still staggered his sensibilities that he'd been so obtuse.

"You thanked me, but I didn't thank you." Her soft words broke his reverie.

"For what?"

"Pulling me from a watery grave. If you hadn't been there, I doubt I could have found my way to air, much less to the bank of the river."

"Or you would have found a way out—I have discovered in the last week that I have underestimated you for too long, Verity. And even when I think I have a handle on what you are capable of, I find I have underestimated you once more."

A soft laugh came from her mouth as she set her chin atop her knees. "Be careful or you will be placing me on a pedestal I have no business atop of."

"What if I don't want you on a pedestal, but here, at the Alabaster?"

She looked over her shoulder at him. "What?"

"I don't want you back at that hovel of a boarding house—ever again. I want you here, with me."

She shook her head. "Dec—"

"I want you, Verity." He studied the green in her eyes, seeing the fear, the denial that flashed rampant.

"Is it that you need me to think about the future? I can do so. For I cannot imagine a single day in the future—a single hour—where I will not want you. Your body and your mind and that soft smile that quirks to the side when I'm driving you mad. I want you. I cannot promise a future I cannot predict, but I can swear to the fact that I will always want you. For the second I think about losing you, like I almost did tonight, the core of me turns into an inferno devouring me from the inside out." He paused, swallowing hard, his palm flattening on the slickness of her

back. "The only thing that quells those flames is the fact that I can touch you now."

She didn't answer him. Instead, her body turned halfway toward him and she lifted her hand from the depths of the water. Silently, she studied his face, lust seeped into the green of her eyes, replacing all fear. She dragged her palm across his cheek as her fingers sank into the back of his hair, then she pulled herself toward him, her lips meeting his in a frenzy.

His mouth not leaving hers, his hands went down to his wet trousers and peeled the fabric from his waist, his legs. Slipping onto his feet, he shoved the trousers down to the floor and moved into the tub behind her, the front of him sliding down along her back.

Bloody hell, his member was already granite hard and ready to burst, so the feel of her back slick against his cock nearly undid him.

His tub was larger than usual, but still a tight fit. It didn't matter, for she lifted herself, settling onto his thighs, the curves of her backside sliding along his shaft, begging it to find home.

Heaven and hell colliding, both pain and bliss to have her wiggling on top of him.

Not trusting his own fortitude in how long this needed to last, he slid his hands around her, one hand going to her left breast, the other deep into the crux of her as his lips attacked her neck.

Slicking his tongue along her skin, tasting her, he found her nubbin, circling it, and she gasped, her hips bucking into his hand.

Hell, he'd never get tired of this. Her voice, the carnal sound of her gasping as his fingers went wicked on her, drawing as much pleasure as he could.

He slid a finger into her, then another, his thumb still working her nub, and her head dropped back onto him, the gasps getting louder. His name. Begging.

So damn responsive to his touch. So damn unrestrained—like an entirely different woman buzzed under the skin of this façade she'd so carefully constructed around her. And all it took to set her free was his touch, his prodding, and she became wildfire.

When her hips started grinding against the strokes of his fingers, he knew she was close. But this one, this one he was going to enjoy.

He pulled his fingers from her core and she shrieked, but then he grabbed both of her hips and lifted her, impaling her from below. Still so savagely tight, like he hadn't just been buried in her two nights ago.

Her frustration faded as she settled her body atop of his, her hips working back and forth, and she leaned forward, bending her legs on either side of his thighs for traction.

She started slow, her breath still panting, lifting herself up and then sliding down his cock. He didn't even try to control her pace with his hands on her hips, instead, grabbing her by the breasts, rolling her nipples hard, then soft. Her hands gripped the sides of the tub and she rode him until her strokes were furious, her mews turning into screams at every descent. Water splashed out of the tub with

every ferocious thrust, like she couldn't sink fast or deep enough onto him. Again and again.

He dropped his right hand from her breast into her folds and found her nubbin, hard and throbbing and he circled it, fast, meeting the rhythm of her plunges.

Her body started to tighten and his other hand went to her neck, his fingers along her jaw and he turned her head toward him. He needed to watch her as she came.

It hit her, her body seizing around his cock, her scream of aching release vibrating through every inch of her.

Bloody beautiful. Destruction and deliverance all at once.

The sight so arresting he was coming before he could react, only pulling his cock from her at the last second before his seed erupted with a force he was not master of. Her hips still gyrating, still riding on his hand, the surges seizing her, he settled his shaft between the mounds of her butt, wave after wave pulsating through him. His head sank down, his teeth biting her shoulder for the raw pleasure ripping through him.

He hadn't ever felt this. Not this hard. Not this fast.

But with her. With her, he was always at the edge of losing control. And then he did. Lose all control. Lose all sense of the world around them and who he was.

Infuriating.

Intoxicating.

She leaned back fully against his chest, her gasps for air making her chest ride swells that sent her breasts bobbing above and below the water.

It took him long moments to move. Long moments to think again.

He dug down into the bottom of the tub, finding the washcloth, and then set it across her chest, taking an inordinate amount of time washing her left perfect breast, then her right one. Her nipples were still raw and taut, and a streak of inordinate pride flashed in his chest.

Her body was his.

She gave it to him freely, unabashedly meeting every one of his touches, his kisses, his thrusts.

His.

The notion settled him, even as a vexing thought festered in the back of his mind.

She never did say a word about the future.

Had he mistaken the hesitancy in her eyes—that she had been worried about the future? Had he mistaken everything about her?

It wouldn't be the first time.

All those secrets he'd vowed to peel away from her?

Time to start.

{ CHAPTER 21 }

With the length of her back pressed tight to the muscles lining his chest and abdomen, the slick of the water between them, Verity watched him curl a wet lock of her hair around his forefinger, twirling, again and again. The motion so repetitive and soothing, she could very well drift off to sleep in the tub, even if the water was slowly losing its warmth. Declan had enough heat for the two of them.

"Tell me about the Guardians of the Bones."

Almost asleep, her eyes popped open. A long beat of silence settled around them. She had been the one to insist he ask her about them, and that request had taken very little time to rise and bite her.

She exhaled a sigh. "What do you want to know?"

"Everything. But one question at a time."

She nodded.

"First, who heads the Guardians?"

She craned her neck, shifting against his chest to look up at him. "Right to the heart of it, then?"

He nodded.

"This goes no further than this room? You won't go digging? Won't raise suspicions that don't need to be raised?"

He inclined his head to her. "I said I would leave it. But I do need to know."

She steeled her spine. She was risking others by telling Declan about the Guardians. But if it meant finally putting an end to the distrust she saw again and again in the stormy grey of his eyes, she would have to chance it.

Declan didn't break promises. She would just have to remember that.

"His name is Hector Samson." She turned, resetting herself against his chest. "He worked in a most discreet division under Wellington, starting before the turn of the century against the French, then in India, and so on. He founded the Guardians in the midst of the wars on the continent."

"Why?"

"He was asked, I presume. He never has said much about his past. What I know, I've pieced together from other guardians. He had access to everywhere and anyone during the wars, and there were certain sons of society that entered the war as soldiers."

"Second and third and fourth sons of peers?"

She nodded, the back of her head brushing against his chest. "Exactly. Young whelps determined to do duty to their country but had no business dealing with the gore of war. Families of the young gentlemen would hire Hector and his network to protect the young men from harm. The men would never know how or why they survived the war, while so many around them died. But it was the Guardians that returned those lucky enough to have coin on their side to their mother's bosoms."

"And after the war?"

"I presume the business only expanded after the war. Too many of those young men either missed the action and surge of raw excitement that came with warfare, or they were adrift with all they had seen and done. The horrors of war—killing, seeing your comrades killed—came back with them after the war. Good choices in life are not made by those with such scars on their souls. So, many continued to be protected by the Guardians. Even these days, there are always young people that need to be protected from their own bad choices."

Declan grunted behind her as his arm slid in front of her waist and tightened. His chin landed on top of her head. "Second question, how did you end up working for Mr. Samson?"

"I was accosted by two ruffians in an alleyway by Charing Cross—they thought I had money and threatened to split my face open if I didn't give it over. Except I had nothing, only my dagger. Hector came upon the scene, but by then I had already put down one of the men and was working on the second. He knocked the man into the wall, then stood, appraising me for a very long moment. He had seen what I did to them."

"Appraising you?"

"Yes, scrutiny like no other. Judging my worth to him. I stood there, staring him down, for I didn't know what his game was—if he was about to attack me as well." Her shoulders lifted. "Then, just like that, he nodded to himself and offered me a job."

"And you took it?"

"Not then. I'm not a fool. What he was offering was too good to be true. But he persisted. He found out who I was, where I lived, what I needed, and he offered me the

very thing I needed to join him. I would have been stupid to turn him down."

"What did you need so badly?"

Her voice crept out, choking on the words, for it still stung her heart, the choice she had to make years ago. "I needed my brother out of the rookeries. I needed him somewhere safe, or he was going to die on these streets. Die because of a stupid choice, or die because he would commit acts so grievous his soul would be marred forever. His heart has always been soft, generous, kind. Until we got to London and he couldn't be any of those things anymore. He had to be tough and callous and cruel. It killed me, day after day, to see him changing, to see the deadened look creeping into his eyes. It killed me to see him like that. So brave in his own destruction. All I wanted was to get him out—get him out of London. Get him someplace safe."

"By giving up your own heart in place of his?" The low rumble of Declan's voice vibrated along the back of her ribcage.

"No. It's not like that."

"It isn't? For I would say that you have that same heart—or had it, before joining the Guardians. There is a kindness in you that cannot be dimmed by the things you've been forced to do."

She fell silent. If only he knew, knew how hardened her heart really was, how deeply her soul was marred. Taking a few more lives to protect Declan would add nothing to the purgatory she was already destined for.

She swallowed hard. "No. I have the cold heart, the spine that can handle this sort of business. You've seen it yourself. Am I ill-suited to the life, to what is required of me?"

"Your body and mind may not be ill-suited for it, but that doesn't mean your heart was meant for it."

Her lips pulled inward, and she bit them between her teeth. How did he manage to needle so easily into the part of her that sat reeking with vulnerability?

His fingers dove into the wet strands of her hair, stroking her head. The touch of it so intimate, so soothing, she imagined she would answer any question he had of her at the moment.

"Was I your first job?"

She curled her head into his fingers. "No. My first job was to be a companion to an heiress in her first season. She was gold dressed in silk, and the men that came after her—constantly trying to entice her into shadowed corridors and deep corners of gardens—were sickening. It was enough to make me happy to play the mute and not have to speak to another male for the last two years."

His fingers massaging her scalp stopped moving. "You were in society?"

Her mouth closed.

Stupid.

She shouldn't have said anything. *Stupid.*

This was why staying mute was important. She didn't lie well. And she talked too long and too much. Hector had told her that long ago.

"Verity?"

"What?" She tried to force her voice strong, unruffled, but the sound came out in a croak.

"Earlier, you said you've been surviving on your own for a long time—what are you surviving from?"

"What do you mean?" Her words offered cautiously, as she could feel the tide of the conversation sweeping her into waters that were too deep to tread.

"It means I don't know where you come from or why. I know you used to wield swords and daggers with the baker's son and the blacksmith's daughter, which makes me believe you grew up in or near a village. You had time to develop those skills, which tells me your family had enough wealth where you weren't needed for household chores or in the fields. You also talk like an educated woman and are extremely intelligent, probably taught by a governess. You would have to have a certain polish about you in order to pose as a companion in society to an heiress."

She squirmed in the tub, her body suddenly uncomfortably caught under his arm over her belly. She'd loved the feel of his muscles as they had slid across her waist, but now his arm felt like a steel clamp, holding her down.

She refused to verify any of his assumptions and could only squeak out a paltry, "So?"

"So what happened between battles with the blacksmith's daughter and where you are now? What exactly was your life before the Guardians? Before the Alabaster?"

Her shoulders lifted in a shrug. "It was different."

"Different how?"

She shook her head slightly, not wanting the questioning to go any further.

He took her silence as confirmation of all he suspected. "You lived a different life before London, and then you came here with your brother in squalor. Yet you knew enough to want him out of life in the rookeries. So why? Why come to London?"

"Someone died."

"Someone died?"

She grabbed the edges of the tub and pulled herself upright and away from him. "Yes."

He grabbed her forearm, his wet fingers slick against her skin. "Who died?"

She looked at him, frozen for a moment when she saw the scrutiny in his grey eyes. She was a puzzle he needed to solve.

A puzzle she couldn't let him solve.

She shook her head, but kept her gaze locked on his. "Don't ask more, Declan. Please. Don't."

He held her stare for a long moment, then exhaled a sigh. "Fine. I'll cease. For tonight. I'll cease." His hand slipped off her forearm. "But I will ask again. And again. And again, until I get answers that satisfy."

She pursed her lips and pulled herself to standing. Stepping out of the tub, she moved to the towels stacked on a wingback chair by the fireplace.

She wrapped one around her body and then stepped back to the tub with one for him. He stood in the tub and the water dripped in sheets off his body, rolling over all the hard planes and cuts of muscles on his chest, his abdomen, his thighs.

She stood, stupefied for long seconds. He truly was an Adonis, cut from the finest marble, beauty in what the human form could be. And for these precious hours, she had reign over that body. It was hers.

The last thing she wanted was for it to end, even if that was the inevitability.

Stifling a sigh, she held out the towel to him. "Did you learn anything tonight, other than to get yourself kidnapped?" She gave him a quick wink. "Jack said you went to the docks on information you squeezed from the man we had captured, but that it was a trap?"

He took the towel and snapped it open. "Aye, it didn't turn out as I wanted. I didn't plan on being crimped, but that was where they made a mistake."

"How so?" She started to dab away at the moisture in her hair.

"That ship they dragged me onto belongs to Bloodwater."

"Bloodwater—truly?"

He nodded. "It does and doesn't make sense. He's always wanted our territory, but during the last few months, I thought he had given up on that dream as he has been working on expanding in the opposite direction. He more than has his hands full with that, so why come after me now?"

"There's more to it?"

"Aye. I just don't know what yet." He stepped out of the tub, sweeping away droplets on his body.

"So, what is our next move?"

"It is time I pay a call upon Bloodwater."

She nodded, her chest tightening. All of this was getting out of hand. They needed to find out who had hired the Guardians, and fast. Declan's life was clearly on the line, whether he was flippant about that fact or not.

He stepped to her, wrapping his hands along her sides. "No frowning. It will be a friendly visit."

"Or a deadly one."

His head twitched to the side with a crooked grin. "It will be what it will be. But it isn't worth the worry until it happens." He yanked her body into his, the heat of him instantly enveloping her. "But before any of that—I plan on taking advantage of a fully naked you." He shuffled her backward toward the bed.

Her hands lifted up, encircling his neck. "Don't tell me not to worry. It is my permanent state."

"Then I will just have to flood your mind with much more wicked things."

With a grin on his face, he attacked, and she fell full force—both onto the bed and into everything he was.

Ceasing her worry, at least for the moment.

{ CHAPTER 22 }

The Fashionable Filly wasn't the worst whorehouse in Bloodwater's domain, but it still had the stench about it of being well-used by sailors—fish and brine soaked into the walls, hanging in every breath.

Declan exhaled, trying to choke the smell out of his mouth. For how long he'd lived at sea, he shouldn't have such a reaction to the smell, but his life in London had taught him one thing—he hated the sea.

Hated the constant motion of a ship under his feet. Hated salted-beef and biscuits and rations of rum. Hated the constant smell of gutted fish.

The only thing he liked about it was the physical work. Hauling ropes, climbing masts, carrying barrels. He could always get lost in the physical work, not thinking for hours on end as his muscles screamed and sweat poured from him in the hot equator sun.

That, he liked.

That, he missed.

The rest of it could go to hell.

Declan crept along the dim hallway, key to the room ahead of him in hand, blade at the ready. Bloodwater wasn't the only one with connections on the opposite side of the river.

He'd left Jack watching the staircase—just the two of them on this foray into Bloodwater's territory. All the better to blend in, not be seen until they wanted to be seen. That

had left Verity back at the Alabaster, much to his relief and much to her chagrin. She'd fought him on it, of course, but after threatening to lock her into his room, she'd acquiesced.

Not that she wouldn't sneak out into the night to follow them—he wouldn't put that past her and his stomach physically roiled at the thought, but at some point, she was going to have to trust him to know what he was doing. And he was going to have to trust her.

Declan paused at the door at the end of the hallway and listened to the grunts inside. Perfect.

He was into the room, his arm wrapped around Bloodwater's neck and his blade at Bloodwater's still flopping balls before the man could turn to see who had made it into the room.

The woman with her legs spread wide under Bloodwater—his favorite whore at the Fashionable Filly—screamed and Declan motioned his head toward the corner of the room. "Move into the corner, but don't you dare think of leaving this room." He couldn't have her escaping the room and running for Bloodwater's brutes.

Holding Bloodwater in place, Declan's stare stayed on the woman as she untangled her legs and jumped from the bed, grabbing a robe as she cowered into the corner.

"Good girl. Stay there, be silent, and you'll be back under his pounding in minutes as long as he cooperates with me."

Bloodwater squirmed, red filling his pockmarked face at his outrage at getting caught balls deep and at the mercy of anyone, much less Declan. But Declan's hold on his neck tightened, even as Bloodwater scratched at his arm.

"I wouldn't do that—my blade could very likely slip and slice off one of your balls with all this wiggling."

Bloodwater stilled.

"That's better."

"What the fuck do you want, Rudderton? Coming into my territory, setting a blade to me." His uncontrolled rage sent spittle flying out the side of his mouth.

"It seems you've been sending people into my territory, so I may as well return the favor. Contrary to your filthy mischief, I am not really seeking to make you bleed, Bloodwater. But I do intend to get some information from you, and if I have to prod"—Declan shoved the edge of the blade deep into the delicate skin of the underside of Bloodwater's ballcocks—"your cooperation along, believe me, I will take great pleasure in doing so."

Bloodwater stilled at the blade's edge protruding into his skin. "What the fuck do you want?"

"You're not working alone on my demise."

"What makes you think that?"

Declan sneered a chuckle. "A month ago, you didn't even blink an eye in my direction. You were off to easier pickings and consumed with the South."

Bloodwater shrugged. "Times change. One meets new people and opportunities arise."

"What kind of opportunities?"

"Lucrative ones."

"Is that so? Tell you what, Bloodwater, I'll leave you with your balls intact if you leave me with a name."

Bloodwater forced a caustic chortle, full of bravado. "From me—from some other cutthroat—this changes

nothing about the unfortunate accident that will happen to you when you least expect it."

"I don't imagine it will." Declan kept his voice steely, menace dripping off every word as he pushed up more pressure on Bloodwater's ballocks. "The name."

"He's so far above you—above me—you'll never get to him."

"I'll worry about that. The name. Last chance, Bloodwater."

"Gunderson." Bloodwater spurted out the name. "Lord Gunderson."

Declan paused for a moment, taking in the worth of the information. Bloodwater could be lying, yes, but he wasn't known for being a lying rat to squeak out of a trap—he usually just killed anyone and everyone around him.

Declan eased the blade from Bloodwater's balls. "Thank you for the name." He pointed the tip of the blade at the woman in the corner, her eyes still wide. "As you were." He flicked the blade toward the bed and she scurried from the corner, keeping a wide berth from his blade as she crawled back onto the bed.

Still not releasing Bloodwater, he nodded to her. "My apologies if the pounding is more…aggressive than it was. But if anyone can soothe him, pretty bird, I imagine it is you."

She nodded, her eyes wide.

He bent to Bloodwater's ear. "Just remember this mercy the next time you think to send cutthroats after me. They die and I come after you. It's as simple as that." He released

Bloodwater's neck and moved toward the door, exiting the whorehouse as quickly as he had infiltrated it.

He had some more investigating to do.

He had never heard the name Gunderson before.

{ Chapter 23 }

Verity pulled the folds of her dark green skirts to the side of the carriage, attempting to make room for the length of Declan's legs as he sat down opposite her in the carriage.

Her breath caught in her throat. Declan was more often than not dressed in just a lawn shirt—an old habit from his days at sea—and on occasion, a waistcoat and tailcoat if he needed to intimidate some unruly patron with deep pockets at the Alabaster.

But this, this was something different. Full crisp cravat above the darkest of blacks that shined along the cut of his tailcoat fitting perfectly over his broad shoulders. The waistcoat underneath lined with the most delicate threads of silver. His black hair neat and tidy, the line of his jaw freshly shaven. She had never seen him more dashing, or oddly, more dangerous looking.

Settle the man in the finest of clothes and it created a wicked air about him, like he would twirl a debutante on the dance floor and in the next minute slit a throat in a darkened hallway.

As usual, Jack drove the coach, and Declan had enlisted two of his guards from his Bedford Square townhouse to act as footmen. Important to arrive with the proper amount of swagger, Declan had mentioned.

Extending his legs and crossing them as he angled them to the bottom corner of the carriage to give the rich silk of

her skirts plenty of room to breathe, he glanced at her, then stopped and looked her up and down for a long heartbeat.

"You look too beautiful." Contrary to his words, a distinct frown set upon his face.

"That is a bad thing?" Her hand unconsciously went up to the side of her hair that had been twisted and braided into an elaborate concoction that she had to admit looked striking. It had taken the maid Declan produced to help her at his townhouse an inordinate amount of time to construct. Time Verity would have grumbled against losing, had it not given her precious minutes to prepare her mind and steel her emotions.

She was about to walk into the unknown, and there was nothing she hated worse than the unknown.

His gloved hand flickered in the air toward her. "You're delectable—something I want to ravage, inch by inch. But I don't want any other man looking at you like that, and they will, and it will be unfortunate for them if I catch them."

Her mouth pulled to a scold. "I look how I look, Declan. I cannot rightly walk into this ballroom with a black cap tugged down over my head and my body hidden under a shapeless black dress."

His finger tapped on his chin. "Except we could have managed that—we could have placed you in with the staff. Maybe we still can."

"And what, you would attempt to be a footman handing out champagne? I don't think so. There are too many in society that know you from the Alabaster. You're too big and too handsome to stand in a corner and draw no attention."

"I could say the same for you in your current dress—except not the big part. And beautiful, not handsome. Either way, you will not escape notice and I'm already cracking my knuckles, ready to punch the eyes out of anyone ogling you."

With a sigh, her eyes looked up at the ceiling of the carriage. "You'll need to, somehow, manage to keep your fists to yourself. You asked me to guide you at this ball, and that will have to be my first rule—no punching the other guests."

"You're going to make rules now?"

"If I must. And apparently, I must." She shook her head as the carriage started to roll along the street. "How is it that you secured an invitation to this function in the first place?"

He shrugged. "It was embarrassingly easy. It's harder to get into the Alabaster than it was to get into this ball. Talen is a viscount now, which handed him a lump of power, not to mention his connections through Ness are wide and varied."

Verity nodded. Ness's father was a Scottish peer descended from a medieval barony, and she knew many in London had dealings or interest in the north. "You said you have a lead on the person that hired Bloodwater, but you didn't give me any details."

"I think the less you know in this situation, the better. I'm having a deuced time keeping you out of the fray of danger, but I do need you to guide me through this Mayfair ballroom without drawing undue attention to myself."

"And that attention could be avoided more efficiently if you told me some of these details. Where or who you need to get to." Her look skewered him—she was getting annoyed at his increasingly intrusive behavior when it came to her person. She had stayed behind when he had ventured into Bloodwater's territory—she wasn't going to be much use for a quick trip into a brothel as it was.

But this—this was her element. Or had been a long time ago. She needed to be with him on this foray.

He wanted her safe, she understood that. But she wanted him safe just the same. Hence the blades and one pistol strapped to her legs high under the silk skirts of the gown he'd procured for her.

He met her glare, and for a moment, she was certain he was going to keep his secrets to himself. "The goal tonight is information gathering—I want to know everything there is to know about Lord Gunderson. He is an earl and his wife should be in attendance as well. Have you ever heard of them?"

She shook her head. The name meant nothing to her. "No, I have never met or heard of them when I was a companion to the heiress—though the circles the Americans ran in were quite different than what I imagine will be at this ball. This address—this is an area of old families, old titles. The kind of aristocrats that don't bother with Americans. It is fine to let them marry into the fold if they come with Midas-worthy fortunes, but they would never be truly welcome in the highest levels of society."

Declan nodded. "That is good, as there is less likely a chance of someone recognizing you from that time."

Her hand swept over the smooth silk across her belly. The dark green concoction fit her frame perfectly, with intricately woven strips of white-and-green-colored silk along the cap sleeves, and a thin mirror of that weave trimming the bodice of the dress. Simple, elegant, it drew attention without demanding it. "I didn't look like this at all when I was with the heiress. I was a prop that wasn't to be even glanced at next to the sparkle that she needed to be, and I was dressed in dullness that befitted that role."

He motioned to her head. "But what did they do with your hair? I would think it was hard to hide the glory of that color."

She chuckled. "Wide, flat hats and caps were plunked down on my head for most occasions. Or feathers that spread and fell everywhere about my hair."

"A sin. But I have something to correct past offenses against your beauty." He peeled off both of his gloves and fished into an inner pocket of his tailcoat.

Verity wasn't even sure what she was looking at when he pulled free a long line of sparkles from his coat.

A lopsided grin on his face, he held up a necklace to her. Diamonds lined the necklace all the way around the loop and in the bottom center, a massive emerald edged with more diamonds. "The dress isn't the lighter green of your eyes, but this I thought matched them pretty well—or at least it should, once light hits it."

Her jaw had dropped open as she looked from the necklace to his face.

Before she could say a word, he leaned forward and set it around her neck, his breath tickling her ear as he latched it closed against her spine.

He pulled away, sitting across from her, a self-satisfied smirk playing about his lips.

She looked down, her white-gloved fingers lifting it, but then pausing, afraid to touch the middle stone. "You shouldn't trust me to borrow such a tremendous piece. If it falls off of me or if something happens and I have to pull a blade and it gets ripped from me or stolen, I—"

"Who said anything about borrowing it?"

Her gaze shot up to him.

"This is just for the evening—as is the dress."

Declan shrugged. "I already bought both of them—what would I do with them now? They're yours."

Her head instantly shook. "No, Declan, this—I cannot accept this."

"You can and you will. Call it insurance. In case of disaster. In case something happens to me. You can sell it, or not, I don't care. I just want you to have it should you ever need it."

Her mouth opened and closed several times, her tongue growing dry. "It's expensive, isn't it?"

"It is." The half-cocked grin was back. "But it would bring you enough to do what you need to should it come to that. Leave London, start a new life elsewhere."

"That expensive?"

He shrugged again.

"No. I cannot accept it." At his instant frown, she recognized the purity of his intention behind the gift and his thoughtfulness sliced into her heart, deep and bleak and sadly hopeful.

"Dec, I know you just want to give me some sense of security, but I can find a way forward. I always have."

"I know you can. I know you will. Your fortitude astounds me sometimes. But you can and you will accept it. Do this for me. It's for my peace of mind, not yours. It may seem like a present for you, but it is actually a present for me. To calm the worry that invades my lungs anytime I think of you in danger, on your own."

"I'm accustomed to being alone."

He grinned like a little child tasting pure sugar for the first time. "Don't get comfortable in that spot."

The sheer silliness on his face made her laugh, and her fingers landed on the emerald. An exquisite cut made the stone catch every sliver of light from the passing street lamps, and it glowed in her hand. Too much, but she wasn't sure the battle to give it back to him would be worth it. Not until she was gone for good, and then she could just tuck it into his desk, waiting to be found.

Her look lifted to him. "Thank you."

"You are welcome, finch."

{ Chapter 24 }

Ten minutes passed in easy banter, Verity giving Declan as many pointers on proper etiquette as she could in the too-short ride to the home of the Duke of Marlton. She could spend the entire night preparing Declan and she would still forget every nuance he would need to know. So the best plan was to stick by his elbow, guiding him where and when it was necessary.

The coach rolled to a stop and one of the guards-turned-footmen opened the door to the carriage. Declan alighted and then helped her down to the walking lane.

Her stomach fluttered as she looked up at the bright lights glowing from one of the largest townhouses she had ever seen.

"I just scanned the walkway ahead and there isn't a woman here that fits this world better than you. Are you sure there isn't something you forgot to tell me about your past?"

He said the words with a teasing grin, yet she winced. A wince she couldn't hide from him, and his countenance sobered, his eyes narrowing on her.

"Now is not the time, but someday soon, I am going to peel every last secret out of you by threat of a very specific kind of torture."

That was exactly what she was terrified of.

Even being here at an event like this was risky enough. But she would find a way to muddle through, her head

down, by his side, with no undue attention upon either of them. That was paramount.

The crush was thick enough with the dancing fully underway that they easily managed to sneak away from the long line of people waiting to be announced by the butler. Slipping in through a side door, they started circulating along the edges of the ballroom.

Declan stood two heads taller than her and easily spotted Talen and Ness on the opposite side of the ballroom by the French doors leading to the terrace. "Talen is across from us, so unless you would like to twirl across the dancing floor, we'll have to weave around the sides to them."

She nodded, then pointed at a footman squeezing through the crowd with glasses of champagne. "Nab two glasses."

"You are thirsty?" he asked as he grabbed two glasses off the passing tray and handed one to her.

"No, I like to keep it in front of my face to obscure my features. It is helpful for that."

He tilted his head to the side, giving her an odd look for a long moment, and then he shook off her comment and offered his elbow to her. They started around the perimeter of the room.

Verity kept her eyes downcast, but took in everything around her. It was an artform—observing and classifying the people, the building, the general mood of the crowd, and the possible threats. All with her head tilted demurely down and making herself as small as the dress Declan had chosen for her allowed her to be.

She noted the impeccable shine of the polished inlaid walnut floor, the fresco painting high on the ceiling depicting the labours of Hercules, and the creamy white Doric pillars anchoring the corners of the room. One of the finest ballrooms she'd ever been in.

Far quicker than she would have guessed his mass allowed him to move through the crowd, Declan found Talen and his wife, Ness.

Ness instantly reached for Verity, drawing her into a hug. Ness had been recovering at the Alabaster months ago after an attack, and Verity had helped her during that time.

Ness paused mid-hug with her lips next to Verity's ear. "Tell me it is true—you could actually speak this entire time?"

Verity's eyes went wide as she pulled away from Ness and she shot daggers up at Declan next to her. "You told them?"

Declan shrugged. "I wasn't going to not tell them. You were coming here with me. Better to experience the shock of your working tongue in private than in the middle of a ballroom."

"But you swore." Reasonable explanation or not, he had no right. Not when the lives of other Guardians were at stake.

Declan shook his head, leaning down to her ear to whisper into it. "I didn't tell them anything about the Guardians—just that you were hired to watch over me and can talk. And fight. That is all they know."

He pulled away, pointing with his glass toward Talen. "I had to tell Talen of you as he's helping me to uncover information on Lord Gunderson."

Verity's look crept to Talen, expecting to see the same ire she saw in Declan when he found out she could talk and had been faking being a mute. Talen had been her boss as well during her time at the Alabaster, and her lies had been just as much to Talen as they had been to Declan.

All she saw in Talen's face was half-concealed merriment at the current situation. Still, she had lied to the man. For *years.*

Her bottom lip jutted up as she inclined her head toward Talen. "I apologize for lying to you during the last years. But it was for Declan's safety."

"If there's anything I learned from our years in London and the rookeries, it is that everyone here has secrets—everyone. Yours is tame compared to many, so do not think further on it." Talen grinned with a glance at Declan. "Believe me, knowing that you were hired to be Declan's guard is restitution enough for the lies. You do not know the joy it gives me to learn that Declan has had you protecting his pretty neck. It is a precious, precious story that I will hold tight to until the end of our days."

"Don't make me punch that smirk off your face," Declan growled.

Talen shrugged.

That went better than Verity expected. Declan had bruised pride, and that was it. She said a silent thank you.

Ness laughed, a musical sound that drew Verity's attention. "I always suspected there was more to you, Verity, but I never imagined this. You're a spy."

"Not really a spy. Just more of a…watcher. And helper when the situation arises."

"Don't be surprised if Scotland Yard—or the Drury Lane Theatre pays a call on you—I never suspected anything this astonishing of you when I was at the Alabaster. There seemed to be more of you, yes—but the speaking was not in my imagination." Ness's finger reached out, tracing along the fine line of silk lace across her shoulder. "And you had such fine features, but it also appears you are gorgeous when you aren't hiding under that black cap and black dress of yours. You wear society well."

Verity's cheeks reddened at the compliment. No one had made a comment on her appearance in a very long time—barring Declan's views and he was more interested in stripping away her clothes.

"What have you learned?" Declan looked from Ness to Talen.

"Several things." Talen glanced about them, his voice dropping low as he leaned in toward Declan and Verity. "Lord Gunderson is a well-respected peer. His estate holds a good portion of all arable land in England, so funds are not a problem for the man. He inherited the title fifty years ago at age thirty with a substantial war chest, and has only built on the wealth of it. His money is all over the place, in land, in shipping, in mines. In parliament, he holds power and sway but doesn't choose to use it very often."

Declan's brow wrinkled. "So an upstanding member of parliament?"

Talen shrugged. "By all accounts."

Verity frowned. It didn't make any sense—why would a man like Lord Gunderson care—even know about Declan's existence?

Declan echoed her frown. "He has no connections to the Alabaster? To the rookeries?"

"Not that I have been able to discern in the short amount of time I've had to inquire about him. If he has vices, he keeps them to his clubs. Though there is one odd thing Ness discovered." He looked down to his wife.

Ness's voice went to a whisper that could barely be heard over the din of the crowd. "He and his wife despise each other. Bitterly. They have for almost as long as they have been married. Why they were originally a match, I cannot imagine. He has humiliated her at events, at balls, at the theater, everywhere and anywhere, as often as he can. And she has returned the favor. Exclaimed in public many times how crooked and useless his"—she motioned downward to waist level—"member is. How he's an idiot. How he stinks from breath to toes. And he has been no kinder to her."

Verity's hand lifted to her mouth, her gloved fingers covering her lips at the awfulness of the story. "That is horrible—to be stuck with someone you loathe like that."

Ness nodded. "It is a peculiar, vile sort of hatred between them that the *ton* has watched with glee for the last forty years. They despise each other so much, that they often tell each other to wither and drop dead, but both of them are clinging to life, determined to outlive the other. It is the only way to win this war." Ness paused, shaking her head. "People say hatred has kept them both alive. And most morbid of all, there are numerous bets placed about town on which one of them will die first."

"What?" Verity's eyebrows lifted high.

Talen nodded. "I verified it at a few of the clubs. Long-standing bets have been placed on who will die first for the last twenty years. The thing is, aside from the status of the money on the bets, no one in the *ton* really cares who dies first. In their separate circles, both of them are well-respected. No one wishes them ill will. They both donate generously to hospitals and asylums across the country and city."

Declan heaved a sigh, his head shaking.

Talen's mouth quirked to the side. "You look as perplexed as I. I take it you know nothing of them either?"

Declan shook his head, his gaze dropping as his hand rubbed along the side of his jawline. "No. Lord Gunderson has never been to the Alabaster or any of our other gaming hells as far as I know." His look snapped up to Talen. "His heir? Is his heir floating about already claiming ownership of the title?"

"No. The title will move off to the son of a distant cousin once Gunderson passes. As far as I was able to discern, the heir lives quite poorly in Ireland and has no inclination he's destined for a fortune," Talen said. "Are you positive you heard the name correctly? Lord Gunderson?"

"Aye. That was the name. Bloodwater could very well be lying, though. I don't put that past him. But how would

Bloodwater even know of Lord Gunderson's existence, unless their paths crossed at the docks, as I cannot imagine Gunderson spends any time in the rookeries."

Talen nodded. "And I doubt Gunderson makes it to the docks very often. He has an army of men handling his affairs."

Declan's shoulders lifted, his look glancing about. "This has been a waste, the whole of it."

"Or maybe it is just something we haven't discovered about the man yet," Talen said, his gaze landing on Verity. "Everyone has secrets."

Declan nodded. "Is he here?"

"Aye." Talen pointed to the far side of the ballroom at a rich mahogany door. "He is in the smoking room."

"Good. Then I want to see this bastard, if indeed, he is the bastard I'm looking for."

Talen nodded and started toward the door.

"Let's go." Declan grabbed Verity's hand and started to tug her through the crowd.

She plunked her glass onto a passing tray and grabbed his forearm, squeezing it to stop him. "Declan, I cannot— only men are allowed in the smoking room."

He paused, looking back at her.

She motioned toward the other side of the ballroom. "Men go in there and women retire into the drawing room with the other ladies for a respite."

His brow furrowed. "No. You need to see Gunderson as well, in case you recognize him."

She shrugged. "It is how it is done. You will just have to describe him to me."

His gaze swept around the room, his look unsure. "Except I don't want to leave you alone in the ballroom, nor do I want you locked away somewhere where I cannot enter without causing a scene."

She would be fine. She could turn around and find Ness and stick to her side until Declan found her again, but she didn't want to be in that ballroom any more than he wanted her in there. Her skin was starting to itch, the bottom of her gut churning the longer she was under the candles of the chandeliers.

She pointed toward the wide doorway at the side of the ballroom that they had entered through. "I will slip back outside and wait with Jack. That will be most prudent."

His lips pursed for one second, and then he reluctantly released her hand. "Fine. I told Jack not to go far, so he should still be rudely holding a spot just outside."

"Perfect. I will see you in a few minutes." She started off before he could stop her, slipping through the crowd with ease because of her size.

She escaped out the front of the house within minutes and found Jack down the street to her left.

A smile pasted on her face as she passed the many couples and groups of gentlemen making way to the entrance of the townhouse, and she was grateful when Jack spotted her and waved.

He stood next to the door of the carriage, leaning against the shiny black side of Declan's carriage, no insignia marking it. Plain. The carriage easy to slip into the night, just like Declan.

Jack's arms were crossed over his chest as he kept a wary eye on the people about the street. Alert and ready as always. Just one of the things she liked in having him as her partner in protecting Declan.

"Where is Declan?"

"In the smoking room. I told him I would meet him out here." She peered around to the backside of the coach. "Where are the footmen?"

"Off with the dice in the alleyway." He opened the door of the carriage. "Do you want to wait inside?"

She shook her head. "No, the air is good, not so suffocating tonight."

He leaned into the carriage, rummaging about until he found a blanket. Unfolding it, he turned back to her, draping it about her shoulders before shutting the door. "Best you stay warm, though, or Dec will likely have my head."

She tried not to grin at that. Declan *would* roll heads if he thought someone wasn't treating her well. His protectiveness wasn't the worst thing in the world. As long as she didn't grow accustomed to it. It would end. It would need to.

Grabbing the edges of the blanket and pulling it across the open expanse of her chest, she moved to stand next to Jack. She looked up at him for a long moment as he had gone back to leaning against the coach with his arms crossed over his chest as he surveyed the crowd outside the townhouse of people both arriving and moving onto the next event at this time of night.

Jack held an imposing stature—dark brown hair, tall, broad shoulders, but he always held an impish quirk to his lips, like he was inevitably a moment away from smirking at something peculiar. That quirk eased the hard lines of his face enough to consider him quite handsome, if one were looking at him for that. She wasn't, so it almost struck her as funny that she suddenly noticed his attractiveness. She was so accustomed to counting on him for covering her back that she had never truly studied him as a stranger would.

Guilt suddenly flooded her chest. It wasn't right, keeping the information she had from him. "Jack?"

He glanced down at her and an easy smile came to his face.

"Declan knows what we do, what we were hired to do." She hadn't meant to blurt it out like that, but she had counted on him for so long, it was inherently wrong to not let him know.

He nodded, his smile turning resigned. "I figured."

"Have you told Hector yet?"

"No."

"Will you?"

He looked to the ground, then out to the lane of people passing by, his gaze on the crowd for several breaths. "No. Not until this business is done. I would rather like to see Rudderton make it through this threat alive, after all the time we've spent protecting him." His gaze shifted to her. "After this, he'll never trust anyone new in his life, so if we disappear and a new team comes in, they won't be able to get close enough to him to do their jobs."

"Then we are in accord on that." A sad smile came to her lips. That was what they had done—made Declan not trust anyone—ruined him in that way.

She reached out and rubbed his shoulder. "You're a good man, Jack."

His head angled to the side with a cocky grin. "It comes and it goes."

She chuckled. "From my vantage it seems to be mostly coming and staying in place." She paused, looking at him in silence for a long breath. "Where did you come from?"

The smile on his face disappeared for a long second, but then reappeared, easy and affable as always. "You know we don't ask that question, Verity."

She nodded. She knew it, just as he did.

"Verity?"

Her name.

Her name wrapped in a voice from long, long ago.

Her entire body tensed as she searched the crowd.

There.

An older man with matching sprouts of brown hair on either side of his bald head pushed his way through the crowd toward her. Far away but getting closer. Closer.

No. Please no. *No. No. No.*

She grabbed Jack's arm, her fingernails digging into the muscles of his forearm. "Get me out of here."

"What?" He looked around, trying to identify the source of her panic.

"Get me out of here," she screamed, giving Jack no choice but to whip open the carriage door, help her vault up inside, and then scramble to the driver's perch.

She heard some yelps, some swearing as he jolted the horses into motion. Hopefully no one was hurt.

She'd landed on the floor of the carriage, but she couldn't pull herself onto a cushion, much less over to the window to look out at the crowd. Instead, her legs pulled up, tucking to her chest, her arms wrapping around her shins as her eyes closed tight and the trembles started.

Her body soon shaking so violently, she couldn't extract herself from the darkness.

From the fear.

{ CHAPTER 25 }

"Declan."

A hand suddenly gripped his shoulder and Declan spun around from where he was talking in a quiet corner of the smoking room with Talen.

"Jack?"

"It's Verity."

For one second, Declan stilled, all the blood rushing from his body as he fought to focus on Jack.

"You need to come."

Declan nodded, his mouth not able to form words, his heart thudding so hard in his chest it felt like he was about to split open in the middle of the Mayfair ballroom as he ran through it.

Onto the driver's perch with Jack so his man could tell him what happened, he had to hold tight to the rail as his carriage took the turns through the streets of London on two wheels, Jack speeding him to the Alabaster as quickly as the horses and busy streets allowed. Three times he almost jumped off the coach, ready to run the rest of the distance.

When they finally turned onto the Alabaster's street, Declan did just that, his boots pounding along the walkway.

Verity wasn't injured, but she wasn't right—that was what Jack said. Someone had called her name outside of the ball and she had crumbled.

Verity didn't crumble. Didn't cower.

She could bloody well handle anything.

His feet skidded as he turned into the Alabaster, and then he charged upward toward his bedroom where Jack had said he'd deposited Verity.

The door slammed into the wall and he heaved into the room, desperate to see her. See her alive and well and whole.

And he was bloody well going to kill whoever had done this to her.

Done what, he wasn't quite sure about yet. But he was about to kill someone. That, he was most assured of.

Sliding to a stop, he searched the room. Bed. Wingback chairs by the fire. Settee along the inner wall.

There.

Shit.

Curled into a little ball in the darkest corner of the room. Only tufts of her red hair peeked out from the edges of the blanket from the coach. She'd pulled it up over her head and hidden underneath.

Silent. So silent.

Was she asleep?

He took a step closer, his eyes adjusting to the dark corner where she'd stuffed herself.

No. Not sleeping. Shaking. The whole of her body trembling ruthlessly. Silently.

Terror lurched through him, setting his veins to fire, his stomach flipping.

He crept closer to her. Closer. The floor creaked and he winced.

Sinking to his knees, he continued shuffling toward Verity, staring at the lump of her, willing her to cease shaking.

Stopping in front of her, he reached out for the edge of the blanket, then paused and dropped himself down further so he would be close to eye-level with her.

"Verity?" A whisper.

He waited, but the quaking didn't cease.

"Verity?" This time he dared to reach out and push the blanket away from the top of her head.

She jerked, her fingers grasping for the edge of the blanket, desperate to drag it back over her head.

Hiding.

She was hiding.

"Oh, hell, Verity," he exhaled, and he set all caution aside and reached out to grab her, dragging her body into his, forcing her onto his lap and curling his body over hers, shielding her from whatever terror she was convinced was in the room with her.

His right arm locked around her body, his left hand buried into the hair at the back of her head, holding her against the tremors ravaging her body.

He held her. Held her for so long he was afraid her body would shatter to pieces in his arms. But then a miraculous thing happened.

The shaking eased, ever so slightly.

When he was sure it wasn't a fluke, he dared to open his mouth, his voice raw. "What did he do to you?"

"Who?" She said the word into his chest, muffling it to where he could barely hear it.

His hand in her hair shifted, his thumb stroking her scalp like he used to stroke the frightened cats on the ships

after they realized they were stuck on a ship out at sea with no escape.

He drew a deep breath, trying to rein in all the fury surging through him at this random man outside the ball. "Jack said a man outside the townhouse recognized you, came at you, and you made Jack take you away from there."

"How?" Her head tilted up and she opened her eyes, blinking, confused. "How did I get here?"

"Jack brought you here. He said he had to carry you in here, Verity." He swallowed hard, not sure what to do with the fact that she didn't remember any of this. "You don't remember? Tell me what happened. Tell me who that man was outside the ball."

"I only remember being in the carriage. I…" Her eyes closed and she buried her head back into his chest. "I cannot…"

"Cannot what? Cannot tell me? Cannot hide? Cannot what? You have to talk to me, Verity." He was drowning with her and he had no idea how to pull her out of the place her mind had gone. It was killing him, slicing him to the marrow to see her like this. "You have to talk to me, finch. Please, just talk to me. Please."

Her head swung back and forth, her brow brushing against his chest. "It…it is just too much. Too much and I am so tired."

His hand shifted to the side of her face and he slipped his thumb under her chin, lifting her look to him. "Tired of what? Just tell me. Please. Just tell me."

No tears fell down her face, but the green in her eyes shimmered in the scant line of light from the fireplace when she met his stare. "I am so tired of men that have no regard for life. No regard for my life. Men that only want pain and greed and hate. And they do all of that without consequence or morality or thinking on what they've done. Just pain. They just want the pain. Want to see it. Revel in it. The pain."

His right hand moved from her back and he captured her face between his palms. "I am not that man, Verity. Do you understand? I am not that man."

She stared at him and he could feel her heartbeat pulsating under her skin. Erratic. Panicked.

She blinked, her look intense on him like never before. Like he could make the sun rise and the darkness set. Like she knew, without a doubt, he had her. Her body and soul to keep safe.

"You aren't. I know you aren't." Her lips parted, a shallow breath exhaling. "I don't want to feel like this anymore."

"I know, finch. I know." His voice rough, the words barely made it out before his lips met hers, hard and insisting and desperate to suck out all the fear that held tight to her bones.

It was the spark to her kindling, and she erupted into a frenzied ball, her hands surging against his clothes, dragging off his coat and waistcoat. His cravat and lawn shirt. His boots. The front fall of his trousers and then she wedged herself off his lap so she could rip the last threads on him from his legs.

She removed the necklace, setting it on his clothes, then came back to him on her knees, ravenous, her hands

diving into his hair with her lips seeking his, but he wouldn't have it—at least not what she was thinking—not yet.

He kissed her, bruising her lips as he imprinted himself on her, leaning over her as he set her long onto the floor and pulled her dark green skirts high. Abandoning her lips, he pushed her skirts out of the way as he dove downward, his mouth meeting her inner thigh.

"Dec. Good hell." The guttural words rumbled from her throat and her fingers curled into his hair.

He smiled to himself, working upward along the sensitive skin until he reached her folds. His hand went under her left knee and he hiked her leg up, draping it over his shoulder and giving him full access to her. His tongue swiped inward, tasting her, losing himself in everything she was. A long stroke down and upward with his tongue and he circled her nubbin, then sucked it.

Her chest jerked up from the floor with the touch, a gargled scream at her lips. Her instinctive reactions were always the perfect guide for how and where to touch her.

His tongue slipped about, playing, teasing, until she started to writhe under him and he slipped two fingers into her, stretching her, curling into the deepest recess of her until his name started to repeat on her tongue. Faster, faster. Her nails dug into his scalp and he kept up the onslaught of tongue and fingers until she twisted, her hips lifting as she came, her body shattering under him.

He didn't stop, forcing her to ride out every wave of pleasure until her body was trembling for the best reason of all.

He looked up at her face, at her mouth ajar, the remnants of her screams vibrating through her full lips and a moment of peace wrapped around him so completely he was dumbstruck for full seconds. Peace that told him this was where he was meant to be, meant to do—his purpose in life. Her.

Her head rolled to the side, and she looked down at him, a wicked smile curving her lips. "You're not done yet. Not until you're deep in me."

He lifted himself, surveying the mounds of silk still wrapped about her body. He could make quick work of that.

He pushed the fine fabric he'd wanted to tear off her body all night up along her torso, seams ripping as they needed to. Stays and chemise torn off and her body was free to the air and to his lips. He traced his way up her skin. Abdomen that curved inward ever so slightly just beside her hip bone. Rib cage that curled up her torso. Left breast that mounded so enticingly, its peak raw and ready for him, that he spent far too long there, tongue swirling, teeth nipping. Gasps from her lips started in earnest again, just as her breath had ebbed into a normal cadence. Upward. The smooth line of her neck, the tang of lemon hitting his tongue.

Her lips. Full and hungry and wanting him.

He slid into her as her mouth opened to him, his tongue matching his cock. Stroke. Play. Retreat. Slow and reveling in every nudge, every squirm her body made beneath his. Her nails raked through his hair and down

along his back, holding him to her, desperate to keep him buoyed to her body.

Her hips rolled, demanding speed, her inner walls twitching as she started to build around him.

Her right leg wrapped upward around his waist, her heel rubbing against his backside and forcing new sensations down into his cock. Hell. The slightest movement from her and he was losing control again. And again. And again.

He pulled out, barely the head of his cock still embedded into her and his face dropped into her neck, inhaling everything about her as he steeled himself. He drove forward. Again. Again. Again. The fourth thrust he sank so deeply she cried out, her legs and body and arms and inner walls clenching, writhing through her orgasm.

It was all he needed, and it took everything from him. All resistance. All thought. All sanity. This was all he wanted. Her.

There would be no pulling out. Not ever again. A growl in his throat, every nerve tensing, he exploded deep within her. His body spasming in wave after wave and she took everything, matching every contraction with her own. Coming like he never had, until every part of his being was lost in the feral sensation.

Before he could even try to breathe again, he flipped them, holding her tight to his chest, their bodies still joined.

It took minutes of blankly staring at the laurel wreath plaster relief on the ceiling before his breath became halfway normal, tiny threads of thought making way back into his brain.

She stayed curled against him. For the heat, for the security, he didn't much care.

Clarity had hit him on that frantic ride back to the Alabaster when he was convinced something beyond horrible had happened—that death was upon her.

Clarity that told him there was only one place in this world that her body belonged and that was pressed up against his. Never anywhere else. Never again.

But she had to tell him what was going on—what was in her past she was so obviously terrified of. It had to do with the Guardians, he was sure of it.

It was time and he would force it out of her any way he could.

A soft moan came from her lips as she shifted her head against his chest, the warmth of her breath heating his skin.

Softer tactics had to be employed first.

He set his chin atop her head, tucking her into his body so not an inch of her felt exposed. "Why didn't you want me to know about the Guardians? You know I can keep council on delicate information like that. You could have told me when I first learned you could talk and that would have saved some turmoil."

A groan rumbled from her throat and she shifted her head to the side, her hand going up so she could trace her fingers along his collarbone. "First, tell me if you found out any information about Lord Gunderson."

"Nothing—nothing of value. I was introduced to the man, stood right next to him in conversation, and there wasn't so much as a blink of recognition in his eyes toward me. He didn't know me from a toadstool, and could not

have cared less to meet me." His lips went to her temple. "You try to divert me, but it won't work."

She chuckled, low and breathy with echoes of her screams from minutes ago.

"Now tell me why you didn't want me to know about the Guardians."

"Honestly? I didn't want it to end. You had me pinned down by my lies and I didn't want it to end. I didn't want my job to end. I didn't want to have to leave you. I didn't want it to be the end of my time with you."

"And telling me about the Guardians would have done that?"

"I was worried about the other Guardians being exposed. But I also know I am about to be taken off of this job, as we haven't found anything of value about the threat upon you. I haven't done my job here. And when that happens, when I have to leave—there is no more of you, no more of us. This job was my way to be near you."

His words rolled slow, cautious. "Do you love me, Verity?"

"It doesn't matter what I feel and I accepted that long ago. If I have feelings in this job, they are at my own peril. They are disposable."

"But do you?"

She fell silent for several long moments, her breath in, out, air heating and cooling his skin. "I do." Her words were soft, defeated. "I have loved you for a long time. Long before you knew I could speak, knew what I was doing here."

His heart stopped in his chest, his next word raw, pulled from the depths of him. "Why?"

He could feel her cheek move across his chest, a smile coming to her face. "Because you are the best of men, even in this life, in this harsh world. You are the best of men in all ways. Not talking for two years, all I did was listen and watch, and I saw everything. And you…you were always the heart of gold here at the Alabaster. Hard but fair. Brutal but compassionate. You have all of these traits that war against each other, but the good…the good always wins out with you."

His throat closed up at her words and he had to draw in a deep breath to break past the clamp of it around his neck. "This doesn't have to end, Verity."

"Except it does." She pulled away from him, cool air seeping into the space between their chests, but she didn't look up to meet his eyes. "I need to move onto my next job, for if I don't, my brother will lose his spot at Harrow. He loses his safety, the only home he's known for the last three years. I cannot do that to him. He is protected there."

"Then he can stay there. I'll pay for his schooling, or if he wants to come to London and live with us at the Bedford townhouse, he can. We'll hire him a tutor so he can still learn. I don't care what it takes. Just stay with me."

Her gaze lifted and her stare sank into his, as though she was trying to understand words that had no meaning. "He can live with us?"

"Yes."

"What are you saying, Declan?"

"I'm saying I want to marry y—"

{ Chapter 26 }

"Stop." Her hand flew up between her and Declan even as her throat choked on the words she had to say. *Had to*, or death would be upon her. "Don't say another word. What you're about to say—it cannot happen."

"Verity—"

"No." The word came out in a half-strangled scream. She pushed herself off of him, scrambling for her discarded dress. "It cannot. It can never happen."

Standing, she picked up her dress and her fingers ripped through the folds of silk until she found the opening of the skirt and she dragged the dress over her head, not bothering with her shift or stays. It squeezed awkwardly onto her body, seams torn in a few places, but she had to get out of here. Had to leave. *Leave.*

By the time her head poked through the top of the dress, Declan was standing over her, glaring at her.

Damn, she thought she had turned away from him.

She spun on her heel to the side, trying to wedge her arms into the short cap sleeves. He moved with her, staying in front of her, trapping her body toward the wall and giving her no escape.

"This cannot happen? What are you talking about—why?" Each word simmered, deadly intention in his voice. "You need to tell me right now who that man outside the ball was, the one shouting for you. Was that Mr. Samson—your boss?"

"No—no—that was not him." Her arms into the dress, she yanked the silk skirt down around her waist so it fell at least half-properly, and then squeezed to the side to go around him, bending to shuffle through the mess of their clothes for her slippers. "I cannot tell you. I have to—I have to leave."

"Does this have to do with your brother?"

She shoved her toes into the right slipper. "It has everything to do with protecting him, yes."

Stop. She had to stop saying more or she would be sure to break.

She shook her head, ducking her face as she jammed her foot into the left slipper.

He moved closer until his body was touching hers, nudging her backward until she was trapped against the wall again. Never mind that he was still naked. The whole of him poised to fight, every muscle twitching. "This has gone on long enough—I haven't pushed you, believing you would tell me—tell me everything when you could finally trust me, Verity. But frankly, at this moment, I don't care if you trust me. You have to tell me what the hell is going on—who are you running from?"

Her breath caught in her throat.

She was so damn close to breaking. Breaking and telling him everything, but that would only spell disaster for her, for her brother. She couldn't do that. Especially to Ned—he'd already suffered so much.

She froze in place for a long second, staring at his bare chest. At his skin twitching with his heartbeat.

His heart. Her heart.

Hell. She couldn't do this to Declan either. Not anymore.

Her chest splintering, she swallowed, straightening her spine. Faking fortitude because she had to make it out of this room.

Her hand landed on his bare chest and she looked up at him, pulling upon every last drop of mettle that she could scrape from the bottom of her very empty, very barren well.

Her voice cut to a whisper, desperation lacing her words. "Except I cannot tell you. You have been… everything." Her head dropped, shaking for a long moment, and then she forced herself to look up and meet his eyes. "You have been everything. But I cannot tell you."

His body rammed into her, his arms going to either side of her as he slammed his palms onto the wall next to her head. Full and well captured. "No. You damn well will tell me."

Her lips pulled inward, her body, her heart fighting what her mind knew she had to do. "Don't do this, Dec."

"Do what? Demand answers? I bloody well deserve them, Verity."

"You do. You're right. You deserve them. You deserve everything, but I cannot give you that." Her right hand lifted, gently going onto his forearm and she pulled it downward. Silently begging him, with just that one desperate motion, to not force her to do what she could never let happen. "It can never happen, Dec, us—for real and for good and for forever. It cannot and it is my fault, not yours. I—I am sorry. I am so sorry I let this go on. Let

my feelings take over what I knew was common sense, what was the right thing to do. I never should have let us get entangled. I never should have stayed once you knew of me. But I couldn't—couldn't leave you."

He heaved a seething sigh and dropped his arm. "Yet you're going to leave me now?"

Her mouth snapped shut.

She nodded.

The most excruciating thing she'd ever done.

She continued to nod as she stepped past him, moving straight toward the door and slipping out into the hallway.

He didn't stop her.

And she didn't stop the silent tears from falling, flooding her vision.

She was done with the Alabaster.

{ CHAPTER 27 }

"There has to be another post."

"There is not one. Not at the moment. But I will let you know."

Hector.

The deep lines across his forehead furrowed deep.

She'd failed, failed miserably. She hadn't found the threat on Declan and this was her punishment.

Her hand clutched onto the edge of Hector's desk, and she leaned forward, not attempting to hide the desperation in her voice. She had no pride left. No bravery. "But I have given up everything—everything for this job. You cannot just discard me."

"I am not discarding you, Verity." Hector's tone softened ever so slightly. "If you are concerned about your brother, his tuition is paid through for the year."

"Thank you." She relaxed backward. She hadn't been expecting that generosity from Hector. But he was fair and straightforward. He always had been. "But what will I do?"

"Find a position well under your skill level until I have something for you, I imagine." Hector folded his fingers under his chin. "I did not anticipate you leaving your position at the Alabaster as you did. And without explanation. Would you care to inform me now?"

Hector knew something happened—something she wasn't telling him and something Jack wasn't telling him. But she couldn't very well confess that she'd fallen in love

with Declan, shared a bed with him, and then left him once her past had reared its ugly head.

All of that would remain unsaid—let Hector think what he needed to in the situation. It most likely painted Declan in a poor light—how she had to leave suddenly. Yet she couldn't tell Hector that Declan was an honorable man that would never dare hurt her. Not unless she was prepared to answer questions on how she came upon that opinion. Declan's reputation would just have to suffer—not that he had ever cared about his reputation—he owned half the sins in the rookeries, for goodness' sake.

Her mouth pulled to a tight line. "There is nothing to inform. I had to leave the post, and I was not close to discovering who the person is that is behind the attacks on Mr. Rudderton." She leaned forward, unable to stop her curiosity. "Has Jack learned anything more?"

"I am not at liberty to discuss a case with you that you are not actively working on."

She nodded, knowing that would be the answer. "Will you be sending in a new person? If it is a woman, I can be available to tell her what I know of the workings of Mr. Rudderton's world."

"There is not enough information in your reports?"

"There are nuances of the Alabaster—how the staff works there—that would be useful, as Mr. Rudderton spends the majority of his time at that establishment. Merely suggestions that would allow her to integrate herself into the workings of the gaming hell faster if she knew of them. If, I assume, you intend to send in another maid."

He nodded, looking at a report on his desk, not giving her his full attention. "I had considered that, or

the possibility of sending in Miss Derrington. But I have
research yet to do on the matter."

Miss Derrington? No.

No. No. No.

Her fingernails bit into her palms. Verity had gone into
the Alabaster as a maid. Miss Derrington had other assets
about her—other glamorous, beautiful, *bosomy* assets, that
she used to every angle set in front of her. While Verity
liked Miss Derrington immensely—had trained with her for
weeks before she took on her first job for the Guardians—
this cut too deeply.

He couldn't do that—couldn't send Miss Derrington in
to seduce Declan.

"No." The word spat out of her mouth before she could
control it.

Hector looked up from the report on his desk, his left
eyebrow high. "No?"

"It is just, if I may be so bold, Miss Derrington—I do
not know that she will be the best course of action."

"Why not?"

"Mr. Rudderton is consumed with his work. I have
observed he spends very little time on the opposite sex. I
only comment, because Miss Derrington would not have
access to him for the majority of the time."

"If she does her job correctly, she should. But I will
take that under advisement."

Verity nodded. "Of course."

He gathered the reports that were splayed across his
desk into a neat pile, tidying the corners of the papers.
"Very well. I may call upon you in another day or two after
I have been given direction on how to proceed."

"Direction?"

"From our employer on the case."

Her heart jumped. This, she hadn't been expecting. She was just trying to scrape what little of her life that she could back together—at least enough so that Ned was safe.

But this—this was too tempting.

Hector was going to speak with the person that had watched over Declan his entire life.

She didn't have another job to attend to, so maybe, just maybe, she could still save Declan—even if she couldn't save herself.

{ CHAPTER 28 }

His eyes bleary, stuck on the empty settee in his office, the ghost of Verity writhing under his hands haunted his skull.

No matter where Declan looked in the room, she was there. Naked on the settee. In her maid's uniform, on her hands and knees cleaning out coal from the fireplace. Standing by his door, defiance in her eyes after he'd discovered she could talk. Quietly polishing and lining up the row of tumblers on the sideboard.

His fuzzy gaze shifted back to the settee. She'd left the necklace in his room, buried under his trousers. He'd gripped the blasted thing for hours, knuckles white, before finally dropping it onto the settee.

It had sat there for the last two days, taunting him.

If Verity were still around, she would have taken the necklace and found a proper place for it.

Always making certain there wasn't a single thing out of place in his life.

She'd doted on him.

Obvious now.

The sideboard in Talen's office had never gleamed like his had. Talen's decanter of brandy was never consistently full like his. Not a stray speck of ash on the floor in front of his hearth, while Talen's had always been swept haphazardly. Verity had always brought food up to him, hot from the kitchens without him asking, and would set it in front of

him, gently reminding him to stop working and eat. Too many times, Talen had been in his office, snitching bites of food away from the plates of food Verity had brought up for him. She never delivered food to Talen unless he requested it.

It wasn't that Talen had ever been neglected by Verity. It was that Declan had been *doted* upon.

So painfully obvious now that she was gone.

But she didn't trust him—wasn't capable of it.

So he couldn't trust her.

The very route he should have taken the moment he found out she could talk. Not trust her, for her very presence at the Alabaster was built on a scaffolding of lies.

Get her out of his life. That was what he should have done weeks ago. That was what he needed to abide by now.

Verity was gone and good riddance to her.

So why, after two days of drinking and trying desperately to avoid it, had the truth not ceased—had not eased from his mind?

He wanted her.

Any way he could have her.

Trust or no trust.

A knock came on the door and from the wingback chair he'd collapsed into hours ago, he thought he mumbled out a, "Come," but there was no ensuring the word actually made it past his muddled tongue.

The door opened and Jack stepped into the room, looking Declan up and down. His mouth pulled to a severe line, or was Declan just imagining that? Jack didn't judge. Jack was always easy. Accommodating.

Paid to be in his life.

"What?"

"Sir, there is a man at the tables below that I think you should be aware of. He has been asking questions of you. He thinks he's doing it covertly—that is, he has been attempting to ask his question covertly over the last few days."

"Why do I give a rat's ballocks about some fellow asking questions?" Declan leaned back in his chair, his arm swinging wide in an exaggerated motion. "People want to know about me all the time—I'm so bloody well interesting."

Jack gave a slight cough. "It is just…you haven't been out of your office in days, sir."

"That seems correct." Declan nodded, eyeing the thin line of brandy still in the decanter on his desk. Verity would have refilled that hours ago. Wait. Had he really just drunk most of the bottle in a day? He shook his head. That also seemed correct.

His look shifted up to Jack. "Is that a problem?"

"No. It does make it easier to protect you, sir, now that Verity is gone. Being in one room sequestered away and all." Jack inclined his head to him. "But there is one more thing about the gentleman below."

"What?" Declan was quickly becoming annoyed with the interruption. He needed to get to those last swallows of brandy.

Jack took several steps forward, stopping directly in front of Declan where it was hard to ignore him. "I cannot be positive, as it was dark, but I believe the man below is

the same man that followed the carriage to the Alabaster from the ball the other night."

That got his full attention. "Someone followed you and Verity?"

"No. He followed us after I returned to the ball to pick you up to bring you here. I believe it was the same man that called Verity's name and rushed toward her outside of the ball." His lips pursed, upset with himself. "I am usually more aware of who is in my vicinity, but after I came back to the ball, I was trying to get you here to Verity as quickly as possible. After you jumped from the carriage, I noticed a man alighting a horse as I pulled into the carriage drive, a man that looked similar to the one outside the ball, and he was dressed in finery that would have reflected the function. But I never got close enough to him to determine if it was the same man."

He wasn't sure how he managed it, for his mind was still fuzzy, but Declan's muddled vision had sobered, his stare now focused pinpricks on his driver. "The man below at the tables. You don't recognize him aside from that night? He's not a part of the Guardians—a replacement sent for Verity?"

"Not that I am aware of. At least not a partner to me. Though Mr. Samson isn't always a fountain of sharing when it comes to the organization."

Declan's hands slapped onto the arms of the chair and with a heave, he pushed himself up onto his feet. Solid—or solid enough. He pointed to the doorway. "Show me the man."

They moved across the hall to Talen's office, which had been little used during the past four months, cool air circling them as they moved into the room. Talen's office had the direct line to the gaming tables below—interior windows that lined the far wall and overlooked the Alabaster's main two-story gaming room.

Declan stopped in front of the center window, searching the rambunctious scene below. When had the place filled in? Had he blacked out? He thought the sun was still high in the sky.

That was why one didn't drink for two days straight.

His look flickered around the gaming tables. "Where is the man?"

Jack moved to stand next to him, shoulder to shoulder. "There. Table five. His back is toward the roulette table."

Declan nodded, taking in the man. Aged. Maybe fifty. Two brown tufts of hair pinching a bald head. Face weathered in the way only aristocrats could manage—aged with time instead of hard work. Nothing remarkable about him. Not imposing. Not dangerous.

"I told the dealers to collect any and all information on the gentleman," Jack said.

"Good man. What did they learn?"

"He is Lord Perrington. A baron of a small estate in Westmorland. Rarely in London."

"Ever been here before?"

"No. He opened a line of credit."

"How much?"

"One thousand."

Declan stared at the man for a long moment, committing every detail of his face to memory. "We don't pull him aside for questioning just yet, but have the men keep him in their sights."

"Will do." Jack took a step away from the windows. "I'll let them know." He turned and walked toward the door.

His eyes trained on Lord Perrington, Declan's mouth opened, even as he tried to keep it closed. "Jack. One more thing. Have you heard from Verity?"

"I have not."

He looked over his shoulder to Jack. "Have you asked anything about her?"

"I was told she dismissed herself from your case. That is all."

Declan nodded, his gaze going to the empty fireplace for a long moment before looking back to Jack. "Is there a new person being sent in?"

Jack winced.

"I assume you don't want me to collapse the whole organization of the Guardians?"

Jack shook his head.

"Then tell me if there is a new person being sent in."

Declan stared at Jack, imparting with his look that this was the moment the man had to make a decision. The moment he had to choose allegiance.

A slight sigh escaped Jack, and he nodded. "There will be."

Just like that, loyalties shifted.

Declan nodded to himself.

He had to sober up.

He had people to visit.

{ CHAPTER 29 }

She expected this, yet she didn't expect this.

One of the largest townhouses on Park Lane, it was twice the size of a normal townhouse in the area. Hector had entered through the front door. He was welcome at this home.

Verity had been following Hector for two days, and he hadn't gone anywhere out of the ordinary. This had to be it—whoever was in that drawing room with Hector had to be the person scrubbed clean from Declan's file.

From her spot hidden alongside an empty townhouse being repaired, she glanced upward at the stream of water surging down in front of her from the broken edges of roof tile. She looked down the street to the townhouse Hector had disappeared into and then ducked her head and ran into the rain.

Dashing across the street, her boots didn't get sucked into the muck of the road that was prevalent in the rookeries. Dung that hit the cobblestones of this street was promptly cleaned up.

At the corner of the townhouse, she veered close to the black wrought-iron fence, then dodged inward at the area, her steps light down the slick stairs to the servants' entrance.

Adjusting her sopping black cap on her head, she knocked on the servants' door. A younger woman with a soot-stained apron opened the door.

Before the woman could say anything, Verity nudged forward. "DeMar's sent me. They said ye needed a new scullery maid." Verity held her breath—all the most fashionable houses used DeMar's to procure household staff.

The woman wrinkled her nose. "They did, did they? I don't think we sent for anyone." She turned around, her head bobbing as she looked for someone, but then she pulled the door wide for Verity. "Well, come inside then, instead of getting soaked to the bone out there. I'll check with Mrs. Lennon to see if she requested ye or not. That place gets the requests wrong all the time."

The woman led Verity into a room that opened into the kitchen and pointed at a rough, long wooden table. "Wait here."

Verity sat on the bench at the middle of the table where she could see the full of the kitchens and all the workers scurrying about. All of their aprons had a crest of a wreath and a lion embroidered into the bottom left corner—no expense spared all the way down to their scullery maids. She focused in on the girl cutting carrots at the far end of the table with bright blue eyes that appeared to see everything about her.

Verity smiled at her. "This house is so large—I hope DeMar's didn't make a mistake."

The girl grinned, friendly. "It is large, and there are a lot of mouths to feed." She leaned toward Verity. "But it is the nicest station on the block. A few years properly trained here, and ye can move into any high-class lady's home of yer choosin'. They all scramble after her ladyship's cast-offs."

Verity's brow wrinkled. "The lady of the house has that much status?"

The girl nodded, grabbing the bowl of carrots in front of her and scooting down to stand next to Verity. "What's yer name?"

"Verity. Yours?"

"Mable." Her attention went down to the carrots. "Ye got lucky if ye got sent here. Lady Gunderson is a fine mistress to the staff. Ye missed Christmastide, but she tries to remember all of us throughout the year. Candles, ripped stockings, lace. She requests it all be distributed up and down the ranks, not just into Mrs. Lennon's pockets."

"Did—did you say Lady Gunderson?" Verity realized too much excitement had just flickered across her face, but she couldn't contain it.

"Heard of her, 'ave ye? Most 'ave. The countess is well-known, especially if you've ever worked close to the square."

"I have heard of her, though I do not know, is there a Lord Gunderson, as well? I have never heard his name spoken."

The girl chuckled, a side smile lifting the right side of her mouth. She leaned down to Verity, her voice a whisper. "There is, but anyone who knows them knows they are fire and ice—and they hate each other with wild, piercing blows if they are captive in a room together. He lives on St. James."

"Two townhouses? That is…"

"Ridiculous?" She nodded, picking up a new carrot. "Those people could crush us with one look if they had a

mind to it—but they only seem to have a mind to crush one another."

"Miss."

Verity looked to her right to find the maid that had answered the servants' door standing next to her. She jumped to her feet.

"I am sorry, Miss, but there has been some mistake at DeMar's. Mrs. Lennon sent for a respectable housemaid. We churn through those faster than butter—everyone moves off to be a lady's maid." She motioned toward the hallway leading to the servants' door and Verity got up and followed her. "You will just have to go back to DeMar's and tell them of the mistake. I am sorry you had to travel all the way here for nothing, and in the rain."

"'Tis no trouble." Verity inclined her head as she stepped out into the area. "I'll let them know of the mistake and they should send a suitable woman here soon."

"Very good."

The maid closed the door.

The cold rain re-soaked her cap within seconds, chilling her head, but Verity couldn't help but skip up the narrow staircase to the street.

Lady Gunderson.

One and the same.

Hector had led her directly to the key to keeping Declan safe.

Now she just had to do some research and then devise a way to meet with Lady Gunderson. A feat that would be easier said than done.

It was time to enlist an old friend.

{ CHAPTER 30 }

One visit done, one more to go.

Declan jumped from the carriage, eager to get the last stop of the day taken care of. Gaming would be starting soon at the Alabaster and he'd already neglected the business for days.

It was a day for righting things, and his earlier visit had gone well.

To his surprise, Ned had been younger than he had anticipated. The lad was tall enough, so from afar, appeared older than he was. Yet up close, Verity's younger brother was skin and bones, having probably just grown a foot or more in the last six months.

Declan remembered that from when he was young—he couldn't eat enough to keep up with his height, his stomach always rumbling.

It was just one of the items he assured was taken care of at Harrow School during his visit earlier in the day. That the boy would be well fed.

Plentiful food, but more importantly, he'd set the fear of God into the headmaster as to the care of Ned. While Declan didn't see anything out of the ordinary at the school to cause him concern, it never hurt to let someone in power know that he was being watched, and that missteps would be noted, consequences doled out.

That visit had gone much the same as he anticipated this next one would go.

Crossing the street, Declan bounded up the marble staircase and, without knocking, stepped into the front receiving room at the offices of the Guardians of the Bones.

A young—but thick and muscular—man sat behind the desk near the front door and looked up from the vellum he was writing upon as Declan's boots thudded onto the wooden floorboards. The man had paused in his writing just long enough to let Declan know he couldn't be bothered—or if he could, it would cost Declan. A man set there to intimidate.

After several silent moments, his head lifted and he looked Declan up and down with cold eyes. He set his quill down. "Sir, are you lost?"

Declan stepped to the edge of the desk, looking down at the man with an overabundance of arrogance that was impossible to ignore. The man was thick, but Declan already knew he was ten times faster and far more experienced at any type of moves this whelp could throw at him. "I am not, as a matter of fact."

Both of the man's eyebrows lifted, the threat in the air Declan brought with him permeating the man's consciousness. "You have business here?"

Declan nodded, his face hard as he stared down at the man. "I do."

"May I ask what that business is?"

"Hector." Declan paused, then slightly inclined his head. "Mr. Samson."

"I do not know if he is taking appointments at the moment."

"He'll see me."

The man gave a snorting chuckle from the base of his throat. "I doubt that."

Declan flipped one finger up, pointing to the hallway and the closed-off rooms behind the man. "You can tell him Declan Rudderton is here."

The man started. It was quick, but the flicker of the tell flashed across his face.

His mouth opened, but Declan didn't let him speak. "Now that we have who I am established, you will be letting Mr. Samson know I am waiting. Impatiently."

For one second, cocky defiance sparked in the man's eyes, but he squelched it and stood from the desk, disappearing down the hallway.

It wasn't a minute before the man was back, his boss in tow.

"Mr. Rudderton, would you be so kind as to step back into my office?" Mr. Samson was nondescript. Medium height, brown hair that was speckled with grey, brown eyes that weren't exactly lifeless, but close to it, spectacles balancing on his nose, not fit but not fat.

The exact sort of man everyone in the room would look past, eyes never lingering very long on him. There was nothing to recommend him. Perfect for a spy during the war on the continent. But they were a long distance from that moment in time.

He nodded to Mr. Samson and the man turned, leading him along the corridor. Thumping echoed down from the floorboards above them, feet fast along the floor, almost like people were fighting or fencing.

Mr. Samson turned to his left, stepping into an office and moving to the side. "Have a seat."

Declan doubted it was Mr. Samson's office. Books filled one wall perfectly, not a tome out of place, a few pieces of paper, quills and an inkwell sat on the desk in the middle of the room, and that was it. Nothing to indicate anyone used this office as anything other than a holding room.

Declan moved to the chair facing the desk, leaning back and pulling his right ankle up over his knee as Samson moved around the desk, sat, and folded his hands, resting them atop the desktop.

"What is it you think I can do for you, Mr. Rudderton?" Samson's voice was smooth. For how unremarkable his person was, his timbre was soothing butter.

The right side of Declan's mouth pulled back in an annoyed quirk. "Let us dispense with the foolery of feigned ignorance. I know exactly who you are, Mr. Samson. I know exactly what you do with the Guardians of the Bones. And you know exactly who I am."

The cool countenance of Samson's face held, and Declan had to admire the steel it took to pull that off.

Samson offered one slight nod, maintaining eye contact. "As you wish. What exactly is it you want?"

"I want to hire you."

Samson's left eyebrow arched ever so slightly. "That is an unusual request."

"Is it?" Declan shifted his ankle off his knee and leaned forward in the chair. "I don't think so. Not when I have need of covert protection around several people."

"Who are these people?"

"Verity Jones and her brother."

Samson took an extended moment. A long inhale. A long exhale. "You would like to hire one of our guardians to protect one of our guardians?"

"I would." Declan's mouth twitched to the side as he picked invisible lint off his black trousers. "I have been assured you are the best."

Samson eyed him, his look seeping into every line of Declan's face, reading intention. Declan had never minded scrutiny—it meant he had the upper hand.

"It is unconventional. You can afford us?"

At that, Declan had to chuckle. The man bloody well knew everything there was to know about him. "You know I can."

"Very well. I'll get guardians on them within the day."

"And she doesn't know about it, understand?"

"Of course." Samson unfolded his hands. "If that is all—"

"It is not."

Samson stopped. "What else is it that you want?"

"I want the file."

"Which file?"

"My file."

Samson's bottom lip jutted up as he stared at Declan. "Fine."

He stood up and walked out of the room. Several minutes passed before he came back into the office with a fat portfolio bound in leather balanced in his hands. "This is all of it."

Declan stood and took the portfolio. "Thank you. Send the bills and the reports to my Bedford house."

"Of course."

Tucking the file under his arm, Declan moved toward the door.

"It's not in there, what you're looking for."

Declan glanced back at Samson. "You don't have a clue what I'm looking for."

He took the last three steps to the door, opened it, then paused, turning halfway back into the room. "Oh, and there is one more thing. I'm keeping Jack."

Samson's jaw dropped for half a second. A half second when the man wasn't fully in control of himself and his surroundings. "No. You cannot take one of our finest—"

"I can, and I will. Jack is loyal, and loyal men are hard to come by. But I imagine you know that. He's mine, as long as he wants it. So, if it's all the same to you, consider this Jack's resignation notice."

Samson's mouth clamped shut, his lips going to a tight line. It looked entirely awkward—probably more emotion than the man had shown in the last ten years.

Declan walked out of the offices, taking note of each and every detail of the layout, the doors, and how the man in the front area was vulnerable to attacks from behind. Years in the rookeries had him attuned to details like that. He would have set up the space differently, but it wasn't his business.

Out onto the street, Declan ran across the street under the misting rain, avoiding puddles that had collected in the last two days.

Into his carriage and he couldn't open the portfolio fast enough. The leather flaps spread wide with the stack of reports balanced on his lap, and he started flipping through pages, stacking them on the cushion next to him after scanning them.

Verity's reports, her penmanship neat and tidy, the swirls on the drops with the slightest bit of flair. Just like everything, she kept the wildness of her spirit tucked away under a thick, straight veneer. But there, in the 'g's and the 'y's and the 'p's she twinkled to life.

He flipped down past her reports. Past Jack's reports. Lewis. Walter. Jordan. Searching deeper and deeper, desperate to find one name in the stack of people that had been paid to be in his life.

Down to the bottom page, the first report from Percy, and then nothing.

He heaved an exhale of relief, his head clunking back onto the wall of the coach.

Talen wasn't in there.

It was what he needed.

His closest friend in the world hadn't been paid to be in his life. Small mercy, for everything he now had to question.

With that, Declan flipped to the top of the stack of papers once more, calmly reading Verity's latest report. Then Jack's. Report after report.

Halfway down the pile, he started skimming the accountings. Notes of scrapes he was in. Fights. Successes. Ships that were taken down by the *Firehawk*, battles that ensued. People he'd killed. People that almost killed him.

By these reports, he should have been dead a good thirty times over if not for the people that had been surrounding him his whole life.

Did he truly live life that perilously?

Or would danger always find a way to him?

{ CHAPTER 31 }

Verity waited on a bench in the quaint octagonal gazebo alongside the tree line of the woods that ran between the landscaped grounds and the cricket fields of Harrow School.

Ned had been gone for at least an hour and a half and impatience had set in. Cold as well.

She tightened her embroidered cloak around her chest. She would wait. Wait as long as she needed to. She had to.

She heard the creak of the heavy iron door along the side of the main structure of the school, just under the row of demon gargoyles still spewing spouts of water from the rain that had ceased an hour ago.

Ned ducked under the sputtering streams and made his way across the expanse of the wide lawn. His growing height had his body all out of proportion—his legs so long it looked for a few steps like he couldn't keep up with his own strides.

The closer he drew to her, the wider his smile cut across his face. By the time he reached her, he was beaming.

"I found it." Breathless, he collapsed onto the bench to her right.

"You did?" She had guessed that the school's archives would be her best option for discovering more about Lady Gunderson, but it wasn't as though her instincts had been stellar as of late. Harrow kept excellent records of the

peerage and the order of precedence, as a number of their students were destined for titles.

Ned nodded, enthusiasm pouring from his smile. She knew he held onto crushing guilt for being here at school, while the toll of what it took to make that happen fell upon her. So to be useful for her had bolstered his pride.

He pulled free a piece of paper he'd folded and tucked into his coat, glancing down at his notes. "Lord and Lady Gunderson married in 1771. There was much pomp about it in the papers, as they were the match of the season. There were a number of clippings on it. They had a son, Geoff, born in 1772."

Her brow wrinkled as she leaned over to look at the notes he'd jotted down. "A son? But I thought the Gunderson heir was a distant Irish relation."

"It is, now. The son died in 1801."

"And the son never married?"

Ned shook his head. "No. But that is where the story gets interesting. At his death, that was the point in which their marriage turned poisonous. In public, at least—it could have very well been vile all those years, but they kept it private."

"How do you know that?"

"That was when the clippings about the two of them started to pile up. Pages of them. There were many more clippings on their public disputes, but after I read four of them, I realized they were mostly the same. Two noxious people working diligently to ruin the other in every nasty way possible."

"That is what I was told as well, but I didn't know it ran so deep and for so long." She worried her bottom lip for a moment. "Clearly, losing the son set something off in one of them—maybe both of them."

Ned nodded. "It appears that way. I can sit down and read through the history of the family more thoroughly, maybe go back a generation or two, if you think that would help? Or do you want me to research anything else?"

"Maybe, but I'm not quite ready yet. This has been an enormous help." Her hand went onto his bony knee and squeezed. Too thin. She looked up at the school building. "Tell me you didn't miss the evening meal because of this."

"No, I still have a half hour. You should go now, before dusk is upon us."

She stood and waited for him to pull himself to his full height before she wrapped her arms around him.

He had just edged past her in height and she held the hug a little too long, singeing into her memory how he felt, how he hugged her back. Still her little brother, vestiges of the boy he once was still present in his smile, in the scruff of his hair along his neck. Things she had to hold onto. She wanted to stop time, hold him here until her legs dropped out from under her out of exhaustion. He was bound to grow so much taller, his shoulders broader by the next time she saw him.

If she saw him.

She clamped down on the thought before it overtook her, clearing her throat and pulling away from him.

A light smile fell across her lips as she pulled away. "Before I go, I just want to warn you—if I disappear for a

while, know that school is paid for through the year, you needn't worry on that. And I will be back before then."

His brow furrowed. "You have to leave London?"

"Yes."

He clutched onto her arm. "You cannot. You cannot leave me."

"I am not going to leave you." She grabbed his hand, pulling it from her arm and clasping it between her palms. "I just have to decide upon our next plan—and you will be safest here while I do that."

"Our next plan? I thought this plan was working fine?"

"It was, but now it is not."

A grumble rumbled through his throat, so similar to Declan's growl that she almost chuckled. Almost.

"But where are you going to go?"

She shrugged. "I don't know yet—that is one of the things I need to figure out. What makes the most sense for us."

He nodded, though the worry in his face had overshadowed all his earlier enthusiasm. His fingers unconsciously traced to the long-healed scar along his face, from cheek to temple. Yet he still trusted her—trusted her to keep him safe. "I don't like it."

She lifted her hand and brushed her fingers across the front locks of his hair. "I know. I don't like it either. I had grown rather content in the life—happy even."

"Then why leave it?"

"Circumstances beyond my control."

Love. Love was what happened.

But that was a story she would tell Ned another time. A time when she wasn't gutted, shattered from her heart on outward. When she could manage to think on Declan without collapsing into a sobbing ball. When she didn't have to force him from her mind just to make it through the day—because she had to make it through the day. Declan's life was on the line and she still had to correct that situation.

Ned nodded, not pressing her. Bless his heart. "You will write?" he asked.

"You know I will. Every week. I will use our cipher if there is information that is sensitive."

They both moved to the steps of the gazebo and stepped down onto the gravel path, walking until it split, one side toward the main school buildings, the other side toward the main drive.

She leaned into him, hugging him one last time before parting. Just as she was set to leave, his hand flew up.

"Wait, I forgot to mention, I talked to your friend a day ago."

She stilled, her feet grinding to a halt in the crushed granite.

"You met my friend? Who?"

"Mr. Rudderton, from the rookeries. I remembered him from one of the areas I started to run in—all the boys looked up to him and Blackstone. We thought they were gods—or as close to it as it came on those wretched streets."

It took a long moment for breath to move from her lungs. "Mr. Rudderton? You met him?"

He nodded, confusion knitting his brow. "Yes."

She attempted to set a benign smile on her face, even as her voice shook. "Wh—what did he say?"

Ned shrugged. "He said he was stopping by to visit with the headmaster, and then he happened to see me, and he remembered you had mentioned me to him. You know him, correct?"

"I—I do. I worked for him for some time."

"He was nice." Ned nodded, not seeming to notice her hiccupped words. "He said he's keeping an eye on you and I told him I appreciated it."

Her lips twisted into a sad smile. How she loved her brother and his caring heart. "You don't have to worry on me, Ned."

"You know I do."

"I know." She pulled him into one last hug and lifted onto her toes to kiss his forehead. When had her brother gotten so old?

She yanked herself away before she dragged him along with her.

"I need to leave. It may be a while, but I will write, I swear it."

"I know you will." He gave her a slight wave and started toward the main entrance to the school.

Verity turned down the main drive, walking toward the street where she could find a hack, her gait slow, deliberate.

With every step, her ire stirring.

What in the hell was Declan doing, visiting her brother?

She reached the main thoroughfare that ran past the school.

Her look lifted from thought, and she searched the
road for a passing hack. She could walk to the main corner
for a hack, but that was several streets over.

Her eye caught a man just down the road, standing
alongside a building with a paper tucked under his arm.

The same man that had been behind her when she'd
been let out of the hack and walked onto the school
grounds.

Her gaze quickly shifted to the street, pretending she
hadn't paused at the sight of him, and she studied him out
of the corner of her eye as she started walking along the
footpath opposite him. One street. Two. Three. She veered
down a side street, then took another.

She paused at the main corner to hire a hack and
glanced behind her as she stepped up into the carriage.

There.

It took several seconds, but she spotted him. The same
man.

Following her.

{ CHAPTER 32 }

The second Verity stepped through the servants' door in the dark corner of the main gaming room, the hairs on the back of her neck spiked.

She'd donned her last remaining intact black dress, apron and cap to make it discreetly into the Alabaster, but at the moment, she wished she were half-naked, her hair falling in bright waves about her shoulders.

Anything to get Declan's eyes off of where they were aimed.

At Miss Derrington's breasts.

Her beautiful, creamy, smooth breasts plumping out of a deep maroon gown, the top shadow of the pink of her nipples peeking out above the rich fabric. Perfect breasts.

Granted, Miss Derrington had just thrust her endowments into Declan's face—Verity hadn't missed the motion—yet still, Declan didn't look away, just smiled and after a long gaze, lifted his look to her face to say something that made Miss Derrington laugh.

The sultry chiming of it echoed into Verity's ears. It hit all the right notes. Sex. Sex. Sex. Readily available. Offering up.

Miss Derrington knew exactly what she was doing and she was unmatched in her work. Golden blond hair, just the perfect length with half of her strands artfully arranged atop her head, the rest dangling luxuriously down her back. The

perfect bosom. And a smile that captured the sun. There wasn't a man that she hadn't been able to charm.

In contrast, what did Verity have to offer? Drab black dress. Even drabber cap wrapped tight around her head, the whole of the black cloth making her look sallow and sickly.

Nothing to offer, except for the healthy dose of rage that had just boiled over in her stomach.

Declan hadn't waited—not even four days before moving on from her.

Four days she had just spent hunting down every clue she could find about his past and who was trying to kill him.

Still laughing, Miss Derrington shifted from standing next to Declan, to wiggle herself onto Declan's lap.

Too much.

A haze of red overtook the room, and Verity shot forward, charging in a direct line toward Declan at one of the hazard tables.

"What in the bloody hell do you think you're doing?" she screeched—a low voice, but still a screech as she bore down on Declan.

All movement at the table ceased, every eye in the near vicinity shifting to her. For all the debauchery the Alabaster held within its walls, a maid attacking a titan of the underworld didn't occur often.

She didn't care. Her glare shifted to Miss Derrington. "Your services are done here. Done."

Miss Derrington started to untangle herself from Declan's lap with a quick smile and a nod at Verity. They were friendly, if not friends—as close as one could get in their line of work.

Declan shot to his feet, pushing Miss Derrington the rest of the way off his lap. His breath seethed as he stared down at Verity, fury in his face. For the lack of color in his irises, his eyes were pulsating with heat, fires exploding so quickly they looked like starbursts in the grey.

"My office."

Two words. Only two, and ground out through clenched teeth.

When she didn't instantly move, he grabbed her upper arm and started toward the back of the main gaming hall, his strides long, boots thundering on the floor as he dragged her behind him.

Bloody barbarian.

She didn't try to twist out of his grip for she knew it would do no good. Keep up, remain upright, and stoke the rage in her belly, for she was going to explode upon him once they got upstairs.

His feet stomped up the steps and into his office, never once looking back at her. It wasn't until he slammed the door behind them, then spun around to her with his fingers still digging into her arm, that he unleashed himself. "Don't you dare ever come into my place and—"

"And what? Yell at you? You're not so mighty you can't stand a little waif standing up to you?"

He scoffed a laugh. "Didn't like what you saw downstairs? Didn't like seeing a woman pawing at my body?"

"What I saw was a fickle piece of rubbish rutting about with the latest tramp that bothered to look his way." Her screech was back in full force.

"You left me, Verity." He leaned over her, his face invading hers, his words fuming. "Do I need to remind you of that? You. Left. Me."

"It doesn't matter." She shoved at his chest with her free hand. It did little good.

"It damn well does. You left. Left me. Were you going to come back? Tell me all about that."

"No, I wasn't coming back. But it doesn't matter—it has only been days since I left your bed and that, below, that—"

"Are you truly jealous?" His brow crinkled, the right side of his mouth pulling back into a sneer.

She shoved at his chest again. "Damn you."

"No, damn you. You're jealous because you want my lips on you. You want my fingers rolling against your nipples. You want my cock driving into you."

"Damn you to everlasting hell, you—"

He grabbed her around the waist, lifting her up, the motion cutting the air from her words.

"Hell is right here, finch." He turned, stalking across the room, and he slammed her backside onto the desk. "You bloody well want me and you don't want any hands except for yours on my skin. But that comes with conditions. Conditions that mean you don't get to come in here and expect me not to touch you."

His hand curved harshly under her jawline, tilting her head up, and his mouth crashed down onto hers, devouring, bruising, and jolting into throbbing motion all the most traitorous parts of her. His fingers moved up, ripping the black cap from her head. He pulled back for a heaving breath. "You want me, don't you?"

"Damn you."

His grip along her jaw tightened. "Say it. Say you still want my cock deep in you."

She huffed a breath, then another, her glare eating into him. "Damn you—yes. Yes, I want you. I will always want you even if I hate you."

It only took seconds for her to rip open the front fall of his trousers and for him to shove up her skirts and impale himself into her.

Hard, rough. Angry. So bitterly angry.

Both of them.

His hands ruthless along her body, pawing at her breasts, and it only twisted the guttural need in her to a pitch. With every breath against his thrusts, she heaved out all the rage in her throat. The pinnacle came at her quickly, slamming into her without warning and thundering along her nerves. A scream—of rage, of pleasure—shook through her throat as her body shattered into a thousand pieces.

He didn't let her ride it, keeping up the onslaught until his body was growling, shuddering, and driving into her with furious intent, marking her soul. Punishing, until he could hold no longer and broke, his seed spurting deep inside of her, filling her with his heat.

Damn him.

Damn that he made her feel like this. She'd come back to help him and all she wanted to do in that moment was

kill him herself. Yet still her body trembled from the blasted aftershocks of her orgasm, heated by his seed deep within her. Still her body burrowed into his chest, her nails digging into his back.

Damn him.

A herculean effort, but she managed to push herself away from him even as she wanted nothing more than to clutch onto him.

"You're still livid." His cock remained embedded deep, not pulling out, still pulsating within her. His hand went under her jaw, his fingers squeezing into her cheek as he tilted her head up to him.

She slammed her hand across his arm, knocking his hold from her face. "This doesn't change a thing." She jabbed her palms onto the desk and shifted to the side to extract herself from him. Jumping onto her feet, she shook her skirts downward into place.

He shoved himself back into his trousers, his fingers fast on the buttons. "Well, it certainly shut your mouth from screeching at me."

"You deserved every single screech."

His look lifted, cutting into her. "Do I?"

Her lips tightened. "You do."

He stepped toward her, invading her space, his words low, eerily calm. "I never even touched that woman down there. She was the one crawling on top of me. She came with a gentleman that was losing a fortune at the tables and I wanted him to continue to do so. I was goading him into not stopping by setting his masculinity at stake. I could not care less about his whore."

"Whore? She has a bloody name."

"She does?" He paused and his eyebrows lifted. A sardonic smile came to his face. "Oh, of course. Your replacement. I should have guessed. What was her name?"

"Miss Derrington."

He stared at her for a long breath, then shook his head, taking a step backward. Distancing himself. "What are you even doing here, Verity?"

"You want the litany?"

"Yes."

"You went to Hector and took your file—the file that keeps you bloody well safe. Yes, he told me. Then you hired a guardian to follow me—you thought I wouldn't notice that? And then you went to my brother—my *brother*. Why? What did you hope to accomplish at Harrow?"

"I was making inquiries, that was all."

"No. My brother is off limits to you—do you understand? Off limits. I will not let anything or anyone harm him—you included."

He started. "You think I would hurt him?"

Her hands flew up at her sides. "I don't know what you intend to do, Declan. There isn't a part of my life that you haven't tried to upend in the last two days—take from me—and you need to stop it. So what is it? What will stop you? What else do you want from me?"

A light flickered in his eyes. "Just one thing."

"Is there anything left?" Her voice pitched into a scream. "I don't have anything left to give you."

He nodded, clasping his hands behind his back as he stared at her in silence for a long breath. "Just the one."

She growled, furious frustration hitting her. "What is it?"

"What are you running from?"

Her head jerked backward, then her feet. Backward, backward until her calves hit the edge of the settee. "No. No. No, I cannot."

He took a step toward her, not letting her escape him completely, though he left an ample amount of space between them. His words came soft, the low rumble of his voice burrowing into her chest. "You didn't trust me before with this—with any of this—but you need to trust me now."

She shook her head, her eyes pleading.

"You said you loved me, Verity, but did you? Do you? Truly?"

At that, all the fight left her chest, her gut sinking.

She was beaten, fair and square by the look in his eye. The look that said volumes. That he was hers to trust. To love. To sink into. To hide within, a shelter from a world that was cruel and vengeful and bitter.

And he needed the same from her.

The look was pure vulnerability, and she'd never seen it on him before. Never. The man wasn't vulnerable. But in this—in her—he was.

Her legs gave out and she sank onto the edge of the settee, her fingers folding together in her lap.

Her defeated voice croaked out just above a whisper. "I did. I do."

He took two steps toward her and sank to balance on his heels, his hands settling over the top of hers, swallowing them whole. "Then trust me. Trust that I am willing to do whatever it takes—whatever that is—to make right for you what haunts you from your past. I will slay any monster. For you, my life on the line—it is where I am meant to be. Meant to do. Because you are *mine*."

The vehemence in his voice cut straight through her chest, carving apart her heart.

Her eyes crept upward to him. "Except I don't want your life in danger. I've spent an extraordinary amount of time ensuring that it is never on the line."

He chuckled and his right hand lifted, caressing the side of her cheek, his fingertips burying into her hair. "Trust me."

She stared at him, silent. Silent for too many breaths. Silent until he exhaled a sigh and stood, moving over to the sideboard to pour a dram of brandy into a glass. He brought it to her, setting it in her hand.

She promptly swallowed the entire splash of it.

The slightest smile quirked onto his face and he took the glass from her, went to refill it, and then set it back in her hands.

That splash went just as quickly down her throat.

This time his devil smile came with a slight chuckle. He pulled the glass from her hand, refilled it a third time and delivered it back into her fingertips. "We're just going to be in here, silent or not, until you tell me."

She stared up at him. "You've effectively kidnapped me?"

"Call it what you want. But here is the truth. You love me, but that love comes with conditions—that you never

have to tell me about your past. That is why you left and that is where there is a gaping difference between us. I love you, but I have no conditions. Whatever you tell me isn't going to change the fact that I love you. It isn't going to untwine our souls."

"You making me sit in here until I tell you of my past sounds like a condition."

He scoffed, shaking his head. "Take it as a suggestion with the utmost importance." His finger flicked out toward the glass of brandy she clutched in her hands. "So drink. Drink up. Stay silent. I love you enough to sit here, waiting until kingdom come."

She looked down, studying the tip of her forefinger mindlessly tracing the fine lip of the tumbler. She shouldn't swallow this dram as well. She did, and she would be slipping down a rabbit hole she could never claw out of.

Her hand shaking, she lifted the glass to her lips and swallowed the liquid, rushing it past her tongue to burn her throat.

She looked up at him. "Two conditions."

{ CHAPTER 33 }

She swallowed the third glass of brandy.

Declan probably should have stopped at handing her two, for if she wasn't going to talk, she was sure to be soused in short order.

His stare bored into the weave of her red hair circling her crown as she focused on the empty glass in her hands. A futile attempt by him to read intention, to strip away all those heavy padlocks she had mired in her head, holding a death grip on her secrets.

She was either going to tell him or she wasn't. The rest of his life, truly, to be decided in this moment.

Hell. She needed to tell him. To *choose* him.

Her green eyes lifted to him, her stare vulnerability laced with steel. "Two conditions."

He inclined his head to her. "You have a lot of them. I expected no less."

She gave him one nod. "Do not touch me. Do not pity me. I cannot get this story out if you do either to me. Do you understand?"

"No." Pity her? Never, for she was Venus—born of marble and sweat and tears. She would not be pitied.

But not touch her? Not comfort her? Not hold her?

That he was not fine with.

Her lips went terse for a second, and she sighed. "Nothing can change the past, no matter what one feels

after the fact. I have to get through this—through telling you—without feeling. And if you make me feel—feel anything—I will break. And I cannot break. Not for what you're demanding of me."

He nodded. "I understand."

Reluctantly, he stepped to the side, leaning his shoulder against the wall next to the mantel of the fireplace. Fully in view, but not close, not an overwhelming presence that would hinder what she needed to say. He crossed his arms to keep them in check and set his gaze on her. "Tell me."

"I murdered someone."

"What?"

She winced.

Damn. Too much emotion, too much surprise in his reply. He nodded her onward.

She exhaled a breath, fingering the bottom edge of the glass in her hands. "Do you remember when we talked about killing? What it does to one's soul? Do you remember how I said I killed those cutthroats that attacked you without mercy?"

"Yes." This time, the word came out deliberate, neutral.

"I lost all of my capacity for mercy long ago. I offered mercy once. I offered it to my father after he beat my mother near to death. She could barely move, bloody, trying to crawl across the floor to escape him. He was beating her, smashing her across her back with the leg of a chair he'd broken. Again and again. Yet she still crawled, even though there was nowhere to escape to." Her words were wooden. Relaying the story, not reliving it.

"He was not going to stop, so I stopped him. I had to hold my dagger to his neck, but I stopped him. And I wanted to kill him, kill him so badly in that moment for all the years he'd made my mother suffer in front of us." She paused, a trembling smile cresting her top lip. "That was what she did her whole life, take every swing from him so that they never landed on us. He never touched me or Ned—only her, and only because she would throw herself in front of us to protect us. All the bruises. The smashed bones. Her broken smile that she always tried to give Ned and me, even though she was in constant pain. My father took that from us—took her real smiles, the ones that would warm my heart and tell me everything was going to be right in the world someday when I could leave that house. In that moment with my knife on his neck, I wanted—needed him—dead. But I couldn't do it. Mercy. Mercy was what my mother had instilled in me. Mercy. Compassion. And I couldn't do it. Couldn't kill him."

She stopped, her eyes glazing over, and he saw her drift into the memories, getting lost.

"What happened?"

"The second I lowered my blade, he picked up the broken chair and smashed it across her head. I sank my blade into his neck at that moment, trying to stop him, but I was too late. I didn't react in time. His blow crushed her head against the marble hearth and cracked her skull. I think she died instantly. I hope it, at least."

"And your father?"

"I killed him. Murdered him. I stabbed the blade into the side of his neck. I didn't even know, didn't understand what I did. I just did it. Ned was behind me because we had just come in from cutting spring flowers and I didn't want him to see it—see any of it—but he did. He was so young. The flowers he'd been holding crushed at his feet. Flowers for our mother to make her happy. Just a little bit of happiness. Tulips and daffodils and lily of the valley, mangled on the floor. And that was when my uncle came into the room, just as I sank my knife into my father."

His gut dropped. "You have an uncle that knows of this?"

She gave a slight nod. "He came in, looked at the scene, my mother, bloody and dead by the fire, my father— his brother—sinking to the floor, blood draining from him fast."

She paused, her fingers around the glass tightening, trying to squelch the shake in them. But he saw it. Saw how even though she tried to stay above the emotion of it, it was overtaking her and he needed nothing else in that moment than to grab her and pull her into his chest and hold her.

He stayed in place, his muscles twitching, angry with bridled energy at not being allowed to go to her.

Her look lifted to him. "My uncle did the calculation quickly. So quickly, I almost missed what he was about to do. He didn't even stop to try to help his brother. No. He jumped past my father, stepped over my mother and grabbed a fire poker from the fireplace. Then he charged at Ned."

"He went after your brother? Why?"

"My brother was next in line before my uncle."

His breath stilled in his chest. "Who exactly was your father?"

"Baron Perrington. The estate is a small but lucrative one in northern Westmorland."

Bloody hell. Baron Perrington. Jack was right. "Your father is a baron?"

"Was a baron. That title now belongs to my uncle."

Declan held back the instant rage coursing through his veins and set his voice to neutral. "How could he have the title? What about your brother?"

"When my Uncle Rupert swung his first swipe at Ned's head—I couldn't believe it, didn't understand what was happening. My mother had just died and I had just murdered my father. Ned managed to duck that first blow, but the sharp tip of the poker still caught him. He has a long scar from cheek to temple of where it cut him deep. Did you see that on him?"

"I did."

"If Ned hadn't screamed, I don't know if I would have moved, but he screamed and I still had the dagger in my hand and I swung—it was weak—but the blade plunged into Rupert's wrist, right between the bones as he lifted the poker for another slash at Ned. The poker dropped and I didn't stay to see how I wounded him. I grabbed Ned's hand and we ran—ran from the house, ran from the estate."

"Your uncle didn't follow you?"

"He did, but he set out to the south, thinking that was where we would escape to—a port, or London—everything was south, so I went north until I was convinced we had disappeared."

"And then you found your way to London with nothing?"

She shook her head. "No. I had something—everything—I had Ned. He was safe. Safe from our father, safe from our uncle. He was safe, and that was everything."

Declan took a moment to let all that information settle, so many holes filling in from what he knew of Verity. "It was your uncle on the street outside that ball, wasn't it?"

She nodded.

"How did he take the title?"

"Ned discovered in the archives at Harrow that Uncle Rupert reported our whole family died of pneumonia. There are graves for all of us in the family plot in Westmorland."

Declan sucked in a breath. "Bastard."

"He knows I'll never come back, knows Ned will never come back. He witnessed me kill my father and he would see me hanged for it—it was what he screamed at me as we ran from the room. That he'd see me hanged for it. I do not doubt it."

"Jones isn't your surname."

She drew a deep sigh. "No. Thompson is. But Ned and I, we can never be known by our true name. And maybe, someday, if I am dead or gone, Ned can take his rightful place in the line, but he is still too young to face our uncle. Ned is brave, but he was almost killed once for the title. And I am his Achilles' Heel—he knows if he comes forth, I will be found and hanged for murdering our father."

"You've killed others."

"Not with witnesses. My uncle saw exactly what I did. He is a peer. There is no getting around it, no escaping it."

He'd had enough. Heard enough.

Declan pushed himself off the wall, walking to her and then dropping, balancing on his heels in front her. His hands started to move toward her knees, but then he stopped and clamped his fingers in front of his mouth as his stare pierced her. "Why didn't you tell me any of this?"

A harsh chuckle bubbled up from her throat. "How could I tell you this? Any of it? That I am a murderer? That I am destined for a noose? Why would I ever do that to you? I'm only telling you now because I have no other way to get out of this room."

His stare turned harsh on her. "You could have told me and I could have helped."

"Exactly. You would try and fix this—fix everything because that is what you do. But there is no fixing this. There is me disappearing. That is how this ends. That was always how this was going to end."

"What do you mean?"

Her head angled to the side and she met his stare. "Why do you think I really work for the Guardians of the Bones, Dec?"

"To keep Ned safe in a school away from the rookeries?"

"Yes. But it is for the future. He's going to need protection in the future, and I am depositing on his future with a guardian watching over him with every day I serve as one. By the time Ned comes of age, I will be gone, disappeared from England, and Ned will have the protection of the Guardians when he sets his rightful claim to the title. He knows exactly who he is and who he will be.

And he will right every wrong ever set forth by my father. Ever set forth by my uncle. But he needs the Guardians at his back to do it. To keep him safe."

"I already hired them for that."

Her head snapped back. "You what?"

"When I visited with Samson—it wasn't just to set a guardian on your tail. I hired one for Ned as well."

"You—you did?" Shock edged along the lines of worry marring her face.

"I did."

"You didn't need to do that. Ned—I will take anything I can get on him, but for me? I don't need a guardian. You didn't need to set that in place."

"Didn't I? I'm not going to let anything—anyone hurt you, Verity. And that includes someone hurting your brother, for if he is hurt, you are hurt. I always knew that."

Her hand lifted to her throat, clutching into the delicate skin along her neck. "I don't…that you have done this for me." She stopped, heaving a sigh. "It is completely overbearing…but that you set a guardian on Ned. For that…for that alone I think I can forgive you anything."

The permission he needed.

He unclasped his fingers and reached for her knees, setting his hands gently on her. "For all that has happened—for all that you have suffered—I want to tear your uncle into little bloody pieces. But I think you know that about me. And I look at you, and through all of this, you have stood, proud and gritty and determined to protect your brother. You've succeeded at that. But you have me now. Let me help with this. And let me start with one question for you."

Her eyes narrowed at him. "What is the question?"

"What is it that *you* want, for *you*?"

{ CHAPTER 34 }

Her mother had been the last person to ever ask her that.

It'd been so many years ago, she almost laughed at the question.

What did she want?

Did she even know?

Could she even imagine it?

She met his look. "I need Ned safe."

He nodded. "That is a given. What else? What is it that *you* want? Are you looking for death, Verity? Is that why you left me? To skulk off and die alone as penance?"

"No." Her bottom lip pulled under her teeth as the one image that had haunted her for years flashed in her mind. "The one thing I don't want is to have Ned watching me swinging from a rope."

She gasped a breath, holding back a sob that came out of nowhere. "To have you watching me swinging from a rope. The drop. My toes twitching. The life leaving me. And you standing there. In the crowd, watching and not being able to do anything." Tears rolled down her cheeks. "That is why I left. I don't want that. Don't want that to be the last image you have of me. I don't want that memory for you. For Ned."

"Hell, Verity." He grabbed her, pulling her into him, crushing her head onto his chest. "How could you not tell

me this? That's never going to happen—I won't let it. Cities will burn to the charred earth before I let that happen."

"I don't think you can stop it. I murdered him. I did it. I have it coming."

"Then you are about to learn just what I am capable of." He heaved a breath, her head against his chest riding the motion. "You were trying to protect your mother. I would have done the very same thing. Hell, I do the very same thing when anyone threatens someone of mine."

His face dipped, his lips on the top of her head. "Tell me, would you do the same thing if Ned's life was on the line?"

"Of course." She wouldn't think twice upon it, wouldn't regret it.

"Then you know how I feel about keeping you safe. There are no bounds. No right or wrong. No morals. You are safe. That is all I care about."

She breathed in the scent of him, spice, sandalwood and smoke, mixing in with the salt of her tears. How she wanted to stay in that spot forever, protected in his arms, the world outside of that room far, far away.

"That is it. I'm no longer vacillating on this decision." He pulled slightly away and she looked up at him.

"What decision?"

His right arm stayed around her body and he shifted onto the settee next to her as his thumb wiped away the wetness on her cheeks. "I need to come up with a plan for the Alabaster, for the other businesses in the rookeries."

"But this is your life."

He shook his head. "Talen and I made a pact long ago—if either of us had something to lose—something to *really* lose, something that could destroy one of us, we would leave this business."

"Why?"

"This place, this life, it is not for people with something to lose."

Recognition sparked in her eyes. "Which is why you've taken over the full of the business since Talen found Ness."

"Exactly. He couldn't—cannot be here anymore." He nodded. "And now I find myself at a crossroads."

"How so?"

"I have something to lose. And I'm not about to lose you, Verity, I refuse it." His knuckles ran along the side of her face. "I'm not about to have you in danger because of me, because I am a target."

"What are you saying?" Her words came out slow, deliberate.

"I'm saying I want to leave this—leave it all. I have more than enough coin and respectable investments to last a hundred years. I would leave it today, but I still don't know why I'm a target."

He shook his head, his brow furrowing in concentration. "The position I hold here in the rookeries—it gets me information that can only be garnered through the service folk—the ones that hear and see everything. Right now, the power I hold can get me into places that I wouldn't have access to. Until this is settled, until I find out who is after me—where the danger has been for years—I'm not safe. Which means you're not safe."

He paused, rubbing his forehead. "The whole Lord Gunderson trail was clearly a folly—Bloodwater sent me on a useless chase and I wasted precious time."

She gasped. "Except it wasn't wasted. It's why I came to the Alabaster tonight—to tell you."

"Not to just yell at me?"

"Well that, and to tell you. Lord Gunderson—there is a connection."

"How so?"

"After I talked with Hector and told him I was leaving the position here, he said he would have to discuss with his employer the next steps for you."

"And?"

A smile came to her face. "And I followed him. For two days, actually. He eventually walked into a rather large townhouse on Park Lane. I made it below floors and chatted with one of the kitchen maids. It was Lady Gunderson's home. She's the one that hired Hector."

His eyes went wide. "You think?"

She nodded and turned more fully into him, grabbing his leg. "Hector didn't go anywhere else that would have been a client's home. And tonight, Miss Derrington was in place, just a day after he met with Lady Gunderson. I also had Ned look in the archives of the peerage in the library at Harrow, and he verified what we learned the other night—Lord and Lady Gunderson hate each other. So, I think this is the lead we need. It is what you said—if we can find out who employed Hector, then we can find out who the threat is."

Declan nodded. "Good. Then I plan to have a chat with Lord Gunderson."

"When?"

"While Talen and I were searching for information on him—there were two opportune times when he would be out in public and I could approach him—one was at the ball the other night, the other is in front of parliament. Talen set up a meeting with him for me under the guise of an investment in a ship headed to the Americas."

"When is the meeting?"

"Tomorrow. I was going to cancel the appointment because I thought Lord Gunderson was a dead end."

"No." She almost jumped off the settee in excitement. "It is perfect. You need to keep the appointment and I need to come with you."

Declan's look turned hard. "No, you don't need to come."

She frowned. "Don't tell me what to do. You know full well I can handle myself in the direst of circumstances."

"No." He shook his head. "It's parliament, Verity."

Her eyes narrowed. What did he care of parliament? "Oh. You think my uncle may see me?"

"Yes. We don't know why he is in town. Parliament would make sense."

She sighed. "There could be a vote he is here for." She grabbed his upper arm. "But this is more important than that, and the likelihood that Uncle Rupert will spot me—it is slim. My father never came to London for parliament, I don't see why Rupert would suddenly take an interest."

"No. He already saw you once outside that ball and I'm not about to risk your life."

Her head snapped back. "So you can risk your life for mine—but I can't risk mine for yours?"

"Yes, that is the crux of it." His head cocked to the side. "The thing about risking your life is that you might just lose it. And I'm not willing to take that chance."

Her hand dropped away from his arm. "Fine."

He nodded, then stilled, interrupting his own nod as his look sliced into her. "You are giving up too easily."

She shrugged. "I can still have my own secrets."

He shifted forward. "No. No, you cannot. Not when it comes to this."

"Fine." She waved her hand in the air. "I'm not yet done with my own investigation. I had planned to corner Lady Gunderson."

"How?"

"I paid a call on my heiress friend—the one that was my first case as a guardian—and her mother is an adherent patron of the Royal Academy, as is Lady Gunderson. There is a showing of a new exhibition tomorrow that Lady Gunderson should be attending. I think I can steal her ear for a moment, possibly ask a few questions."

"Good." He exhaled an exaggerated sigh of relief. "I would much rather have you in an art gallery than in front of parliament."

She smiled. "We just may uncover the mystery of this yet."

"And then onto setting the rest of your life right."

She nodded. "One thing at a time."

Hope.

True hope, for the very first time in years, flickered to a faint glow in her chest.

A future, a real future, might just be hers.

{ CHAPTER 35 }

Verity looked at the painting in front of her in the Exhibition Room. Men and women, naked, being dragged—or falling—into hell. Serpents and demons devouring them. Turning them into monsters.

She liked it and she didn't.

Hell was coming for her. Sooner or later, there was only one place her immortal soul was destined for. At least Declan would be with her. She'd take hell to be by his side for all eternity.

"This one is gory." Prudence took a sip of punch as she stopped next to Verity and handed her the second glass in her hand. She turned to soak in the painting. "But there is something so real about it, it is hard not to be entranced."

Verity kept her eyes trained on the painting. "Deep down, everyone is fascinated with carnage, even as they try to look away. It is both an invitation and a cautionary tale in one."

Prudence drew in a deep breath, then looked to her. "Lady Gunderson arrived."

Verity's eyes flickered to her friend. "Where is she?"

"In the Hall. It is holding a menagerie exhibit, both sculptures and paintings. It is mostly empty at the moment." Prudence nudged her head toward the adjoining room at the far end of the gallery.

Verity forced a smile. "No time like the present."

The two friends walked along the length of the gallery, not hurried, even as Verity wanted to sprint down the length to set herself next to Lady Gunderson.

She kept up light conversation with Prudence, even as they entered the Hall.

Prudence edged closer to Lady Gunderson, then walked by, seemingly to take an interest in a bronze sculpture of wolfhounds Lady Gunderson was studying. "Lady Gunderson, it is so good of you to make the exhibit—my mother was most excited you were attending today. She always mentions what a steadfast support of the Royal Academy you are and that you are one to emulate."

Leaning on her cane, Lady Gunderson shifted her attention to Prudence. "Lady Soderton, you are such a bright addition to these shadowed halls. And this whole place has been lightened with your mother's addition to our rank of supporters. She doesn't take to the cynicism that is so prevalent in the old crows that squawk about and have pecked at the members for years. Myself included."

Prudence chuckled, glanced back at Verity, and then turned to Lady Gunderson. "Lady Gunderson, may I present to you my good friend, Miss Verity Jones."

Verity stepped forward next to Prudence with a bright smile on her face as she looked at Lady Gunderson.

She gasped.

A full, jaw-dropping gasp.

Entirely rude. Entirely warranted.

"Child, is there something amiss?" Lady Gunderson shuffled a step forward, leaning heavily on her cane.

Verity almost jumped a step backward, but managed to stay in place. "No, my apologies, Lady Gunderson, I was just struck by the beauty of your silver necklace. It sets off your eyes so prettily."

Eyes that were exactly the same as Declan's. Irises that were void of color, molten steel. Even aged, the color, the shape of them were unmistakable.

Shit.

Lady Gunderson smiled, confused. "Wh—what was that, dear?"

Had she just sworn out loud?

Her hand slammed over her mouth. "No. Apologies, my lady." She turned to Prudence. "I am so sorry, I must excuse myself."

Verity fumbled past several people on her way to escape the room, and then ran in a full sprint down the length of the gallery.

Drawing stares and sneers of disgust.

She didn't care.

She had to get to parliament.

No matter who saw her or the consequences.

{ CHAPTER 36 }

Declan walked across the Old Palace Yard, pushing through the many men jostling about before the start of parliament for the day, his stare locked on a specific carriage across the way. His boots thudded on the flat stones and he was across the yard in no time, looking into the window of the carriage.

Lord Gunderson sat inside, as expected, and as Declan approached, a footman opened the door to the carriage and Declan climbed inside, taking a seat opposite Gunderson. The carriage started to move before the footman closed the door.

Taking off his top hat, Declan inclined his head to the elderly gentleman. "Thank you for meeting with me on such short notice, Lord Gunderson."

Gunderson gave him a nod. "You will have my attention for five minutes, Mr. Rudderton. Lord Youngston said his investment with you and Lord Washburn has gone well? How many ships do you have in your shipping fleet?"

"Five, at the moment, my lord. We are awaiting the return of two ships from the Handover Company that we may soon purchase as well." Declan fell into easy talk on the legitimate side of his business with Talen. Though much of their wealth came from the seedier nooks of London, he and Talen had worked hard to expand into reputable ventures, all of which had become much easier with Talen's inheritance of a title.

As Declan talked about the latest shipments, he studied Lord Gunderson. The heavy wrinkles on his face were odd, as the man had one of the whitest complexions he'd ever seen, almost translucent skin. If it wasn't for the freckles and age spots dotting his face, Declan could almost swear he saw blood pumping through the veins. Most of the man's hair was white, with occasional shocks of faded red hair. His eyes, a dull blue. Dull with age or just unenthusiastic about life, Declan couldn't discern.

Why in the world would this man have any interest in him at all? Again, Gunderson looked at Declan like he didn't know him, much less had ever heard of him before meeting him at the ball several nights prior.

Declan glanced out the window only to see they were passing Charing Cross. This wasn't a simple five-minute carriage ride about the streets around parliament.

He looked to Gunderson. "My apologies, was I keeping you from something important? I left my carriage by parliament, but can be let out anywhere."

"No, that won't be necessary. We will turn about shortly, I presume." Gunderson grabbed his cane and used it to knock on the roof of the carriage. The response of, "Yes, mi'lord," came down from above.

Enough jabber on business, Declan could see his time with Gunderson was quickly coming to a close. Best to get right to the matter of it. "Forgive me if I am being presumptuous, my lord, but do you know of me?"

"Of course, I know of you. I wouldn't be meeting with you if I didn't."

Declan's eyes narrowed. "Yes, but beyond our meeting the other night. Have you ever heard my name before?"

"Rudderton? No. I don't know that I've ever had acquaintance with a Rudderton before." Gunderson stared at Declan for a long moment, his blue eyes vacant, and then he leaned forward, looking out the window of the carriage. "I think we are done, Mr. Rudderton." He lifted his cane and knocked on the roof of the carriage once more.

"We are here, mi'lord." The carriage stopped.

Here?

Declan looked out the window. They'd driven to a wide lane between two warehouses. Not exactly empty, but not exactly a busy alleyway.

His eyebrows lifted. "Shall I depart, Lord Gunderson?" He was ready to escape the man, as it was rather clear, once again, that Gunderson had no connection to him. As suspected, a false end no matter what Verity had discovered. Gunderson was just a waste of his time at this point.

Lord Gunderson gave him one nod. "I would rather appreciate that. Except, wait one moment. I do have something for you." He leaned his cane on the cushion next to him and reached into the inner pocket of his coat.

The silver of the pistol flashed in Declan's eyes just as quickly as the distinctive sound of the trigger being pulled back.

A bloody pistol, aimed right at him.

Declan froze, his head tilting slightly to the side. It wasn't the first time a cocked and loaded gun had been aimed at his heart. "Lord Gunderson, have I offended you in some way?"

"Fool boy. Never get in a carriage with a better. It doesn't bode well for you."

"A better? What are you talking about?"

"I needed plausibility and this is it. When you accosted me outside of parliament and had me forced here, threatening me, I was beholden to shoot you."

Declan's head snapped back. "Shoot me?"

"I am holding a pistol at you, you imbecile. Shooting you is a likely outcome with a criminal such as yourself, and I become a hero for clearing the streets of dung like you."

"Dung like me?" Realization hit Declan. Bloodwater had been telling the truth. "You do know me, don't you?"

"I do."

"You're the one trying to kill me."

"With the most inept cutthroats imaginable. So I will take care of this personally." Gunderson lifted the gun, leveling the aim of it at Declan's chest.

There was no way the man could miss him, not at this close range. Even if Declan sprang him, the man would clip the trigger and a bullet would still hit him.

He needed time. Time for what, he wasn't sure.

His hands lifted slowly, palms to Gunderson. "Why? Why me?"

A twisted smile, evil, crossed the old man's face. "Simple. You never should have existed. That is why. I am merely correcting history on that mistake."

His forefinger on the trigger twitched, pulling back the trigger.

{ CHAPTER 37 }

"Declan!"

Verity screamed, but even to her own ears, her voice was nothing but a breathless warble, her legs cramping, threatening to collapse under her.

Too late. Too many men. Too much noise.

Too far away. Too much space in Old Palace Yard.

"Verity. Verity Thompson. Verity."

Her name. Her *real* name.

Her head swiveled to the right.

The devil.

Uncle Rupert running toward her from the steps of parliament. Yelling her name. Fury. Death in his eyes.

Her look swung back to Declan as he stepped up into a carriage and it started moving before the footman fully closed the door, the servant having to run to his perch hanging off the back of the slick black coach. The coat-of-arms on the door. The same family crest she'd seen embroidered onto the apron of the girl cutting carrots in Lady Gunderson's kitchens.

"Verity, don't you dare move!" From across the yard, madness echoed in the shriek of her uncle.

Her stomach roiled, threatening to upend the contents of her belly, but she choked it back. Not now. Not when she needed to catch that carriage.

To the hell with her uncle. If he caught her, he caught her. But he wouldn't catch her before she found Declan and

saved him. He was more important—more important than her life. He would protect Ned, she knew he would—he'd protect her brother better than she ever could.

Her look went frantic about her. There. A chaise. She could handle a chaise.

She hoped.

Her legs were in motion before thought could enter her brain and she shoved past the purple-coated fop standing next to the bright blue chaise, chatting with a group of men. She leapt up into the two-wheeled gig, dropped the brake, and set the single horse into motion before the man could scramble up after her. He swung his cane at her legs until she kicked down at the wood, knocking it from his hand onto the floor of the gig.

He held onto the side of the chaise for an admirable amount of time, his feet stumbling, half dragging, until she took the corner onto the street Declan had disappeared on and the whole gig threatened to roll over. The fop fell off.

"So sorry, sir," she screamed over her shoulder. "I will return it posthaste."

If she was lucky.

If she was alive.

Flicking the reins, she pushed the horse faster. Faster.

Through the Charing Cross mayhem that sent the side of the chaise scraping along a wagon and the wheels crunching over the end of a tomato cart.

Faster.

Finally, there—Gunderson's carriage.

Her brow wrinkled, her eyes squinting. The carriage was turning into a lane by a warehouse? That lane could go nowhere. She knew this area well enough to know the next road over dead-ended in both directions.

Panic exploded in her chest and she screamed at the horse to go faster, then yanked hard at the reins as she got to the turn.

She looked down the lane only to see Gunderson's carriage at a standstill. The lane was wide enough for traffic both ways, but was eerily empty. A wagon and donkey at the other end of the lane, a few men—sailors—walking along the road and then turning into one of the warehouses. No one else.

Grabbing the cane from the floor of the chaise, she jumped from the gig, sprinting toward the carriage and past the footman.

She wedged a foot onto the iron stair collapsed under the edge of the coach and looked into the window.

A pistol.

A bloody pistol aimed at Declan. And the old buzzard—the bastard of a man lifting it, pulling the trigger.

Her hand came up, smashing the heavy metal handle of the cane through the window and aimed directly at the pistol.

The shot filled her ears, the blast stunning her for a second, and in the next instant the door slammed open, the handle smashing into her gut. Falling, falling, falling.

She hit the ground hard, flat on her back, all air whooshing out of her body, pain everywhere at once.

Her vision left her for one second, two.

"Verity Thompson, you are dead."

Her body curled, still fighting for air as her head rolled to the left.

Uncle Rupert advanced down the alleyway. Coming fast. Silver. Silver in his hand. A dagger.

The ground vibrated under her with heavy feet—Gunderson's driver, the footman—closing in on her.

Uncle Rupert almost to her and he lifted the blade, ready to strike.

Attacking. So close.

She couldn't move. Not a muscle.

Boots. Sudden boots tumbling down from the carriage. A body flailing, falling in front of Verity just as Uncle Rupert slashed down at her with the dagger.

The sound she heard distinctly.

The squish of a blade slicing through flesh. Blood. Muscle.

Except not her flesh. Not her blood.

A body dropped to the ground next to her just as boots and boots and more black boots crowded around her.

Boots and legs and a skirt and she couldn't see anything.

She gasped, gasped again and again for air, a dying fish, trying to not let her body shut down on her. Another gasp and there—air. Another gasp. More air.

She flipped onto her hands and knees, but still couldn't see anything through the wall of legs around her.

But she could hear.

An inhuman growl, fists hitting flesh—hitting a face, bones crunching, and the primal scream only grew louder.

Breath finally in her lungs, allowing her to move, she jabbed a hand between the legs surrounding her and wedged her head out past two of the black boots.

Declan on top of a body, swinging, the head now bloody pulp.

Her uncle.

Jack jumped away from the wall surrounding her and tackled Declan around the chest, yanking him upward. "There are too many people around—too many, Dec. He has to live. You have to stop."

Declan fought off Jack, his arms still swinging. "No— he's going to fucking hell."

Jack set his mouth by Declan's ear, yelling, "Not if it means you get taken away from Verity before you even have her."

Declan kept swinging, his raged look still fixed on her uncle.

"He just bloody well killed Lord Gunderson—he's going to hang, Dec. He's done."

Declan's arms swung, once, twice more, and then fell down by his sides.

His breath heaving, Declan looked over at Lord Gunderson, at the side of his gut soaked with blood.

His gaze flickered past Lord Gunderson, searching for her.

He found her, her head sticking out from the fortress of legs, and he stilled.

One heartbeat and he shrugged Jack's hold off of him and lunged to her, jumping over Lord Gunderson and skidding to his knees. The legs around her parted and he

grabbed her, his arms iron clamps yanking her into his body. "Tell me you're not injured."

She wedged her arms upward, her hands running across his face, needing to touch him to make sure he wasn't shot, wasn't dying.

"Tell me you're fine, Verity." The words came out furious and strangled and desperate.

"I—I'm fine." The breath still not fully making it into her lungs cut her words to a whisper. "Jus—just can't breathe yet."

His hands clasped onto the back of her head. Clutching her so hard to him she was sure she would never be able to peel away from his torso. A new home for her, happily living melded to his ribcage.

Except she could smell blood. Her hands ran along his shoulders and upper arms and her right fingers dipped into something sticky and warm. "You're bleeding."

"It's just a nick."

She should be tearing off his coat and shirt to look for herself, but for once, she believed him. There was no way he could have pummeled Uncle Rupert as he did if a bullet had just shattered his arm.

His body shifted against her as he looked upward. "Where did Gunderson's footman and driver go?"

"Ran off," Jack said.

Declan grunted. "Then we tell the authorities exactly what happened here. That man killed Lord Gunderson."

"Aye," Jack said.

Verity pulled her head back, looking at Lord Gunderson's body and then up at Declan. "What? How?"

He shrugged, his lips going to her forehead, his voice low. "I didn't have anything else to throw in between you and your uncle. Gunderson was the closest thing."

Great Zeus. Declan really was capable of anything. Especially when it came to keeping her safe.

To that end, Verity wedged her head to the side, her thoughts finally settling enough to be curious as to who all the legs that had surrounded her belonged to. She looked up to find four men and a woman scattered around them and Jack.

She jerked away from Declan, her gaze flying to him. "How many guardians did you hire?"

Declan shrugged, sheepish. "Just a few more after yesterday."

Her eyebrows lifted.

"Well, maybe four or five...and Jack."

Jack looked down at her and smiled. A goofy, wide smile that made her want to pull his ear. The bugger.

"How in the hell did you get away from them all?" Declan asked.

"Oh, that." She winced. "We have a chaise to return." Her head turned the opposite direction toward the main street and she pointed. The scratched side of the chaise had scraped harder than she realized, the bright blue paint now torn to shreds of wood. "Ugh. Or maybe we have to buy that gentleman a new one."

Declan laughed, full and hearty, and never in her life had she felt more at home, more right, than she did in that moment.

{ CHAPTER 38 }

"What are we doing here?" Verity looked across the expanse of green in Hyde Park, feeling a light breeze that wasn't bogged down with the thick London air making way into her chest.

Their feet crunched along the gravel pathway. They had been following the edge of the Serpentine for fifteen minutes and Declan hadn't said a word about what they were there for.

He motioned around them. "This was as close to the countryside as I could get in London. We still have unfinished business in town, so cannot leave just yet, but I wanted you in air, in space you could breathe in, and this was the closest spot I could think of."

Her arm nestled into the crook of his elbow and she pulled herself tighter to him. It had only been three days since the scene outside of parliament and she was still coming to grips with the weight that had been lifted from her shoulders.

The threat upon Declan was gone with the death of Lord Gunderson.

Uncle Rupert was still alive, barely, but not coherent and about to be hanged for murdering Lord Gunderson. Another day, and easy breath would be hers once more. The threat on Ned gone.

Declan pointed toward the lake. "Come, let us stand here by the water."

They veered off the footpath and strolled across a stretch of lawn to the water's edge. Ducks and geese and four swans puttered about in this corner of the lake, darting close to shore where a little boy was tossing bread crumbs into the water. The giggle of the boy as the fowl pecked each other for the crumbs rang in the air. Pure joy on his little cherub face.

In silence, they both watched the boy for minutes and Verity realized she hadn't stood still in a long time. Even in the last few days spent at Declan's townhouse, she had fluttered from room to room, dusting, cleaning fireplaces, scrubbing silver, anything to keep her hands busy as the authorities sorted out Uncle Rupert's fate.

She cleaned, even as Declan had asked her to hire kitchen staff and a crew of maids to do all that work. That had resulted in the few maids that she had initially hired walking a wide berth around her, looking at her strangely for days.

"When was the last time you felt innocence?" Declan's voice was soft.

She looked up at him. His gaze hadn't moved from the boy. She wasn't sure if he was asking the question of her or of himself.

Her look drifted back to the boy. "I don't know."

"Think."

She stared at the swans in the water, searching her memory. And then, there it was. She stumbled upon it even when she didn't think she could find that emotion again.

"It was summertime. I was eleven, maybe twelve, and I was with Ned. He was four and so curious about

everything. We were walking along the edge of the forest
where the bluebells grew. We were picking the flowers for
my mother. She had been in pain that morning, so we
thought to bring some home to cheer her. But then she
appeared and she had on the prettiest blue dress, and for
once, she didn't have bruises on her face. She said the pain
had stopped and we had hours—hours where we plucked
flowers and lay in the grasses with the sun on our faces.
We weaved a crown of bluebells for Ned's head, which he
loved—king of the flowers. And we laughed. I couldn't even
tell you what we laughed about. But we laughed—the kind
of laughter that made our bellies hurt and tears stream from
our faces. There were no worries that day. It was innocent,
and I felt that. She gave me that, and I don't know how she
did it."

Verity paused, shaking her head. "When I think back
on it, that was the time father had broken several of her
ribs. How she managed what she did, I don't know. But she
never let me see the pain that day. Only laughter."

Her mouth closed for a long moment as she stared at
the boy across the water. "Innocence always comes with a
price."

"It does. But she loved you enough to pay that price."

She nodded. "She was so strong, but so weak. But she
knew how to love us—that never wavered."

He looked down at her, a soft smile touching his lips.
"You miss that innocence?"

"That feeling?" Her mouth pulled back in a sad smile.
"I do. Like nothing else. I had moments like that with
my mother, and I just want to preserve as much of that

innocence for Ned as I can. He was too young to remember her like I do. But I want him to have a few more of those innocent moments before the world devours him, like it does to everyone. Before the jading. Before the loss. Hope was so easy back then. Everything was going to be right. I tell him that same thing now and he sees how I lie to him. How I tell him everything will be fine, even when I know it will not be."

Declan turned fully toward her. "Then you need to find the innocence again—that is the only way he'll believe you."

She shook her head. "That is gone, gone forever."

"Or it can start anew, today, with me."

Her brow wrinkled. "What?"

He grabbed both of her hands, clutching them. "What is it you want, Verity?"

"Ned safe. You safe."

"You have that." He smiled. "So I want you to think on the question again, truly think on it now that the threat upon Ned's life, your life, is gone. What is it you want next?"

She looked away from him, studying the water for a long moment. "I want…" She didn't need to think on this, for in a thousand years her heart would never change on the matter. Her gaze shifted to him, searching for home in the grey of his eyes. "I want the exact same thing as I did a fortnight ago. Six months ago. A year ago. I want you."

"And?"

"I want a life together. I want Ned to live with us—I miss him so much."

"Anything else? You do not wish to return to your old life now that it is an option?"

"My old life was never my own—it was surviving, pretending not to see the things I couldn't bear. Pretending not to feel the things that gutted me." She drew a deep breath. "It wasn't real. But you…you are real. Real and raw and everything that is home to me." Her shoulders lifted. "That is the world I want to be in, anything beyond that, I cannot even begin to imagine."

"I think it's time you expand your imagination." A mischievous grin crept onto his face. "So how about we start with that clergyman under that tree over there." He dropped her right hand and pointed to a man standing under a tree by a carriage. "And in that coach behind him, Talen and Ness and your brother are waiting."

Her eyes flew wide, her look shooting to him. "For what?"

"For us to marry, if you will have me."

"Marry? But we cannot—what about banns?"

"We can and we will. Do you not think, after everything, that Talen and I cannot get some things done when we need to?" He nudged the tip of her nose with his knuckle. "Special license, finch."

She felt it. The tiniest spark flashing into a real flame in her chest. Hope.

He smiled at her. "That, I need to nurture."

"What?"

"I daresay, I just saw hope flash across the green of your eyes. Something I plan on nurturing until it is the only thing shining in the green."

Her bottom lip pulled under her top teeth. If that was what he was looking for in her, he was sure to be disappointed. "I don't know if I'm capable of that, Dec."

His hand lifted, his fingers going under her chin as his thumb brushed against her lips, relaxing the worry in them. "I'm not so naïve as to think all that has jaded you will leave your soul. But I want it to fade, to be smothered under the shadow of all the light and love our life together will be."

She stared into the silver of his eyes, devoid of color, but not life. So much life. A life she wanted. Needed. "I like that thought."

"Tell me you'll like being my wife even more."

"I will."

A smile, carnal and wickedly satisfied curled across his lips. He looked ready to drag her over to a bench and take her in the middle of the Park. Best to get married first. Scandal—lots of it—could come later.

Weaving her hand into the crook of his elbow, she turned and waved at Ned's face peering out of the carriage behind the clergyman.

She would show Declan just how hopeful she could be. She only had to say "I do."

Hope personified, in that one simple, tremendous act.

{ CHAPTER 39 }

The man was buried.

And now he'd been summoned.

Lady Gunderson had waited until her husband was buried and the bulk of the affairs set in order before calling Declan to her home.

Declan had sent requests to see her multiple times. Requests that had gone unanswered until this morning when he'd been summoned to her home at half past one.

Jack had circled the carriage about the row of houses four times, as Verity had insisted that Lady Gunderson would demand promptness of them. Not early. Not late.

They still had no information on how he was connected to Lord and Lady Gunderson, even though Verity had her suspicions.

Suspicions that were only theories until they heard the truth directly from Lady Gunderson.

Declan looked around the drawing room he and Verity had been shown into. It reeked of wealth—cough-inducing wealth that crept around him, threatening to suffocate. Anything that could be gilded, was. Any surface that could hold elaborate carvings, did. Every fabric was the finest silk.

Whereas his neck grew hotter by the second under his cravat, Verity sat on the settee angled toward the fireplace, her hands folded in her lap, a serene smile on her face.

She hadn't grown up in as much wealth as this, but still, she fit. Fit in this room—her posture, the way she

carried herself, how she didn't look at every artifact in the space, calculating how many barrels one would have to roll down the docks just to own a gilded…monkey statue, was it? Yes. A monkey with emerald eyes.

Eyes that had nothing on his wife's.

Verity looked up at him, willing him to calm with her gaze. Calm when the answers he needed were somewhere in the rooms above them in this blasted townhouse.

Both doors to the drawing room swung open, and the butler stepped into the space announcing his mistress. "Lady Gunderson."

Verity stood, aligning herself next to him as the butler moved to the side and an elderly woman, dressed in black and leaning heavily on her gold tipped black cane, shuffled into the room.

The butler closed the doors behind her.

Lady Gunderson looked to the round table at her left. "Good, I see Mary brought in tea." Her gaze flickered over Verity and then she looked to Declan.

There they were. Grey eyes. Grey eyes very similar to his, if Verity was to be believed. He wasn't quite sure at the likeness, as he didn't spend a great deal of time studying his own eyes.

But Verity had insisted—it was the only reason she had reached him in time to stop Lord Gunderson from killing him.

Lady Gunderson stopped in the middle of the room and her forefinger flipped up from her grip on the raven's head of the cane to point at Verity. "The one from the exhibit. This was the one?"

Declan's brow furrowed. "The one?"

Lady Gunderson's voice was pert while her body was not. "The woman that was outside the carriage when my husband was killed?"

Declan nodded. "She is."

"Then she is also the one that saved you." Lady Gunderson's look shifted down to Verity and she studied his wife for an awkwardly long moment.

"She is," Declan repeated.

Lady Gunderson's lips pursed and she looked to Declan, her face a battle ram. "What I have to tell you is private. She is not welcome in this conversation. What is she doing here?"

"I asked her to come."

"This is private."

"She stays."

"She is not welcome. The invitation was for you alone."

Verity fidgeted next to him, looking up at him. "Dec—"

"She is my wife." Declan's glare stayed on Lady Gunderson. This woman was the last person he would ever allow to order him about. "She stays."

"Your wife?" Lady Gunderson's dark eyebrows lifted, the color of them punctuation on her face, while the rest of her hair had long since gone white. "You wrapped that up fairly efficiently."

Declan shrugged. "There was no reason to wait."

Lady Gunderson turned her canny eyes to Verity. "You, girl, you were hired to do a job. You weren't supposed to be this pretty. I was told you would be plain."

"You know I am a guardian?" Verity asked.

"Of course, I know. I know about everything and everyone that has touched Declan since he was a babe."

"How?" Verity's voice was strong, inquisitive. She wasn't about to be cowed by this woman any more than Declan was.

"Hector told me." The wrinkles about her eyes deepened as she examined Verity. "That uncle of yours was taken care of at Newgate, I was told. Hanged? Three days past?"

"He was slipped a pistol before the actual hanging. Peers wanted him to go out honorably, rather than by the noose. He took care of it. I was witness to his body," Declan said without emotion, even though the mere mention of Verity's uncle curdled his tongue. Torture was what the man deserved, and he got off far too easily.

Lady Gunderson harrumphed. "Good riddance to rubbish—to both that atrocious man and my husband." She moved toward the wingback chair that sat closest to the fire, but then paused as she passed Verity and Declan. She leaned in, studying Verity's face closely. "Well, there is no reversing the marriage, so I will need to move past the future I imagined and accept what is in front of me. That was my husband's failing—the man couldn't move past anything." Her feet started to shuffle toward the chair. "Pour me tea, dear girl, if you would be so kind. Three spoons of sugar—it is the only thing that keeps these bones going."

Lady Gunderson sat heavily into the chair for how frail she looked, and settled back into the cushions.

Verity poured her a cup of tea and brought it over to her.

"Thank you, dear. The both of you must sit now."

Verity glanced at Declan. He could only offer her a slight raised eyebrow without being rude. Lady Gunderson had walked in and commandeered the room, something he wasn't quite expecting, though he should have, after reading about the earl and the countess's rows over the years.

He sat next to Verity on the settee and waited until Lady Gunderson took a long sip of her tea. "Do you mind if we come right to it, my lady?"

She scoffed a laugh, took another sip of the tea, and then set her gaze upon him. "Ask what you need to."

He nodded, the thousands of queries in his mind boiling down to one question. "Why did you hire Hector—the Guardians—to watch over me?"

"Hector told you that?"

"No. We have surmised that much."

Her look flickered to Verity and then landed back on Declan. "It is no secret in society that I despised my husband. I assume you know that?"

"Aye. We do."

A twinkle sparked in her right eye. "I imagine many bets were finally settled about town after his demise?"

Declan coughed, then chuckled. "Yes, quite a bit of money has exchanged hands during the last week over the matter."

She nodded. "Always bet on the one with something to lose."

"You outlived him because you had something to lose?"

"Of course, dear boy, why would I ever have wanted to live this long? Life is exhausting, but I had you to lose, Declan, and I was not about to let that happen."

He leaned forward, setting his forearms on his thighs as his hands clasped together. "Who exactly are you to me, Lady Gunderson?"

"I am your grandmother."

Her words were not a surprise, but nonetheless, slammed into his chest, taking his breath away.

He thought he was prepared for this.

He was not.

He had family. He had them all along.

Verity's hand slipped under his arm, her fingers moving forward to curl over the whites of his knuckles. He could feel her eyes on him, but he couldn't look at her, couldn't move, couldn't speak.

He had *family*.

Squeezing his hands, Verity cleared her throat and looked to the countess. "Forgive us, but we don't understand how that can be. Your son died in 1801 before Declan was born and he was never married."

"Was he not?" Lady Gunderson implored, her grey eyes canny.

Verity shook her head. "There is no record of it."

"Except my boy, Geoff, was married. He took vows a month before his death, and you, Declan, were born three months after. Your mother died in childbirth."

Declan stared at his grandmother—or this woman who claimed she was his grandmother. This could very well just be the ramblings of a confused old woman.

He shook his head. "My mother was with child when they married?"

"Yes. And my husband and Geoff fought about it for months. Your mother was not of our class, and my husband would not have that in his lineage. Though I do believe your father loved your mother, which is why he fought so hard for her."

She paused, looking to the fire for a long breath before continuing. "They eloped to Scotland. And when they returned, the earl was furious. My husband always hated Geoff—he'd spent thirty years doing so—and this was the thing that finally snapped his mind. He went after my boy. Both of them, at the top of the stairs, struggling against the other. They both fell down the stairs. Arms, legs, and bodies tangled, and I watched the whole thing. My husband lived. My boy did not."

She took a sip of the tea, her hand shaking ever so slightly.

Still, Declan could not speak. Could not manifest words.

"Why did the earl hate his son?" Verity asked in a soft voice.

The countess's gaze shifted to Verity and she studied her for long, silent seconds. "This goes no further than this room."

Verity nodded and leaned into Declan's side.

"Geoff was not his son. I cuckolded the earl. Unforgivable, and I will pay my dues when I meet my maker, but what is past is past. My husband discovered the truth a month into our marriage, but by all accounts, he

had to claim Geoff as his. He has hated me, hated Geoff ever since."

"And he killed him." Verity said the words plainly, untarnished.

Lady Gunderson nodded. "With that, the earl took the opportunity to wipe every trace of Geoff from the world. He refused to acknowledge the marriage between Geoff and your mother, Mable. He cast her out of the estate, threatened her with hanging if she ever appeared on the estate again, and she had you in a room above a tavern in Southampton."

Declan found his voice, words spitting out. "You knew and you didn't help her?"

"Of course, I helped her." Her voice snapped. "I loved my son—he was my world. No matter what hopes I had for a match for him, I could not fault the lass for finding herself in the same position I had been in myself. With child, unmarried. She carried my grandchild, for goodness sake. How do you think she afforded the room in Southampton?"

His hands curled into fists, his words punctuated with fury as his glare sliced into his grandmother. "Did my mother die alone?"

Lady Gunderson blinked, her mouth clamping shut, the first indication that she felt anything. Anything at all. She took a sip of the tea, swallowing, her throat working hard under the wrinkled, crepe skin of her neck. "Mable was not alone. There was a midwife. Your mother held you. Named you."

His head dropped forward, hanging, searching for breath that wouldn't move into his lungs.

His mother held him. Named him.

And then he was set adrift. A babe onto the sea.

"Why, in the heavens, did you not claim him?" Verity asked, her words sharp.

"The earl killed my son—he'd been looking to do so for thirty years. So no, I was not going to let him know Declan existed." Her voice snapped. "I was not about to let him ever find out you were born. You were alive and healthy."

She stopped, exhaling a sigh, shaking her head. "I just never imagined the earl would live this long. He had so much hatred layered in his bones, in his blood, and I thought it would kill him long ago. Devour him up from the inside out. I thought he would die and I would be able to bring you home. Bring you into your rightful place. I have the documentation on your parent's marriage from the man that married them across the border."

He wasn't hearing her right.

His head snapped upward, his look cutting into her. "You mean this?" He yanked his right hand out from under Verity's grip and swung it about him. "This isn't my rightful place."

His gaze followed his hand around, a sour taste slipping onto his tongue. "My father was not of the earl's blood. I was not of his blood. This is not my rightful place."

"But it can be. You are of my blood. You are my grandson. This, the title, the earldom, it is yours. It is your rightful place."

Declan stood and Verity jumped up onto her feet next to him. He glared down at his grandmother. "My rightful place is the place I've carved out in this world on my own.

This—you—all of it is just an inconvenience that has made me question every single person that has ever been in my life." He gave her a slight bow. "It is good to know you exist, Lady Gunderson. Thank you for shedding light on my parentage. Good day."

Declan turned and walked out of the room, not able to suffer another second in his grandmother's presence.

~ ~ ~

Verity followed Declan from the settee. She wasn't about to stop him from leaving, for everything he was feeling at the moment had its place. Yet decency made her stop halfway to the drawing room exit and turn back to his grandmother.

Before she could say a word, Lady Gunderson cut her off. "You need to get him back here."

A frown crossed Verity's face. "I do thank you for the employment these last two years, Lady Gunderson, but my job is done. I have retired from the Guardians. My allegiance is to my husband and if he feels the need to leave this place, then I am one step behind him."

The countess's grey eyes narrowed at her. "I don't intend to give up that easily, Mrs. Rudderton."

"No, I don't imagine you do. I imagine you've spent the last twenty-five years looking out for Declan from afar. Worrying about him, maybe, maybe not." Verity shrugged. "The thing is, all he really needed all those years was to not be afar. It was to be close. To have a place in the world. You didn't offer him that, so he created it on his own. I am a part of that. The Alabaster, everything in the rookeries is a part of that. I am his home, and that is his world. I don't know that he will ever give that up. I don't know that he should."

The countess's lips pursed, the wrinkles deep. "I expected more of him. I expected him to have the steel spine he was born with and step into his place in the family."

Verity guffawed.

Openly and awkwardly and she wasn't ashamed of it. "A steel spine? That man has a spine that can move mountains. He has done more—accomplished more in his life than anyone I have ever met. Including you and your husband."

She lifted her hand, palm to the countess, her voice softening. "I understand the position you were in—what you would do to protect him. You loved him, even if you could not reach out to him. I understand that. I admire that. I am in awe of your iron will on the matter. But this… this will just take time. And you have to be prepared for him to never be what you want him to be."

Lady Gunderson glared at her, her pursed lips not wavering.

Verity gave her a slight bow. "Good day to you, my lady." She turned to leave.

"I would…"

Verity stopped, looking over her shoulder, eyebrows raised.

"I would accept just a grandson. A grandson without any expectations of taking on the title. Just a grandson."

Lady Gunderson wasn't a delicate matron of society. She'd outlived a man with the goal of making every day of her life miserable. Obstinate, cunning, hard, but there, at the edge of her left eye, a tear.

Verity stared at the wetness working down the rows of wrinkles and sighed. "A grandson…being a grandson…I think he will come around to that. He is just coming around to the idea of me. Of being a husband. Of having a home. Of having permanence." A soft chuckle escaped her. "I am just coming around to the idea of that as well. It may take some time, but I think Declan will come around. Don't give up." Verity smiled. "And don't die. Use all your stubbornness on my husband. He'll appreciate it, even if he never acknowledges it."

Lady Gunderson laughed. "I plan to keep breathing, child." She paused, nodding to herself. "Thank you. Thank you for taking care of him. I think he always needed someone like you in his life."

Verity smiled, genuine. "I think so as well. But as it turns out, I always needed a man like him in my life. And now I have him."

The smallest smile slipped onto Lady Gunderson's lips, her voice cracking. "Keep him close, then, dear. Keep him close."

Verity nodded. "I intend to."

{ EPILOGUE }

"You are positive this is a good idea?" Sitting on the peach wingback chair in the open area of the conservatory at Perrington House, Lady Gunderson fussed with the white cap atop Landon's head, ignoring his tiny hands wiggling maniacally in the air, fighting her as he squirmed on her lap. Only six months old and Landon had entered into a battle of wills between him and his great-grandmother.

Verity hid the chuckle ready to breach her lips. Battles her babe would win every time, as his great-grandmother had a spine of jelly when it came to her great-grandchildren. Verity had just watched three years of Lady Gunderson melting into a pile of mush every time Annelise would make her great-grandmother play with her. Her three-year-old daughter loved everything—dolls, blocks, ponies, worms—and it didn't matter what, if Annelise wanted to explore it, she had a partner in her great-grandmother.

Verity bent down and reached past Lady Gunderson's arms to intervene, tugging the cap fully onto her babe's head as his chubby fingers latched onto her pinky. It wasn't cold yet in the conservatory, even though the chill of the fall air had taken to the countryside, but Verity did want them all to look presentable for what was to come.

Landon's cap straight, Verity's eyes met Lady Gunderson's. "I am positive. I am. I hope."

Not the iron clad reassurance Lady Gunderson was looking for, but Verity couldn't give her that. She could only hope and trust in her husband.

As stubborn as he could be, he could also see reason.

Lady Gunderson's aged grey eyes narrowed. "But I maintain that we do not talk about such things openly. It is easier that way. More refined."

"I know, Grandmother." Verity kissed Landon on the nose and then stood. "But I think that needs to change. I think it has to change."

Lady Gunderson's mouth opened, then closed as she bit back her next words.

Verity nodded to her, trying to set optimism into her face. It had never been her natural state, but ever since Annelise was born, and then Landon, she was finding that elusive feeling easier to come by.

Even in the last years, after they moved up to Perrington House in Westmorland, life had gone better than she had hoped.

She had wanted to move to Perrington House so they could wipe all traces of her father and uncle from the estate before Ned came of age. To make it feel like a real home to him. His, to take pride in and make into whatever he wanted with his own family someday.

Verity needed her brother to feel comfortable at Perrington House, for it was to be his to make decisions upon in another year. To that end, she felt accomplished. They had brought light and happiness into this world that had once been a sad place for them, and now Ned didn't want them to leave, even if Declan had already built them a home several miles away atop the most beautiful hill, where she could see Perrington from the south terrace.

She imagined it would only be a matter of time before he changed his tune, but until that happened, she took every day he still wanted to see his older sister as a gift.

"They're coming, they're coming, they're coming!" Excited squeals came with the energetic bundle of two wee boys running into the room, their arms flailing and giggles at their lips. Thomas and Valance ran over to their parents by the sweets table, where Talen and Ness stood talking to Ned. Laughing, Talen turned to the boys, scooped up a son in each arm and squeezed them. They screeched giggles and he dropped them back onto their feet.

With a grin, Ness shook her head and stepped to her left, where their two-year-old, Headon, had his fingers deep in the dirt of the planter holding lemon trees. She brushed the dirt from his fingers and lifted him to her hip, moving next to Talen's side. He kept a hand on the shoulder of each of the wiggling boys, so they didn't run off madcap.

Verity smiled at Ness, and Ness gave her a nod in support.

She didn't know what she would do without Ness, who had become her closest confidante over the years. She needed all the support she could get in this moment.

She could have invited more friends for this occasion, but her optimism would only allow her so much margin. Talen, Ness, Ned, the children and Declan's grandmother. That was it. Only the ones very closest to them in case this didn't go well.

Footfalls echoed along the wide stone pavers that led into the conservatory and Declan appeared a moment later, a smile on his face, carrying their daughter in front of him.

She had both of her hands fully over his eyes, blocking his view of everything.

Declan laughed at whatever Annelise had just told him. "How many more steps, wee one?"

"Four." She giggled, her butt wiggling in his arms as she looked over her shoulder at the room. "Step high, Papa. High, so you don't stumble. Don't look."

Declan exaggerated his high steps per Annelise's command. "You're not taking me into the river, are you, Lise?"

She laughed hard, falling to the side in his arms, and her hands almost fell away from his eyes. "Papa, no. Step higher. Higher."

He did so and uproarious laughter overtook her again. A ride for her, just as much fun as the game of getting her father into the solarium without his peeking ahead.

At her laughter, he chomped his teeth, trying to nibble on her squirming arms. She squealed, her entire body shaking in glee as they moved into the conservatory.

Verity's heart swelled to impossible proportions, as it always did when she saw them laughing together.

"Stop, Papa, stop now."

Declan's feet stopped.

Annelise looked over her shoulder at her mother, her mouth pulled wide in a smile that asked for permission.

Verity nodded at her.

Her little hands flew away from his eyes. "Surprise, Papa!" She slapped her palms onto the sides of his cheeks. "Surprise, it's your birthday. Surprise!"

"What?" A half-smile stayed on his face as he looked from Annelise around the room, taking in all the faces and the spread of sweets and treats on the table.

"Surprise Papa! Mama says we get to celebrate you today. It's your birthday and we have a party for you."

"What?" A deep line appeared between Declan's furrowed brow and his look centered on Verity. He was warring between staying happy for Annelise's sake and the confusion overtaking him.

Verity nodded at him with as much enthusiasm as she could muster on her face.

His look shifted down to his grandmother. Lady Gunderson nodded. "I had the date verified."

Annelise squeezed his cheeks, flopping about in front of him to make him look back at her. "Octo—" She stopped, confusion on her chubby face, and her head whipped around to Verity.

Verity smiled and nodded. "Yes. October."

She turned back to Declan. "October three." She held up three fingers. "Three, just like me, Papa."

He smiled, laughing, and caught her forefinger with his teeth. "Three, just like you. Unless I eat one of those three."

She screeched a laugh and yanked her hand away. Still giggling, Declan put her wiggling body down onto the floor. She ran over to the table stuffed full of every treat imaginable, her eyes big on the sweets.

Declan looked to Verity, the smile he'd forced fading. "But how?"

Verity set her hand on the tall back of the chair Lady Gunderson sat in. "Grandmother has been working to verify the date for years. For her sake, for yours. She never told you in case she couldn't discover the real date. She had to track down an old sea captain to do so."

Declan shook his head. "But…"

Lady Gunderson cleared her throat. "I found him, finally, in Belize."

"Papa, here, this is special for you." Annelise ran to him, holding up a bite-size sweet cake for him. He bent down and let her pop it into his mouth with a giant chomp that made her giggle.

He poked her belly. "Thank you, sunshine. Off to play with your cousins."

Annelise ran off to where Thomas and Valance were still being held in place by Talen, and the three of them started jumping about the wide table of treats, jibber-jabbering and pointing out all the sweets they planned on eating.

Swallowing, Declan stood and turned to Verity and his grandmother, his look going to pinpricks on Lady Gunderson. "Holding my babe in front of you isn't going to protect you from this."

"No?" Lady Gunderson shifted Landon on her lap with a grumpy exhale. "I thought it would help."

Declan crossed his arms over his chest. "Talk."

Across the room, Ness cleared her throat as her hands corralled the backs of her children. "We can take the children into the music room."

"No, stay, Lady Washburn," Declan's grandmother said. "I know there are no secrets between the lot of you. It will save Declan and Verity repeating all of this back to you. I have nothing left to hide on this account. I am proud of my grandson and his wife. Proud of my great-grandchildren."

Talen looked to Declan and raised his brows. "Dec?"

Declan nodded. "Stay."

Ness squatted down to the height of the children. "Can you three please go and find Cook and tell her we are in desperate need of more sugar plums, since you little snitches ate it all before Uncle Declan made it in here, and it is his party." She pointed to Annelise. "Take your cousin with you, since she didn't get any while you two were sneaking pieces. And ask if you can help Cook or Miss Mary with anything."

Thomas and Valance flanked Annelise, each grabbing one of her hands, and they ran out of the room. The two older boys took great pride in their responsibility for protecting Annelise from any and everything.

Declan waited a long breath, watching the wide entrance the children disappeared from. His gaze finally shifted to Lady Gunderson. "Grandmother, why now? It has been years. Years."

"I wanted to give you this, give you this for real. The date of your birth. Since I first met you, I wanted to give this to you. I just did not think it would take this long. It took far too many years to verify everything. I wanted it

to be real, not a random date I picked to soothe my guilt, but the true and proper date. I did not anticipate it would be this hard to find one old sailor. But he was across the ocean."

"Why did it hinge on him?" Declan asked.

"He was the one that took you in the day you were born, he and his wife. She couldn't bear children. Tabis and Hannah Rudderton. Captain Rudderton. They were fine, honest people. You lived for a number of years in the West Indies. But then she died of marsh fever when you were four. Tabis fell ill as well, and you were shuffled onto a Royal Navy ship, bound for England. But then the ship was diverted to the continent."

"So I stayed on the ship?"

She nodded, a frown on her face. "You did. It was easier. Safer."

He rubbed his hand across his forehead. "October third?"

"Yes. And I have a gift for you." Lady Gunderson paused, looking around the room, looking flustered for a second when she was never one to be flustered. "Or not a gift, truly, as that would be awkward. A person. I have a person here that I brought for you."

"Who?"

"One that knew your mother."

His brow furrowed, confused.

"She was the woman I hired to protect your mother. She was with her until your birth. You once asked me if your mother died alone, and I said no, but it wasn't the full truth. Your mother, Mable Casson, had Miss Simone

Bannerson with her. Miss Bannerson was the one that held her hand, that knew her best, at least at the end. She was not positive on the date because the birthing went on for days and then your mother died, so I had to find the captain."

Verity stepped forward, setting her hand on Declan's forearm. She could see he was reeling from all this information, but she wasn't sure if he was reeling in a good way or a bad way. "Miss Bannerson was kind enough to make the journey north. Please, will you talk with her?"

Declan looked around the room. "Where is she?"

"In the library."

It took a long breath before Declan nodded.

"She's waiting for you, if you want to go now."

He stared at Verity for a long second, then nodded and turned, exiting the conservatory.

Verity stood in place, watching him leave.

"That was horrible," Lady Gunderson exhaled. "Just as I suspected, he hates me again, hates me for all of it."

Verity turned around. "He doesn't hate you, Grandmother. He never hated you. He hated what happened, what was lost. You know he adores you."

Lady Gunderson's thin shoulders lifted in a defeated sigh and she looked down at Landon. "Hard-won adoration now lost."

Verity glanced back at the entrance to the conservatory over her shoulder, staring at the empty corridor.

She hoped not.

~ ~ ~

Declan stared at the open doorway of the library.

Ten minutes, he'd been sitting alone, digesting all that he'd just learned.

It wasn't a surprise when Verity appeared in the doorway, though he thought she would have been quicker to hover her way into the room.

"Miss Bannerson said you asked lots of questions?" Verity asked, her hand clutching the edge of the doorframe.

Declan nodded. "I did."

"Did it help?"

"It did." He didn't have more of an answer for her, as he was still trying to place all he had just learned of his mother into his mind.

She took a step into the room, her hands wringing. "Are you angry? At first I thought something smaller with just your grandmother to tell you the date, but then Lise heard us talking and she found out it was your birthday and she wanted a party for you. And I thought it would be fine, but I didn't mean to ambush you with the information and—"

"Finch, stop." He held his hand out to her. "Come here. I am not angry."

Relief flashing in her face, she came to him, and he grabbed her hand and hauled her into his lap.

He pressed a kiss to her forehead. He would never tire of the way her body instinctively curled against his. "I'm not angry. Overwhelmed, but not upset. And not expecting what was waiting for me when I walked into the conservatory—as I haven't given a thought to the matter of my birth in years."

"I know. Your grandmother insisted on discovering the truth. She thinks this is still a wedge between you and her."

"But why now? She knows I've forgiven her for the past."

"I don't know if she actually believes it. Or has allowed herself to believe it." She curled her hand along the back of his neck, her green eyes raking over his face. "This date—this means something profound to her."

"Why? I had gotten past it."

Verity pursed her lips for a moment, then met his look. "Do you know that feeling, how when you look at Lise or Landon and you want to give them everything—the world and everything in it?"

He nodded. "Too much so."

"You are that to your grandmother. She wants to give you the world. Including your birthday."

His chest squeezed hard. For all his tumultuous past with his grandmother, he was grateful now for her presence in his life. She'd become family to him.

His head angled to the side. "How did you get Miss Bannerson here to Perrington? How did you even find her? Grandmother said she thought she had disappeared and she lost any trace of her long ago."

A mischievous smile came to his wife's lips. "I called in an old favor."

"With who?"

"Hector. Miss Bannerson was one of the first guardians."

He scoffed a laugh, shaking his head. "She left that part out."

"Did you ask her about it?"

"No, I only asked questions of my mother. We know there is no one left of my mother's family, so to talk with someone that knew her. It is…it has been a blessing. I feel I know my father through Grandmother, about his love of horses, his intelligence, his devotion to my mother, his stubbornness." A slight smile came to his face, his head shaking. "I even know the Ruddertons through my letters with the captain. But my mother has always been a mystery, so this, this brings her alive for me in a way I never knew I needed."

"Good. Miss Bannerson said she would stay for a few days more so you can get all your questions answered. She has been most forthcoming with me, and I am curious about her early days as a guardian."

"Don't open that door again."

Verity shrugged. "Mere curiosity. Plus, it is always good to know people."

He patted her leg. "I am ready."

"Ready for what?"

"To celebrate." The smallest smile, genuine and with a hint of bashfulness curved his lips. "As much as I dislike having all of your eyes on me at once, it is my birthday."

Her eyes went wide, a smile as bright as the sun spreading across her face. "Yes. Thank you—we want to celebrate you. You are the bedrock at the core of all of us. Let us look at you. Be grateful for you. You make me feel like I am the only person in the world every time you glance at me, so let me—us—give you just a little of that back."

"You are the only person in the world, aside from Lise and Landon, of course." He kissed her lips, nearly getting sucked into another matter entirely that only involved him and his wife.

Knowing where this was headed, she smiled into the kiss and then pulled away, shaking her head.

His stare met hers. "Thank you for giving Grandmother the fortitude to give me this piece of me. I don't imagine she would have done so without your prodding. But more than that, thank you for opening your mouth and speaking to me those years ago."

She chuckled. "I don't think I had a choice."

"You always had a choice. And I'm glad it was me."

"It always was." She stood from his lap before he could draw her into another kiss and reached down for his hand. "We have a party to attend. Your daughter has been guarding the last sugar plum from the boys for an hour now that she's keeping safe for you."

Declan let her pull him to his feet and they started toward the door. "Good thing she can be fierce, that one."

Verity looked over her shoulder to him with an impish grin. "Remember that when she opens her palm and produces the hot gooey mess to put on your tongue. The safest place was in her hand."

Declan winced with a chuckle.

Yet still, melted sugar plum or not, life was more than he ever could have imagined, and that was because of this woman in front of him.

He may be the bedrock, but she was the world above it.

It was time to celebrate.

~ About the Author ~

K.J. Jackson is the *USA Today* bestselling author of the
*Hold Your Breath, Lords of Fate, Lords of Action,
Revelry's Tempest, Valor of Vinehill, Box of Draupnir,
Exile, Guardians of the Bones,* and *Flame Moon* series.

She specializes in historical and paranormal romance,
loves to travel (road trips are the best!), and is a sucker for a
good story in any genre. She lives in Minnesota with
her husband, two children, and a dog who
has taken the sport of bed-hogging
to new heights.

Visit her at www.kjjackson.com

~ Author's Note ~

Thank you for allowing my stories into your life and time—
it is an honor!

Be sure to check out all my historical romances
(each is a stand-alone story):

Hold Your Breath
Stone Devil Duke
Unmasking the Marquess
My Captain, My Earl

Lords of Fate
Worth of a Duke
Earl of Destiny
Marquess of Fortune

Lords of Action
Vow
Promise
Oath

Revelry's Tempest
Of Valor & Vice
Of Sin & Sanctuary
Of Risk & Redemption
To Capture a Rogue, *Logan's Legends*
To Capture a Warrior, *Logan's Legends*
The Devil in the Duke

Valor of Vinehill
The Iron Earl
The Wolf Duke
The Steel Rogue
The Christmas Countess
The Devil Baron

Box of Draupnir
The Heart of an Earl
The Blood of a Baron
The Soul of a Rogue

Exile
Exiled Duke
Wicked Exile
Dangerous Exile

Guardians of the Bones
Discreet Destruction
Shadows of Scandal

Paranormal Romance:
Flame Moon
Triple Infinity, *Flame Moon #2*
Flux Flame, *Flame Moon #3*

Never miss a new release or sale!
Be sure to sign up for my VIP Email List at
www.KJJackson.com

Connect with me!
www.KJJackson.com ~or~ kjk19jackson@gmail.com

Printed in Great Britain
by Amazon

42533208R00192